NO-TIME for LOVE

NO-TIME for LOVE

A Novel

NANCY CAMPBELL ALLEN

Covenant Communications, Inc.

Cover image © 2000 PhotoDisc, Inc.

Cover design copyrighted 2000 by Covenant Communications, Inc.

Published by Covenant Communications, Inc.
American Fork, Utah

Printed in the United States of America
First Printing: May 2000

07 06 05 04 03 02 01 00   10 9 8 7 6 5 4 3 2 1

ISBN 1-57734-652-1

To Karin and Julie,
the original Cynic Sisters;
To Sydney, who's well on her way;

and

To Nina and Anna—
May the legend live on . . .

Acknowledgments

I need to thank Jed Brian for his techie expertise. I now know everything I need to know to hack my way into a high-tech computer system. And my thanks also to Robbyn Estes. You were definitely right—too many raised eyebrows.

Lastly, I need to thank Marti Frasier for letting me borrow her name, even though I used it for the bad guy.

Prologue

The hands that gripped the steering wheel were bruised and bleeding; all traces of the expensive manicure administered mere hours before had been obliterated. Her breathing was harsh and shallow, and one eye was already beginning to swell shut. That she had escaped at all was a miracle. She only hoped she had enough of a lead to make it to the airport before they noticed her absence.

She cursed as she was blinded by light reflected in her rearview mirror. Stepping on the accelerator, she squealed around a sharp bend in the road, her thoughts in disarray as she realized they were rapidly gaining on her.

She skidded dangerously close to the guardrail along the side of the mountain road, her limited knowledge of the terrain no match for the frayed state of her nerves and her battered, exhausted body. Her head snapped back against the headrest as a large black Suburban smashed into the small Jeep from behind.

She couldn't stop the terrified laugh that erupted from her throat and filled the interior of her car. Then she thought of her fiancé and felt a twinge of guilt. She'd been holding on to the relationship as a backup, trying to be someone he wanted so he'd hurry up and set a date, thereby allowing her to become someone *she* wanted: Mrs. Wealthy and Secure.

Ethically, she knew she should have broken the engagement weeks ago. They were ill-suited, and she doubted he'd ever figure it out, the fool. The fact that she'd been stringing him along in case her first choice didn't follow through hadn't bothered her until recently. The shrill echoes of her laughter died and she sobered, thinking of the box she'd stashed in his attic less than a week earlier. *They'll finish me and they'll go after him,* she realized with a sudden, horrifying intensity. He was innocent. She didn't want to be responsible for his death.

The Suburban rammed her again, this time sending her Jeep crashing through the guardrail and plummeting into space. She closed her eyes, suspended in the moment, waiting for impact. *I guess I'm the fool . . .*

* * * * * *

Connor O'Brian pulled to a stop at the curb and leaned his head against the seat, closing his eyes. The tears seeping from the corners were a surprise he hadn't expected. She'd been playing him like an idiot for months; he had known that and had planned on ending the thing before she'd ever left town. He supposed the reason for his sorrow was due to the nature of loss; he'd been mourning the end of the relationship since he'd found out she'd been seeing someone else. Her boss, no less.

It hadn't been right; it had never been right. He'd been looking for something he should have known he wouldn't find with her. Something about her had seemed familiar, and he had jumped on it with an impulsiveness that had surprised even him.

He sighed. Well, at any rate, it was over in a very real, physical way. He turned to open the door and straightened his shoulders as he stood. It was time for some moral support. He approached the door of his good friends, noted the late hour on his watch, and rang the doorbell anyway.

Chapter 1

Elizabeth Saxton opened the door to her Seattle high-rise apartment, nudged it closed with her elbow, and locked it. She dropped her purse and keys on the floor and wandered over to the large living-room windows that overlooked the nighttime skyline of the city. *It's amazing,* she thought to herself as she watched the cars driving on the streets below. *All these people—making commitments to other people and not bothering to keep them.*

Turning away from the window, she walked slowly into the bathroom, where she shrugged out of her black evening dress and kicked off her heels. She methodically removed the wires strapped to her midsection and stared for long moments into the mirror. Her brows furrowed as she gazed objectively at the beautiful honey-blonde hair and flawlessly made-up face, the intense green eyes, the small nose, and full, perfectly shaped mouth. "Men," she finally said aloud to the woman in the mirror. "They can't be trusted."

She was just stepping out of the shower when she heard the phone ring. The machine picked up before she made it out of the bathroom.

"Sigrid Elizabeth, where are you?"

Liz smiled as she recognized her mother's voice and ran to pick up the cordless receiver before the woman on the other end could hang up. "Mom?"

"Well! You're home! I've been trying to reach you for two days now. Haven't you heard my messages?"

Liz sank into a comfortable overstuffed chair and pulled her bathrobe securely under her chin. "Sorry. I've been really busy."

"What's wrong? You don't sound good."

Liz laughed. "Thanks, Mom." Only her mother would be so blunt. She sighed, her smile fading. "I'm just tired, I guess." Tired of following other women's cheating husbands around. Tired of having to tell the wives their suspicions were confirmed.

"Oh, honey. Why don't you do something else? You know this isn't your only option."

"It pays well." She paused. "It's disillusioning."

"Sweetheart, you'll find someone wonderful and forget all about the cheating masses. Someone who's active in the Church."

"Oh, Mom," Liz said quietly. "That's just it. The guy I scouted out tonight *is* a member of the Church. His wife has been suspecting for weeks that he's up to something, and sure enough, I followed him to a hotel where he met his girlfriend. Tomorrow I have to meet with the wife and give her the gruesome evidence."

Liz stared pensively into space as the silence on the other end lengthened.

"Honey, you've got to get out of this," her mother finally stated. "You have a degree in computer programming, for heaven's sake. What are you doing?"

Liz smiled bitterly. "You wouldn't believe what wealthy women in this city are willing to pay to get proof. I can't afford to quit. Besides, I'm getting a valuable education."

"That's ridiculous." Liz could picture the impatient expression on her mother's face. Sigrid Saxton was never one to mince words. "If this is your idea of an education, you haven't been paying close enough attention to your dad and me all these years. And how about your sister? She couldn't have found a better man."

"Exactly. She got the last good one. I don't harbor any high hopes for myself."

Sigrid sighed impatiently. "Liz, this is a personal vendetta. It's been a long time now. Let go of it. I don't think it's a matter of your broken heart anymore. It's your pride, so swallow it and move on."

Liz smiled. Her mother always made everything seem either black or white, and the solutions so simple. "Yes, Mother. Whatever you say."

Sigrid laughed. "Ha! If only you'd been so agreeable when you were younger, my life would have been much simpler."

"But not nearly as exciting."

"Liz, I just think you'll be happier when you shift your attention somewhere else."

Liz pursed her lips into a grim smile. "Well, I'll keep you posted. I love you, Mom. Kiss Dad for me."

"I will. I love you too, honey."

Liz sat with the phone in her hand for a long time after her mother hung up. Maybe she *was* holding onto bitterness as a means to repair her battered pride. She shook her head slightly in disgust as a blonde-haired, blue-eyed face swam about in her memory. She'd thought she was so in love with him. Their interests had been so similar, their scholastic pursuits the same. What had started as a casual friendship had evolved into a serious relationship that had spanned nearly a year.

She closed her eyes at the image of him locked in an amorous embrace with a certain buxom university lab assistant. Then she snorted in amused disdain and wondered when the pain had turned into anger, and the anger to derision. Maybe her mother was right. She certainly wasn't in love with him still; she knew she never really had been. He was companionship. He also had professed commitment. Perhaps that was what stung the most. She had indeed watched her parents through the years, and she knew what love was all about, having witnessed it firsthand.

There was someone, though—someone she'd always been able to envision herself with. Someone she laughed with and silently adored, never having admitted to him or anyone else that she really, *really* just wanted him all to herself. When they were together, he always introduced her as "my good friend, Liz." She had taken that as a broad hint and never tried to further the relationship. *Connor.* It always came back to Connor. He'd spoiled her for anyone else.

Liz sighed and made herself leave the comfort of her chair. She turned on her computer to check her e-mail and smiled as she saw her sister's address splashed across the screen. "READ THIS NOW!" was the subject line, and Liz obediently clicked in the appropriate spot.

"Hey Liz," the message began.

> *"Where are you? It's been a week! I'm starting to get a little concerned, here! I may just have to have Mom check up on you."*

Thanks, Amber, Liz thought with a rueful smile. Her sister was obviously not averse to pulling out the big guns.

The message continued:

> *"Tyler and I have been talking, and we think you should come for another visit. A longer one this time. Just do it—put your stuff in storage, break your lease, and sponge off us for a while! I miss you, and I think you need a break. Don't say no until you've at least thought about it for a while, okay? I know you have a life and everything, but you know how much I want you to come out this way. Humor me, will ya? My only companionship when I'm home during the day comes from a three-year-old and a one-year-old. They're sweet, but I now know Tarzan verbatim and am developing a deep and abiding hatred for Barney the Dinosaur. If you possess any kind feelings for me, you'll drop everything and get here . . ."*

Liz laughed out loud. Tag-teamed by her mother and sister. Did she really stand a chance?

Chapter 2

Connor O'Brian dropped the phone back into position on his desk and rubbed his eyes. That blasted audit was going to kill him. The company was fine; there was absolutely nothing to hide. But people were still panicked, and somehow it had fallen on his shoulders to keep tempers even and fears allayed. It didn't make sense. He was vice president over sales, not the company's human resource person. Yet no matter how hard he tried, he could never say no, and he couldn't stop himself from taking on the problems of his colleagues as though they were his own.

He gritted his teeth as the phone rang yet again, then he picked it up. "Yes?" He closed his eyes and nodded. "Yes, I'm on my way. No, I canceled my other afternoon meetings." His boss was the worst of the lot. The man was a heart attack waiting to happen.

Connor again dropped the phone into place and leaned back into his chair for a moment, gathering the mental energy he knew the remainder of the day would require. He stood and retrieved his suit jacket from its draped position across the back of one of the plush chairs in his office. He shrugged into it, barely registering, as he might have in leaner financial days, the smooth cut and expensive feel of the fabric as it slipped into place over his broad shoulders.

A mildly frustrated sigh escaped his lips as he gathered his ammunition: paperwork on every sale the company had made in the last year, showing that each was legitimate and clean. He raked a hand through his short black hair, shaking his head at the fact that through the years his boss had managed to create a multi-million dollar company, but couldn't hold his fears at bay when the IRS poked its nose into his business. Making his way to the conference room, he tried to concentrate on keeping his brows from furrowing, of their own volition, into a fierce frown, and even managed to exchange smiles with a few colleagues he passed along the way.

His life had been busy of late. He'd worked nonstop to reach the position he had with the company. His forte was people: he understood them, liked them, and knew how to sell to them. His meteoric rise through the upper echelons of the sales division for the country's largest medical supply company had come as no surprise to his colleagues. Amazingly enough, no one seemed to resent the fact that he'd entered the company as a twenty-five-year-old kid, fresh from college, and in five short years had risen to sit comfortably as the vice president over sales. He was too darn nice to resent, and he knew it.

Had been nice, he corrected himself grimly as he continued down the hallway. He didn't feel so nice anymore, although he managed to mask that fact at work and church. His associates still saw the same carefree man they'd come to know, and if they noticed a certain edge to his demeanor of late, they respected him enough not to comment on it.

What he needed was a change of pace. Maybe when this infernal audit had run its course and he was free of its clutches, he would take a nice, long vacation and sort through his life. One thing was certain: he wasn't sure how much longer he could keep running at his current pace before finally spontaneously combusting into a ball of frustrated fury. It was an image that had him ghoulishly grinning in spite of himself, and he almost laughed out loud.

It wasn't as though he had no idea why he'd become slightly embittered; he merely chose to avoid thinking about it. He rubbed the tensed muscles on the back of his neck and turned a corner.

The conference room was full when he entered. He tamped down an irrational urge to scream at the lot of them, and instead pasted on his "people face." It was his best asset, and one that usually didn't require energy to summon. He enjoyed his job and the associations he had formed through the years. If only he could distance himself from the problems he faced at work, he might find it a bit easier to master his irritability. Unfortunately, work followed him home, to the grocery store, to the gym, to church, on his dates. He was never free from the stresses of his job.

He smiled and took his seat. Straightening his tie, he made joking reference to the fact that he felt as though he'd just entered the jungle of death. Everyone laughed, the mood relaxed a bit, and his colleagues sat back to let him work the magic he did so well, putting people at ease and making tense situations seem a bit less dire. He was their strongest advocate; no one doubted it for a moment.

* * * * * *

Connor smashed the racquetball into the wall with such force that when it came back and imprinted itself in his forehead, he hadn't even seen it coming. It was odd, he thought as he lay prostrate on his back, that life's moments of greatest clarity came at such inopportune times. He wasn't content; that was the problem. Aside from work-related concerns, he had a great job, a great house, a great car, great friends, great parents and siblings, but no contentment. No real peace. Sure, he was at peace with who he was, with his work ethic and integrity, but something vital was missing.

He was lonely.

He'd always planned on having a family of his own someday, but he wasn't about to go out wife-hunting merely for the sake of having a wife. He didn't want just any wife. He'd tried going after that once before.

The image of his boss's face swam above his head. "Are you okay, O'Brian?"

Connor slowly sat up and ran a hand across his forehead. A perfect ending to a less than perfect day. He nodded. "I'm fine." His eyes narrowed in confusion. "I think I saw this happen in a movie once."

His boss, Dan Fernatelli, placed a hand under his arm and helped him rise. "I think you should go home now, O'Brian. You've been putting in a lot of time here, and I appreciate it. Go get some rest."

Connor nodded absently, making his way toward the door of the racquetball court. Home. There's no place like home. That was from another movie, wasn't it? He reached for the doorknob, his hand brushing past it on his first attempt.

"Here, let me get that for you," Dan said, leaning forward.

"No, no, it's okay. I'll just grab the one in the middle." Connor blinked fuzzily, reaching again for the elusive doorknob.

"I don't think you should drive home," Dan stated definitively. "I'll take you there myself."

"Oh, I don't think so. My house is a bit of a mess, and I'm really not in the mood to entertain tonight," Connor replied, grinning crookedly and stumbling across the threshold of the racquetball court and into the hallway.

"Easy there, friend," Dan replied, a worried expression finally crossing his features. "I think we should make a stop on our way home."

* * * * * *

Connor pushed his front door open with two fingers. It wasn't locked. The cold chill that he felt in his soul had nothing to do with the fact that he was the recent victim of a mild concussion. He stepped inside, his boss close behind.

"Wow. You weren't kidding. It *is* a mess!"

The entire house had been trashed. Completely and utterly dismantled. Connor stepped unsteadily inside, unable to fully absorb the shock at the wreckage his home had become. "I . . . I . . ."

Dan stared. "This isn't your doing?"

Connor squinted at the man. "Are you kidding?" Reality finally assaulted his senses, making him see red. "Why would I do this to my own house?!" He kicked and shuffled his way to the kitchen, where he found the portable phone on the floor. He picked it up, only to realize it had been dropped and the batteries were missing. Rather than sort through the mess, he instead pulled his mobile phone from his attaché case, his head throbbing and fingers trembling in a mixture of disbelief and fear.

He punched the three magic numbers and put the phone to his ear, surveying the wreckage. His home. His belongings. His *life*. He felt utterly and completely violated. The impotence and vulnerability he felt on top of it all compounded his anger tenfold.

Dan stood uncertainly to the side, watching his employee with growing alarm. "Do you know who did this?" he finally asked.

Connor shook his head, his eyes closed. His call was finally answered. "Nine-one-one emergency."

He sucked in a breath. "Someone broke into my house." He didn't recognize the sound of his own voice. It was wooden and flat, even to his own ears. Had someone asked him an hour later about the details of his conversation with the woman on the other end of the line, he'd not have remembered a word. He must have said something right, however; the police arrived within minutes.

Dan hovered around Connor until he was finally asked to get out of the way. "Are you sure you'll be all right?"

Connor nodded. "I'll be fine. I'll see you tomorrow."

His boss hesitated. "Do you think this has anything to do with the audit?"

Connor looked the man in the face a full five seconds before answering. "I'll let you know. And thanks for your concern."

"I didn't mean . . ."

"I know you didn't." Connor rubbed a hand along his aching head. "It can't have anything to do with the audit, Dan, because the audit is inconsequential. If you had done something wrong, then I might wonder."

Dan patted Connor awkwardly on the shoulder and mumbled an apology. Making his way to the door, he stopped, looked back once, shook his head, and finally made his exit.

Connor closed the door behind him with a flourish and barely resisted a literal snarl. His home had been virtually destroyed, and all Dan could think about was that it might be connected to the audit. He leaned against the closed door and hung his head, rubbing the bridge of his nose between his thumb and forefinger and wondering if he'd be able to sleep when the time came. He didn't know why someone had broken in, but he knew one thing with certainty. It had happened once before, five months earlier, right after Allyson's death.

Chapter 3

I can't believe you're actually leaving me."

Liz smiled. "It's only temporary. I'm going to attempt saving my sister from insanity." She looked around at the "office" where Bump housed his company as though committing it to memory. She loved the beautiful old Victorian-style home that had been completely renovated and restored to its splendor of days gone by, but decorated with masculine appointments and furnished with large, contemporary overstuffed furniture in rich earth tones. She had enjoyed her time spent in these surroundings—until recently, at least. She'd miss the place.

The man seated at the computer snorted. "Yeah. And you'll find a job at a PI company in Virginia that pays you better than this one. I'll never see you again."

"You'll just be missing all the money I've been bringing in. I don't flatter myself into thinking you'll be missing me for my charm."

The man known to his friends as "Bump" sighed and pushed back from his computer screen. "I'll miss your money *and* your charm. Are you sure this is what you want to do?"

Liz regarded her friend with her head cocked to one side, taking in the dark, shoulder-length hair that was pulled into a ponytail, the intense amber-colored eyes and the powerful, sculpted physique. In addition to his striking appearance, he was, quite possibly, the smartest person she knew. He was brilliant with electronics and gadgets, and had an uncanny sense at sniffing out the unknown, which made him perfect in his role as the head of Seattle's fastest-growing private investigative firm. "Why don't you find yourself a nice woman and settle down, Bump? Don't you think you've broken enough hearts for one lifetime?"

"I've been after you forever, but you just won't have me." Bump grinned and folded his muscled arms across his chest. "You've spoiled me for anyone else."

Liz laughed and leaned forward to land a playful smack on his leg as she sat in a chair opposite his. "That's a lie and you know it. You couldn't settle on just one woman if your life depended on it."

Bump's smile slowly faded as he closely examined the telltale signs of fatigue marring Liz's otherwise impeccable beauty. "Are you okay, hon? What's going on with you?"

Liz sighed. "I'm tired of doing this. I need a break, and Amber offered to share her husband and kids for a while." She drew her knees up to her chest and hugged her legs. "I don't know what I want."

Bump regarded her quietly for a long time. "You've been miserable, and you've never said a word to me about it." He paused, speculatively studying her in concern. "I should never have let you talk me into letting you take over Crystal's position when she left."

Liz shrugged. "It was my own choice. There was no reason I couldn't have done her job."

"You're different. I've never been comfortable having you do her job."

Liz quirked the corner of her mouth into a jaded smile. "I've been making enough money to live in a great apartment and dress well. What more could a girl want?"

She raised her eyebrows as Bump swore derisively at her. "Give me a break, Liz. You're not some shallow woman who can't think beyond climbing the steps of a social ladder. Don't insult me by suggesting I don't know you any better."

Liz dropped her head to her knees and closed her eyes. "I'm stagnating. I'm frustrated and I'm lonely. I need my sister's company for a while." She raised her head and looked bleakly at her friend. "Maybe it'll help."

Bump nodded slowly as he tipped back on his chair. "Maybe it will. You know you'll always have a job here if you need it. A job doing what you were *originally* hired to do." He paused and looked at her closely. "If you need anything at all, I'll be here. Keep my number programmed into your cell phone."

Liz smiled. "As always." She rose and offered her hand. "I'll miss you."

Bump stood and brushed her hand aside, gathering her into his arms and squeezing for a moment. "I respect you, Liz. I don't say that to just anyone, you know."

She smiled softly. "I know."

* * * * *

Connor rang the doorbell when he tried the door and found it locked. He smiled broadly at the woman who opened it.

"Dr. Montgomery. I brought you something." He held out a box of Godiva chocolates to his friend and kissed her cheek.

"Oh!" She hugged him fiercely and drew back with a huge grin. "You know me too well. And do I ever need this tonight." Motioning him into the house, she closed the door behind him. She was dressed in her scrubs from the hospital, and her curly hair was pulled back into a ponytail. "I am so tired," she sighed. "So is Tyler. He had the kids today while I worked, and he looks worse for the wear than I do."

The subject of her discussion materialized as they entered the kitchen at the back of the house. He was wiping down the counters with one hand, a dishrag over his shoulder and several *Star Wars* action figures in his other hand. He turned to Connor and rolled his eyes.

"Izzy threw up twice today, not because she's sick, but because she's got a gag reflex that would kill a horse."

Connor laughed. "What are you feeding her that she's gagging on? She's only a year old."

"Eighteen months. She's old enough to eat like a regular person, and she's making me crazy." Tyler ran the sponge under a stream of warm water and wrung it dry. He attacked another spot on the counter with the languid energy of one who has spent an entire day with two or more children. "And Ian refuses to pick up his toys. He strings them all over the house, and when I tell him to pick them up, he says his legs hurt and he has to sit down." He gestured angrily with the action figures he clutched in his fist. "Well these, I tell you, are going in the garbage. Then maybe he'll learn."

Amber gently pried Qui-Gon Gin and Obi-Wan from his grasp, rescuing them from certain annihilation by placing them in a cupboard above the sink, well out of reach of a three-year-old's clever and wandering fingers. "Leave them up there for a while, then when he's grieved enough, you can give them back to him. He'll be much wiser and more considerate for the experience, trust me."

Amber kissed Tyler on the cheek and gestured for Connor to sit on a stool next to the island. She brushed her hair off her forehead and sighed. "Can you stay for a while? I'm going to hop in the shower now that the kids are down; Tyler and I were planning on getting some pizza. Have you eaten?"

"Yeah, but there's always room for pizza. Are you sure I'm not interrupting an intimate evening or something?"

Tyler snorted. "Are you kidding? Where would we get the energy?" He gestured toward a small box Connor had carried into the house. "What do you have there?"

"I don't know. Some stuff my mom sent and said you might be interested in. She remembered the O'Brian you were doing research for and thought you would want to see this."

Connor didn't miss the look his friends exchanged. Amber cleared her throat. "You mean the friend that led us to you?"

"Yes. I think that must be the one." Connor had met Tyler and Amber Montgomery shortly after the two had married and traveled to Utah to do some research for a "friend" by the last name of O'Brian. He had never met the friend, and they had spoken of him only in the vaguest of terms. It was something he'd always wondered about, but he had never found the right time to ask for more details. Well, enough was enough. *There's no time like the present.*

"So when are you going to tell me more about this guy?" Connor watched his friends squirm. Amber pursed her lips, and Tyler continued wiping a spot on the counter that didn't require further cleaning.

Amber turned to her husband. "How about I shower first. You call out for pizza. We may need strength." She patted his hand with a wry smile and turned to go upstairs. "Oh," she looked back. "Have you heard any more about your house?"

Connor shook his head. "No prints, nothing left behind, nothing at all to suggest who might have done it."

"Was anything taken?"

"No. It's just like last time. Everything was dumped from shelves and drawers, things ripped off the walls, but nothing was stolen." He shook his head again, one eyebrow quirked. "I don't get it."

Amber turned again to leave the room, calling over her shoulder, "Well, maybe it's time you came to live with us."

Connor laughed. "I don't think so," he said. "I worked long and hard for that condo. I'm not going anywhere."

Thirty minutes later found the trio seated in Tyler and Amber's family room, snarfing pizza and guzzling diet drinks. "I really needed this," Amber said on a sigh. "I'll finish it off with the chocolates and be in absolute heaven."

Connor smiled. "Do you work tomorrow?"

"It depends. Define 'work.' Technically, no. I don't go to the hospital tomorrow. I'm home with the kids."

"Yes, while I get to go on vacation. To my office." Tyler smiled and took a large bite of his pizza, pulling at the strings of cheese that tore loose from the mother ship but didn't quite make it into his mouth. He chewed and swallowed, winking at Amber. "I'll call you every hour, on the hour, to monitor your distress."

She shook her head. "You're so kind."

Tyler laughed. "Connor's going to think we don't like our kids. We really do, you know. We've just both realized that being a full-time caregiver is harder than being a doctor or a CPA."

"It's so true," Amber interjected. "We wouldn't trade it for the world, but it's not easy. We're lucky, though. At least one of us gets to be with the kids every day. Not every couple has such flexible work schedules."

Connor nodded. "You guys are lucky. Your kids are cute. You've got a great family." He felt a familiar pang of envy and shoved it aside. "So," he said, setting his plate down on the coffee table and wiping his hands on a napkin. "Should we open this box?"

Amber nodded and patted the seat next to her on the couch. "Come sit here. Tyler, you sit on the other side."

"Are you expecting something huge here?" Tyler asked as he set his own plate down and moved to follow her directions.

"I don't know. I feel all antsy."

Connor picked up the small box his mother had sent and positioned himself between his friends. Taking the pocketknife that was attached to his keys, he began cutting the tape. "My mom called yesterday to say this was on its way, and that I should open it with you. She thinks you'll really appreciate what's inside, given your interest in Civil War stuff and genealogy."

He finished cutting the tape across the middle of the box and put away his knife. Carefully opening the flaps, he dumped the foam peanuts onto the floor. He cast a look over his shoulder to Amber, who sat at his right. "Breathe," he said with a grin.

She took a large breath and smacked his shoulder with the back of her hand. "Just show me what's in the box."

Connor lifted all four flaps back to reveal two small books, which appeared aged. The sharp intake of breath on either side was unmistakable. He looked first to his left, then his right. His friends were staring transfixed at the book lying on top.

Tyler was the first to move. He lifted the top book with a shaking hand and held it tightly, as though it might disappear at any moment. Amber leaned forward and stared around Connor at her husband. She was the first to find her voice.

"Is that what I think it is?" she whispered.

Tyler nodded. Connor stared in disbelief at the tear forming in Tyler's eye that soon spilled over and traced a lone path down his handsome cheek. He'd never seen his friend cry. *What the . . .* was all he could think.

Tyler cleared his throat and wiped at his face. "Sorry," he said, glancing at Connor, who turned at Amber's sniffle and looked at the woman beside him.

"What is all this?" he finally asked.

Amber rested her elbows on her knees, massaging her temples with her fingers. "We, uh . . . " She wiped at tears of her own, then reached into the box Connor still held in his lap and picked up the second book, carefully opening it and leafing through the first few pages. After a soft exclamation of surprise, she turned to Tyler. "It's Ian's journal," she murmured.

"You're kidding."

She shook her head. Thumbing through the book, she paused here and there until she reached a page where she stopped completely. She slowly turned to Connor, who appeared completely baffled. "Who else has seen this, do you know?"

Connor lifted his shoulders in a shrug, one brow arched. "My mom, probably. I don't know of anyone else. Do you mind if I take a look at it?"

Amber hesitated, then handed him the book, still open to the page that had given her pause. Connor glanced down at the neatly written script, the pages yellowed with age and the ink faded.

> *Much has happened recently. I handed the evidence of General Montgomery's treachery over to General Grant last week. I am much relieved to have rid myself of the burden. I think often of Amber and Tyler, and wonder where they are. I spoke to young Boyd two days ago, who is mending well. He sorely misses the good Doctor Saxton, and I must admit, his feelings are a mirror of my own.*
>
> *Boyd told me that no one has seen Tyler or Amber since the night I left for General Grant's camp. Supposedly, General Montgomery and Major Edwards have sworn on their lives that one moment Tyler and Amber were with them, and the next they were gone. Of course, nobody gives their words much credence anymore. Their ramblings have been dismissed as lunacy, and their credibility concerning anything substantial has been ruined beyond repair in light of all their illegal and horrendous activities.*
>
> *I alone know the truth. Tyler was right. He told me he and Amber might suddenly disappear. I hope they've gone safely home . . .*

Connor stared dubiously at the writing before him. Tyler had been looking over his shoulder, and leaned back as he finished reading the words on the page. Connor pursed his lips, biting the inside of his cheek in scrutiny as he read the words again. Tyler and Amber remained silent until he looked up, waiting for answers they didn't seem ready to give him.

"Well?" was all he managed.

"Well." Amber's response came out on a sigh. She scratched her forehead and wrinkled her nose. "Hmm. Where to start."

"I don't suppose the fact that there's an Amber and a Tyler mentioned here is a freak coincidence?"

"No, it's not a coincidence."

Connor nodded slowly, continuing. "And what year was this written? Let's see . . ." He flipped back a page to the dated entry. "December 29, 1862." He looked up at his friends. "So you two are what, immortal? I'd look for sharp fangs, but then I've seen you out in broad daylight."

Amber snorted and Tyler laughed out loud. "No, bloodsuckers we're not. We . . . um . . ." He paused, sobering, then held up the book he still clutched in his hand. "Connor, this is the book that converted me. That, and witnessing one very special blessing."

Connor glanced at the cover. "The Book of Mormon. It converts a lot of people."

"No. *This very copy* is the one I read." Tyler shook the book gently back and forth. "I read this exact book."

Connor looked from Tyler to Amber and back again. "What are you saying—that you hopped in a DeLorean and went for a ride?"

Tyler looked at his wife for help. She took pity on him. "Connor," she began slowly, "we don't know how it happened. We think we know why, but the actual 'how' of the whole thing is still a mystery."

Connor said nothing. Amber took a deep breath and continued. "One night when I was working a shift as a resident at George Washington, I saw this guy come in with a gunshot wound. It was Tyler, and he was dressed in a Civil War Confederate Army uniform." She gestured toward her husband. "I'd never met him before, and the chief resident told me to go back to the lounge and get some sleep. As I walked back down the hall, I got hit in the head with a door and knocked out. When I came to, I was in a Union Army hospital and the date was October 16, 1862."

She stopped, closely scrutinizing his face.

Connor still said nothing.

She took a deep breath and continued. "Tyler had been attacked in his office that same night and knocked out as well. When he woke up, he was in the same place I was. We met, and well, weird things happened . . ."

Connor shook his head, finally finding his voice. "Are you guys in league with my mother or something? I mean, she's never been one for practical jokes, but is this supposed to be funny or something?"

"What, are you kidding?" Tyler's voice bordered on sharp. He gestured again with the book he still held. "You think we'd joke about something like *this?*" He stood and began pacing in front of the hearth. "I've never really understood all of the experience," he said as he walked. "I've mulled it over a million times, Amber and I have talked about it, and there are things we'll probably *never* understand." He paused and ran an agitated hand through his hair. "One thing I'll never do, though, is discount the fact that it brought me to Amber, and it brought me to this." He held the book in front of him. "This book brought me peace, and Amber is my life. I'd do it again in a heartbeat if I had to."

Connor shook his head, his brows furrowed in a deep frown. "I don't get it. I'm sorry, but I don't. Okay, it's not a joke, but . . ."

Amber interrupted. "Would you like to hear the whole story?"

"Yes, I think I would."

Chapter 4

"Tyler, sit down. We've done this once before."

Tyler's jaw clenched. "I'd rather stand."

"Fine. But quit pacing. You're making me dizzy." Amber turned to Connor. "That journal was written by your ancestor, Ian O'Brian, probably about five or so generations back. We met him and became friends. He's the reason we looked up your family in the first place." She paused, her eyes filling with tears. "We wanted to meet his descendants." She touched the back of her fingers to Connor's cheek, a tear spilling down her face. "You look so much like him. Your eyes are exactly like his. I've never seen such blue eyes."

Tyler and Amber talked late into the night, sharing their experiences with Connor and telling him a tale so wild and unbelievable that he could only shake his head. Had he been listening to anyone else, he'd have thought they were insane. Completely and certifiably insane.

But they weren't insane; that was the problem. He knew the Montgomerys like he knew his own family. And in the end, when the hour was way past midnight, all he could do was believe them.

The three sat sprawled on various pieces of furniture, looking for all the world as though they'd survived an atomic blast.

"I don't want you to think," Connor commented, turning to Tyler, "that I was mocking your conversion, or ever would." His mind's eye shifted to a small cottage near London, where he'd witnessed the conversion of two of the sweetest elderly people ever to walk the planet. No, a person's relationship with God was something he respected. "When I asked if this whole thing was a joke, I didn't mean your testimony or anything . . ." He trailed off.

Tyler brushed it aside. "No big deal. I know what you meant. It's not exactly an easy story to swallow."

"You said you'd done this once before," Connor commented to Amber. "When?"

"You mean explaining the story?"

He nodded.

"We told my parents and Liz right after it happened." Amber smiled softly. "They thought we were nuts."

Connor raised one eyebrow. "I can't imagine why."

She laughed. "Come here," she said, standing. "I want to show you something." She led the way to her and Tyler's bedroom. The two men followed behind her. She walked into the spacious closet and reached into a far corner, high on a shelf. Retrieving a large box, she hefted it down and walked back out into the bedroom. She lifted the lid and proceeded to lay clothing on the bed—one black dress with a large white apron, and a gray Confederate Army uniform.

"This is what we were wearing when we came back," she said. She picked up the edge of the white apron and rubbed it through her thumb and forefinger, gazing at the dress as though she couldn't really see it. "Every now and then, when I look at these clothes, I can smell the place and hear the marching." Her words were hushed, sending a chill down Connor's spine.

Amber shook herself. She laughed, apparently trying to dispel the mood. "I keep trying to tell Tyler we should wear these to a costume party someday, but he won't set foot in that uniform."

Tyler shuddered. "No thanks. I don't even know why we're keeping it. I hate that thing."

"You hated it all that much?" Connor studied his friend with curiosity.

"Yeah. It reminds me of the general."

"That bad, huh?"

"He was an evil man. It wouldn't have surprised me if he had sprouted horns and found a pitchfork to carry."

* * * * * *

It was late when Connor left. Tyler wondered what his friend really thought of all they'd told him. He seemed to believe it, but who knew? It wasn't exactly a plausible story. He sat on the edge of the bed, taking his socks off and balling them together, throwing them into the hamper just inside the doorway of the walk-in closet. He wandered out of the bedroom and into the hallway, spying Amber as she entered Ian's bedroom. He followed her inside and watched as she bent and kissed the sleeping child, giving him a small squeeze as Ian turned restlessly in his sleep. "Mommy loves you," he heard her whisper.

Approaching Amber, he put an arm about her shoulders and squeezed. Then he moved forward and kissed the sleeping boy himself, feeling the love swell in his heart, wondering how he'd ever been impatient with the child earlier in the day. He turned to Amber and whispered, "I think I'll get the *Star Wars* stuff out of the cupboard."

"No you don't!" She pointed at him in reproach. "You leave them there! He's cute while he's sleeping, but tomorrow he'll be dropping toys all over the house again." She smiled at her husband. "You're pathetic, you know."

Tyler heaved a sigh and straightened. "I know."

The couple wandered into Isabelle's room and kissed her as well, touching her soft skin and inhaling the delectable scent of bathed child. Amber nuzzled the spot just behind her ear and whispered again, "Mommy loves you, sweet girl."

Tyler followed Amber down the hallway. She picked up toys as she walked, humming softly to herself. He smiled. The tune was "All Through the Night." She was strong in ways his own mother had not been, and she was a fun and loving mother to their children. She was the other half of his soul; had he not found her he knew he'd be living a lonely and bitter existence.

He reached for her wrist as they entered their bedroom, pulling her close and resting his head on hers. "I love you," he murmured.

He felt her smile. "I love you, too."

He glanced over at the bed where the Civil War clothes still lay, and released her with a sigh. "You get ready for bed," he said. "I'll put these away."

Tyler heard his wife brushing her teeth in the large bathroom adjacent to the closet. He carefully folded the clothes and placed them back in their former resting place. He shuddered involuntarily as his fingers touched the uniform he'd been wearing when he nearly lost his life. Clenching his teeth, he shoved it firmly into the box and placed the lid on tightly. As he made his way to the closet, he spied Amber in the bathroom. He felt himself relax. Shoving the box back onto the high shelf in the corner, he reflected on thoughts he'd often encountered since meeting his wife.

Whatever the price, it had been worth it.

* * * * * *

Connor walked slowly into his living room, carefully placing the box his mother had sent on the couch, where he sank down with a sigh. He really was long overdue for some rest. The story he'd heard from his friends had left him feeling drained. He couldn't seem to stop thinking about it, and no wonder. It was a fantastic tale, and he was sure it would play itself out in his head for a long time to come.

His thoughts of their experiences kept mingling with memories from his mission in England. So many people, so many different lives—he'd been touched and blessed in many ways by them all. His mind again came to rest on the image of the Holmes cottage. It really was time to write to the sweet old couple. It'd been months since he last had contact with them. He checked his watch and mentally counted the time difference between Virginia and England. Maybe in the morning he'd give them a call.

He finally stood and surveyed the state of his home as he moved to the kitchen to check his messages. The bulk of the mess had been cleaned up, and his insurance company was promising money shortly to replace what had been destroyed. He shook his head, wondering again about the purpose behind the break-in, and was unable to conjure up any further possibilities. He sighed and began rummaging through his pantry for a snack.

A big chunk of chocolate would be nice, he mused as he scrounged through the shelves, although he knew it was time to grocery shop and he'd probably not find anything edible. It was wishful thinking, at best. When was the last time a chunk of chocolate had magically appeared in his kitchen? His hand brushed across a smooth piece of paper, and he pulled it out to examine it under the kitchen light.

He caught his breath as he viewed the photograph he held. It was a picture of him with his arm draped around the shoulders of his now-dead fiancée. The shock of seeing it unexpectedly was enough to send him slowly sinking onto a chair by his kitchen table. He did nothing for a long moment, staring at the faces of the man and woman who were as much strangers to him as any he might encounter on the streets. Her face was that of a person he thought he'd known, but hadn't, really. The image of his own face staring back at him was one he barely recognized. The smile was strained, the lines around the eyes more than a little telling.

The picture had been taken at a company picnic, about two weeks before she'd taken a last-minute trip to Colorado—a family reunion, she'd told him before she left—where she'd lost her life. He shook his head. That picture should never have been taken. He should have broken the engagement *weeks* earlier. No, he should never have proposed in the first place. That was the most obvious fact of all.

His teeth were hurting. He attempted to relax his jaw, which had clenched of its own accord when he'd realized what he was holding in his hand. Standing, he ripped the picture clean in two and tossed it in a waste basket as he made his way down the hallway and into his bedroom. He walked into the adjoining bathroom and turned on the shower, waiting as steam enveloped the room before returning to the bedroom and plunking himself unceremoniously onto the bed. He pulled off his shoes and threw them in the general direction of the closet. It wasn't as though he was making a mess, he reasoned numbly, fighting a surge of irrational laughter.

His mind groped for something to divert itself from its current unpleasant train. What was it he'd been thinking about before he'd found the picture? Ah, yes. Time travel. Nothing like a little bit of impossibility to take one's mind off one's troubles.

* * * * * *

As Liz's plane made its descent into Virginia, she stared out the window at the green countryside below. The early-morning sun slanted through the airplane windows, making her squint in response. She closed her eyes and clutched her armrests as the plane dipped. Her stomach protested at the movement, and she regretted the insane impulse that had convinced her she didn't need to bother with motion-sickness pills this time. She only hoped the plane would land before she disgraced herself in front of two hundred other passengers.

When the plane finally came to a stop at the gate, she took her time collecting her bags and waited until nearly everyone else had disembarked before she ventured forward herself. The sight that greeted her in the terminal nearly brought tears to her eyes. There stood her sister's children, holding balloons and jumping with excitement. A few yards away stood her sister, looking as beautiful as ever. Her chestnut-colored hair fell in curls to her shoulders, and her eyes, the same exact shade as Liz's, glowed as she smiled.

Liz stooped to envelop both children in a huge embrace and smiled, misty-eyed, at Amber. "I've missed you guys," she said, hugging the children tightly.

"Aunt Liz," began her three-year-old nephew, Ian. "We got these balloons for you. Can I keep them?"

Liz laughed and tweaked his little nose. "Sure you can, buddy." She leaned over to kiss the beautiful little girl who was the very image of her mother. "How are you, little Isabelle?" Her niece smiled and patted Liz's face with her chubby little hands.

"Not at all shy, are they?" Amber came to stand behind her children and hugged Liz fiercely as she stood. "You look good," she said as she pulled back, still holding Liz's shoulders and looking into her face. "Tired, but good."

Liz laughed. "Glad I pass your inspection. Let's get out of here," she said as she reached down to pick up her niece. Amber hefted Ian up on one hip, and the women made their way to the baggage claim.

"The clothes and other stuff you shipped came yesterday. I put everything away for you in the guest room." Amber watched as the suitcases came barreling down the conveyor belt.

"Thanks. I really appreciate this." Liz ran a hand through her hair. "I needed a vacation more than I thought."

"No problem." Amber grinned at her sister. "It's more of a favor to me, you know. This mom stuff is harder than I ever dreamed it would be."

Liz reflected on her sister's past drive to finish medical school and establish herself as a respected physician. So many things had changed for her when she met the man who became her husband. Their story was an odd one, to be sure. But one thing she knew from simple observation: Tyler and Amber loved each other completely and without reservation. All else seemed secondary. The children had brought a dimension to Amber's personality that seemed to have deepened her appreciation for life.

"You look happy," Liz said, putting an arm about Amber's shoulders and pulling her close.

"I am happy." Amber smiled and kissed Liz's cheek. "Twice as much, now that you're here."

Amber sat down at the kitchen island with a sigh and smiled at Liz, who was seated at the table perusing the newspaper and eating pretzels. "Finally," Amber breathed. "I think they're asleep. Every single night Ian comes up with fifty million different ways to prolong the inevitable."

Liz smiled. "They're sweet, Amber. I can't believe how much they've grown." The last time she'd seen the children was a year earlier, when Isabelle had been blessed.

"Yeah, it happens fast. Next thing you know, I'll be a grand-mother." Amber grinned and looked at her watch. "Tyler ought to be home soon. His company's helping with an audit on a medical supply company, and he's been putting in some long hours."

Liz nodded. "How are things going with you two?"

"Really well. The kids have stressed him out, but in a good way." Amber laughed. "He never really saw himself as a father, so it's been a real eye-opener for him."

Liz decided to pry. "He never thought much of his own father, did he?"

Amber shook her head. "That man was evil. How Tyler ever made it into adulthood intact is a credit to his mother's early efforts and his own will." She stopped talking as the sound of the garage door opening reached the kitchen. "Speak of the devil," she smiled.

Tyler opened the door connecting the garage to the kitchen and stepped through, plopping his briefcase unceremoniously on the countertop and heaving a huge sigh. He ran a hand through his hair and began loosening his tie when he glanced up and saw the women looking at him expectantly.

"Well, look what the cat dragged in," he said, grinning at Liz. He moved around the island in the middle of the kitchen to embrace her as she stood to greet him. He hugged her tightly, then pulled back holding both her hands in his. "You look great, as usual, little sister." He leaned forward to plant a kiss on her cheek.

Liz laughed. "Always the charmer, aren't you Tyler?"

Amber snorted. "He wasn't always so charming, trust me." She hid a smile as Tyler looked at her with a scowl on his face.

"A fat lot you know, Mrs. Montgomery," he scoffed as he released Liz's hands and approached his wife. He planted a familiar kiss on her lips and leered. "I was charming when I needed to be."

"Hmm. Whatever." Amber placed her hands on either side of his face and kissed him again with a comically loud smacking sound.

Liz laughed. "Man, you'd think two old married people would get tired of that after a while."

Tyler turned his head to look at her over his shoulder. "Never," he grinned. He winked at Amber and moved to the fridge, where he began pawing through its contents. "Don't mind me," he said. "I'm starving. So what's new with you, anyway?" His voice was muffled and directed at Liz.

"Nothing, really. I guess that's why I'm here. You guys are supposed to provide me with some excitement."

Tyler backed out of the fridge and absently replied, "Excitement huh? Right now I'd settle for some food that looked edible." He dove into the fridge again to attempt another round at foraging for food.

Amber looked guiltily at Liz. "I need to go grocery shopping. It's still my least favorite thing to do, so I always put it off until the last minute."

Tyler reemerged, holding a bowl and looking bemused. "What is this? Wait—let me rephrase that. What *was* this?" He looked at Amber, an expression of patient speculation covering his features.

Amber moved from the stool and snatched the bowl from his hand. "Nothing," she hastily replied. "I need to clean out the fridge." She dumped the whole bowl of frightening green fuzz into the garbage can and slammed the lid.

Liz laughed out loud. "Amber, you haven't changed." She turned to Tyler. "You should have seen the stuff we'd find in her fridge when she was in college. Talk about yuck!"

Amber made a face. "Yeah . . . Amber was always the messy one, and Liz was always the clean one. Well, clean is boring and predictable."

Liz grinned. "Predictability isn't such a bad thing, especially if it helps you find food in the fridge." She winked at Tyler.

Tyler shook his head and reached for the phone book. "Well, honey, I suppose it's comforting to know you've stayed consistent, at least." He flipped through the pages while Liz laughed at her sister who was scowling at both of them. He stopped turning pages and grabbed the phone. "Chinese, anyone?"

Forty-five minutes later, the threesome sat at a table overflowing with Chinese take-out cartons. Liz piled more food onto her plate than she'd allowed herself to eat at one sitting for ages it seemed, and she relaxed, propping her feet up on an empty chair. She was dressed casually in gray sweatpants and a white T-shirt, her hair pulled back into a ponytail and her face scrubbed clean from any traces of makeup. She sighed with contentment.

"I can't remember the last time I felt this good," she mused aloud.

Amber nodded. "I figured as much. You've lost a ton of weight, and you're eating like a starved woman. What have you been doing to yourself?"

"Nothing." She sounded more defensive than she'd intended. "Nothing, really." Her tone softened as she picked her way through some shrimp fried rice. "My job was really demanding, in an odd way. I've been stressed . . . my appetite hasn't been what it usually is."

She caught Amber's scowl and returned it with one of her own. "I'm not stupid, you know. I've been eating. I just . . . haven't eaten as well as I probably ought . . ." Her voice faded, and she looked back down into the food she'd been restlessly stirring. "I haven't much felt like it."

Amber was quiet for a moment. "I know, Liz. It's just that I know you, and I know you weren't happy. I didn't like your job because *you* didn't like your job."

Tyler had remained silent. "Well, now we're all happy, aren't we," he interjected. "We're getting full on the best kind of food to ever grace this fair planet, and then we're going to watch videos until the wee hours of the morning." He paused and grinned at Liz. "That's what we old married people do for fun now. Throw kids into the mix, and the concept of a 'night on the town' changes just a bit."

Liz laughed. "Actually, your version of fun sounds really good right about now. I've had nothing but 'nights on the town' lately, and they haven't been all that great."

Amber smirked. "You were with the wrong people, my dear. Following cheating husbands around would put a bit of a damper on the evening for anyone."

"Isn't that the truth," Liz muttered. "You have no idea . . ."

She was interrupted by a knock at the front door. Tyler stood to answer it, and returned with a couple dressed in elegant formalwear.

"Connor!" Liz's heart constricted as she recognized the man standing before them in a tux. He held his arms out to her and she laughingly returned the embrace. "Look at you! Where are you going?" She glanced at the beautiful woman who stood back a foot or two and was sizing Liz up and down the way only women can do to each other. Liz stiffened at the perusal.

Tyler interceded. "Connor, would you like to introduce us to your friend?"

Connor O'Brian cleared his throat and held his hand out to the woman who stood near his side. "This is Brenda Matthias. She's an associate of mine. Brenda," he turned to his date, "these are the friends I was telling you about. Tyler and Amber Montgomery, and Liz Saxton, Amber's sister."

"Charmed." The woman practically purred the sentiment and offered her hand to Tyler. She had apparently decided not to bestow the same privilege upon the two women; when Tyler released her hand, she promptly wrapped both of her arms around one of Connor's as though he were the only available life raft on a sinking ship.

Connor behaved as though the woman clinging to his arm was not present. "So Liz," he said, "are you here on vacation?"

Liz smiled. "A vacation of sorts. I'm going to stay here for a while and help Amber and Tyler play with the kids."

"Well, it's good to see you. We'll have to double up again and beat these two in tennis." He motioned toward Tyler and Amber with his head. "It's been a while."

"Ha. That was sheer luck. You'd never be able to do it twice." Tyler laughed and nudged Amber, who was viewing Ms. Matthias through narrowed eyes.

"Yeah. Sheer luck," she finally acknowledged, exchanging a quick glance with her sister.

Liz bit the insides of her cheeks to keep from openly smirking. She knew exactly what Amber was thinking of the willowy woman who seemed to be attempting to occupy the same space on the planet as her date. If she pushed any closer to him, she'd knock him to the floor—a prospect the woman might not have found entirely disappointing.

"Anytime, anyplace. Luck had nothing to do with it." Liz did her best to ignore the woman who was currently shooting daggers with her eyes in Liz's general direction.

The corner of Connor's mouth turned up in a smile and he nodded. "Too true," he acknowledged and turned to Tyler. "I'm sorry to bother you on a Friday night, but I was wondering if you had those papers ready for me to show Dan."

Tyler nodded. "Right here, in fact. I finished them today." Tyler reached for his briefcase sitting on the countertop, extracted a folder, and handed it to Connor. "I hope this works for you."

"Thanks, I'm sure it will. The powers that be are getting restless." He smiled at Amber and Liz as he and his appendage made their way toward the front door. "Let me know when the re-match is on. I'll be there."

The door had barely closed behind the pair when Amber and Liz burst out laughing. Tyler came back into the room, having escorted Connor and his date to the door, shaking his head and smiling. "People should know better than to mess with the Cynic Sisters. You two are like a pair of cats. There was enough glaring going on in this room to kill someone!"

"Well," Amber finally managed between guffaws, "Connor should have told her Liz was an old friend, nothing more. Did you see the way she was scuzzing you while you hugged him?"

Liz nodded, trying to avoid the subtle pain she knew was inevitable. Always an old friend. She shook it off. "A woman that beautiful shouldn't be insecure. There she was in a formal gown, hair done, makeup on, and here I am in my sweats." She shook her head. "Unbelievable."

Tyler looked at the women in amazement. "Apparently you two don't realize that even dressed the way you are, you both put that woman to shame."

Amber and Liz exchanged a wry glance. "That's very nice of you, honey, but we've both looked better and we know it." She turned to Liz. "Am I right?"

Liz nodded. "Absolutely. She had nothing to worry about. The fact that she was so obvious in her paranoia, I find particularly pathetic."

Tyler shook his head and resumed his seat at the table, diving back into his dinner. "Well," he finally managed over a mouthful of sweet and sour chicken, "it's all in the eye of the beholder. And right now, I am beholding beauty in sweats."

The women grinned and picked up their food as well. "To us," Liz stated, raising her water glass. Amber clinked her glass against Liz's and nodded. Tyler looked on in amusement, pitying the poor fool who dared cross the pair.

* * * * * *

Connor turned off the ignition and sat in his car, staring straight ahead at nothing in particular, and thinking. The frustration was manageable. What frightened him was the ambivalence. Then there was the emptiness he felt when some well-meaning Church member would ask him if he'd ever get married. He always managed a smile and an appropriate response—usually the requisite "One of these days . . . ," but the smile never reached his eyes and his voice lacked conviction.

He hated coming home from dates that left him feeling as though he'd wasted several hours that he'd never quite retrieve. Hours that were filled with inane conversation and endless babbling about nothing at all. Such occasions only served to remind him of how empty he often felt at the end of his day, with nothing to keep him company but the television and a DVD player. The sad part was, given the alternatives, he'd rather be alone.

He finally left the car and entered his partially cleaned condo, wandering through to the kitchen and tossing his keys on the counter. Careful to avoid the incriminating pantry that had given him grief the night before, he instead rummaged through the fridge, finding leftovers that looked marginally edible. Shrugging out of his tux jacket, he sat down to yet another solitary meal.

Marriage was overrated, he mused, removing his gold cuff links and dropping them on the table with a solid *clunk*. He thought of his date for the evening and nearly laughed in derision. She was one in a long line of women who wanted his money. Not to mention his collection of stocks and bonds. He'd created a diversified portfolio any financial planner would love. The concept was as old as the stars, and it wasn't one he'd ever dreamed he'd encounter. He'd grown up in an upper-middle-class home, well enough off but not extravagantly so.

He'd found joy, of late, in sharing some of his monetary blessings. One of the few bright spots in his life was sharing his resources with some of the families in his stake that were low on funds of their own and lacking the finances necessary to support a son or daughter on a mission. He donated generously and anonymously, and was grateful he had the means to do so.

He sighed and brought himself back to the present, mentally putting a check mark next to Brenda Matthias' name and dismissing her as a source of future companionship. She'd been entirely too agreeable. About everything. He knew for a fact from her uncle, his boss, that she hated stock car racing, yet when he mentioned he'd attended the races at Daytona some months earlier, she'd gushed on and on about how much she loved "that sort of thing." It was with no small amount of surprise that he'd seen the red flags signaling disaster, and had listened, with weary resignation, to her chatter as the night had grown progressively worse.

There was something, though, that hovered at the back of his mind. Something good had happened that he couldn't quite place. He smiled slowly as an image came to the forefront. *Liz.* It was always good to see Liz. She made him laugh. Watching her interact with her sister was a treat in itself. They saw each other so infrequently that they talked continually when they were together, laughing over funny childhood memories and throwing out one-liners from their favorite movies. They stopped laughing together only to take time out to sleep and shower, it seemed. He couldn't think of an occasion when he'd left the company of the Saxton sisters without a smile on his face.

He stretched out in his chair and closed his eyes, a genuine smile manifesting its presence for the first time in months. Maybe life wasn't so bad. Liz was in town.

His thoughts were interrupted by the shrill ring of the phone. He scowled at the offensive object, hanging innocently in its cradle on the wall. The noise continued. Connor reluctantly made his way to check his caller ID, and was rewarded for his efforts by seeing his sister's name. He picked up the phone.

"Claire?"

"Hi! I've been trying forever to reach you—you're never home!" The voice on the other end was a welcome surprise. Connor settled back into his chair with an easy grin. What was it about family? Merely hearing his sister's voice brought back the ease of many years of love and familiarity.

"Well, I can't just sit around and wait for you to call, you know." Connor's grin deepened at his sister's laugh. "Some of us have places to be."

"Ha! The rest of us have places to be, too. We just know how to maintain family ties, that's all." Claire's laugh was like a balm to his weary spirit. "Anyway," she continued, "I have some exciting news."

"Let's hear it."

"I did it."

Connor sat forward in his chair. "It's all done? It's official?"

The thrill was evident in her voice. "Can you believe it? I'm finished! You are talking to Dr. Claire O'Brian. I'm a full-fledged archaeologist. And not only that, I leave tomorrow to go to the ruins in Guatemala—the ones I've been telling you about that I've been trying to get funded for almost a year now. We just got the money, and now it's actually going to happen."

"Where did the money come from, all of a sudden?"

There was a momentary pause on the other end of the line. "Darren's doing it," she finally answered.

Connor gave a low whistle. "Really? Are you okay with that?"

"Yeah, I am. He's thousands of miles away in Paris, and I'll be across the ocean. What can he do?"

"I don't know. Nothing, I guess." The thought of his little sister being even remotely connected to her manipulative ex-boyfriend had his hair standing on end. "You're a big girl," he admitted gruffly. "I suppose you know what you're doing. Just so you're happy . . ."

"I am. Happiest I've been in a long, long time."

Connor sat back in his chair, emotion clogging his voice. "Ah, Claire. I'm so proud of you. I wish I were there—why didn't you call sooner? Did you walk through your graduation ceremonies?"

"I did. Mom and Dad insisted. And if they hadn't pressed the issue, Paige would have. It was a last-minute decision. I really didn't care, but you know how the family is."

Connor smiled. He did indeed know how the family was. Proud, close-knit, and feisty. His parents were both of Irish descent, which didn't always mean what people thought it meant, but in their case, the stereotypes held true. The only variation on a typical Irish theme was the absence of quintessential red hair. Their family trademark was instead the unmistakable black Irish hair, coupled with startlingly blue eyes. His youngest sister, Paige, had such deep blue eyes that they were more aptly described in shades of purple.

"Still," Connor cleared his throat, "I wish you'd called. I could have been there in a few hours."

He could hear the gentle smile in her voice. "It's okay, Connor. Really. I know how busy you are."

"Not too busy for you."

"I know. Anyway, I just wanted to let you know I'm leaving tomorrow, and I'll write when I have time."

"Okay. You'll be careful?"

"Of course."

He paused, not sure of the wisdom of broaching his intended topic. "How are you doing? I mean, really doing?"

"Fine."

"No, Claire. I mean, are you eating? Are you healthy and all that."

Her laugh was short, but thankfully lacked the traces of uncertainty he'd heard from her in the past. "I really am okay. I've done my therapy, the whole nine yards, and I'm feeling better than I have in years."

He released a breath he hadn't realized he'd been holding. "I'm glad to hear that. You take it easy, okay? One day at a time. Don't stress yourself out."

Her laugh was longer this time. "That's a fine bit of advice, coming from you!"

He had to smile. "Well, at least when I stress out, I'm not endangering my life."

"That's a matter of opinion, brother," she snorted. "You might want to have your blood pressure checked."

His eyes filled with an unfamiliar mist. He didn't want to hang up. "You just be careful, okay? Get some sleep so you'll be rested tomorrow."

"I will. You sound like Dad and Mom, you know."

"I know. I figure that's a good thing."

"Yeah. It is."

Chapter 6

Connor squinted against the bright sunlight and prepared to return Tyler's first serve. He and Liz were in good form and had all but clinched the match. He grinned as Tyler's efforts produced a groan when the ball bounced off the net. "One more just like that, buddy," he couldn't resist calling to his friend on the other side of the court.

"Hey, shut up."

Liz grinned at Connor as she rocked from side to side, wiping sweat from her brow, her breath coming out in a small puff to lift her damp bangs from her forehead while she waited for the final serve. The volley that resulted was quick and definitive on the part of the victors, causing Amber to fall to the court in mock exhaustion while Tyler threw his racket into the net.

Liz laughed and crossed the court to flop down next to her sister. "Good match, you guys. You've gotta get a handle on that competitive spirit, Tyler."

"Don't I know it," her brother-in-law replied as he took a long swig from his water bottle. "Oh well," he sighed when he finally came up for air. "We gave it a good shot, Am." He sat next to the women on the court and ruffled his wife's hair.

Connor joined the trio after retrieving his own water bottle and gulping the majority of it down. "We are, and always will be, the champions." He raised Liz's hand high above her head and shook it back and forth as she laughed.

"Let's not be bad winners," she said. "I have to live with the losers, you know."

Tyler rolled his eyes in disgust. "You just caught us on a bad day."

"A bad day that repeats itself every time we play, apparently," Connor couldn't resist adding with smile.

Amber rolled over, groaning. "I'd like to see you guys set a fractured bone or remove an appendix," she said with a snort.

"I'll leave that to you, Dr. Montgomery," Connor replied, inclining his head in deference. "The sight of blood makes me sick."

"Well, good. I'm one up on you there," Tyler remarked with a smirk.

Amber pushed herself to her knees. "We need to check on the kids. I told the baby-sitter to put them down for a nap, but I doubt Ian cooperated. Where's the cell phone?"

Tyler stood and pulled Amber to her feet. "I left it in the car. Come on, we'll go call and leave the two smug winners to themselves." He threw a wink over his shoulder at Liz as he and Amber walked to the parking lot.

Liz stretched and took a drink from the water bottle Connor offered her. She regarded him casually, reflecting on their first meeting. Tyler and Amber had recounted their amazing story to Liz and her parents shortly after they married. While it was the most unbelievable thing she'd ever heard, she'd had no choice but to believe it. Amber was one of the most honest and practical people Liz knew, and she trusted her implicitly.

During the first year of their marriage, Tyler and Amber were both immersed in genealogy work, trying to track down the descendants of a man they'd met in the "Twilight Zone," as they'd referred to it. Their searches had finally led them to Connor's family in Logan, Utah. They met, immediately struck up a friendship with Connor, and offered him a place in their home in Virginia while he looked for work after college.

On Tyler and Amber's first anniversary, they were sealed in the Salt Lake Temple, and Liz had come down from school in Seattle for the occasion. She'd met Connor at the breakfast following the ceremony, and had been immediately set at ease by his friendly nature. Had he not been so friendly, she might well have been intimidated by his physical appearance.

He was, in a word, stunning. His hair was black and his body was, in her opinion, sculpted perfection—the result of good genes and four years of college rugby. His face was the most aesthetically pleasing one she'd ever seen in her life; he possessed full lips that made for a charming smile, a straight nose, a rugged brow that bore its share of rugby scars, and eyes that she herself envied. They were cobalt blue, and piercing in their intensity. He was exactly the sort she was attracted to, and those attributes, coupled with a fun personality, had sucked her in from the first few moments.

She looked at him over the tip of the water bottle and noticed the subtle changes in his face. Five years had passed, and he was aging well; the small lines around his eyes only enhanced his appearance. He was still as large and fit as ever, and every bit as appealing as the day she'd first laid eyes on him. She'd seen him on several occasions since Tyler and Amber had been married, and he only grew more attractive with time.

He grinned. "What are you thinking?"

"I'm thinking that for a man who just turned thirty, you don't look a day over, well, twenty-nine."

"Gee, thanks. And might I return the compliment."

She grimaced. "Please don't. I turn twenty-five next month, and I'm trying not to think about it."

"I'll remind you of that when you turn sixty or so. You'll wish you were only twenty-five."

Liz had to smile. "I know. I'm not usually so shallow, either. I've been indulging in a fair amount of self-pity these days."

Connor stood and offered her his hand. "Let's go sit under the trees. It's getting hotter out here by the minute."

She took his hand and stood, gathering her tennis racket and an athletic bag that held her equipment and water bottle. They strolled to a shady area near the courts, and she sank gratefully onto the cool, dark grass.

"So what's all this about self-pity?" he asked as he sat, leaning against a tree trunk.

"I got sick of my job, basically, and I needed a change of pace. Amber offered me the guest room, so here I am. I'm trying to figure out what I want to do now." Liz's gaze was pensive.

"You were with that PI company for what, two years?"

"Three. It was hard to leave, in some ways, but a relief in others."

"Amber mentioned you were doing a lot of surveillance stuff."

Liz yawned. "Yeah. The first two years I did a variety of fun PI work for the man who owns the company. Then this last year, one of the women who did some specialized work quit, and I moved in as the replacement."

"What was the specialized stuff?"

"Well, basically I followed cheating husbands around town, getting the evidence of their infidelity on tape, both audio and visual. Hidden cameras and wires, all that."

"Wow." He whistled through his teeth. "Well, wow."

"I know. Their wives would go to my boss, tell him they'd been suspecting their husbands of cheating, and ask him to provide evidence. I'd trail the husbands and get proof that they were being unfaithful, and then the next day, the wife would come into the office, I'd give her the tapes, and she'd hand me a fat check. Along with a whole bunch of tears and heartbreak." Liz rubbed her eyes. "So many of those women hated me as they sat there, listening to the proof of their husbands' infidelity. I was doing a job they'd hired me to do, but I felt like a home wrecker."

Connor patted Liz's foot, which was next to his hip on the grass. "Hey. It wasn't your fault. You said it yourself; you were just doing your job."

The memories weren't pleasant ones, and they filled Liz with a sick depression. It was with some relief that she saw Tyler and Amber approaching from the car.

"It's a miracle, but both kids are asleep," Amber called out. "Let's go get lunch."

Liz was on her feet in a second. "Great. I'm starving."

* * * * * *

Liz sighed with contentment as she sat curled on the living room couch. She wondered at the fact that she hadn't thought of such an obvious solution to her dilemma earlier. What she'd needed was some time with her sister. The day was coming to a deliciously relaxing close; her niece and nephew were down for the night, and Tyler was in his study, working at his computer. She sniffed appreciatively as

Amber entered the living room. "Smells good," she offered with a smile.

"Nothing like a big plate of nachos." Amber handed Liz a napkin, set the plate and two drinks on a corner of the coffee table, and settled herself in a chair close to the couch. "I'll tell ya," she said, reaching for a chip smothered in cheeses and salsa, "if I didn't have that treadmill upstairs, I'd be in trouble."

Liz grinned as she pulled a chip of her own toward her napkin. She closed her eyes at the delicious taste and chewed slowly, savoring the sensations. "I think I'll be making use of that treadmill myself," she finally said after swallowing.

Amber laughed. "So tell me," she remarked after a few moments of quiet, companionable munching, "what's your assessment of life these days?"

Liz sighed. "My assessment, huh?" She frowned slightly. "I'm not exactly sure. That's what I'm trying to figure out. I've felt really good here with you guys; I think one of the biggest things I needed was a change."

"You think your job was the main problem?"

She nodded. "Yeah. Just the last year or so. You wouldn't believe the stuff I saw. Made me doubt my faith in mankind. And I mean the 'man' part literally."

Amber smiled softly. "I've heard some pretty scary stats about women, too. Something like forty percent of married women cheat. I think that was the number."

Liz nodded soberly. "I wouldn't be surprised. I never saw any of that, though. All I saw was the woman being cheated on, after which I had to tell her that her husband was a class A jerk. Of course," she admitted, "I went into that portion of the job with my defenses up. I took over Crystal's position just shortly after that fiasco with Nate blew up in my face."

Amber scowled over a mouth full of nachos. "That relationship was a mistake from the word go," she muttered and took a swallow of her drink. "He was never any good for you. He had 'cheat' written all over his face."

"Well, then, I must have been pretty stupid, because I never saw it coming. It's okay, though. Now I'm glad."

Amber nodded. "You're not the only one. Mom, Dad, and I were trying to figure out a way to have him bumped off without you noticing. None of us liked him at all."

Liz laughed, the incredulity obvious on her pretty face. "You might have said something," she choked out. "What, were you all just going to let me marry the guy, then secretly shudder every time I brought him to a family reunion?"

"Well, we'd have probably said something before it went that far. As it was, he took care of things himself." Amber's smile faded. "I didn't want you to be hurt, Liz, you know that. I'm just glad things worked out the way they did."

"Me too." Liz reached for another chip, pulling at the cheese stringing from it. Her brows again furrowed in a light frown. "I'm tired of being alone, though." She popped the chip in her mouth and chewed, motioning with her hand before swallowing. "I mean," she said, waving at their surroundings, "look at what you have here. You have this beautiful house, a great career, a husband who thinks you walk on water, and two wonderful kids."

She paused for a breath. "Now, let's look at what I have. A degree in computer programming I don't use, one serious relationship in my past that ended in disaster, and a career history of catching married men in compromising situations so their wives will be proven correct in their suspicions. We'll pull any woman in off the street and have her take her pick. Your life or mine."

Amber winced. "It's not that simple, Liz, and you know it. Some women have no interest at all in marriage and kids. Your life would seem pretty glamorous to a lot of them. I confess," she made a quiet admission of her own, "there have been times when the kids have thrown fits in the grocery store or at church, or Tyler and I have fought over something stupid, that I've wondered what I've done with my life. I really, truly, wouldn't change a thing. But it's not always perfect. I don't think it was meant to be." She paused and rubbed her eyes. "It's a learning process. Anyone stepping into marriage thinking it's all a walk in the park is in for a rude awakening. Sometimes the day starts out crappy, it's crappy all day long, and the ending is crappy, too. That's when I think to myself, 'Okay. I'm done for the day, and I'll start over again tomorrow.' Usually after I've had a long, hot soak in the tub and bawled for a good ten minutes."

Liz laughed. "I know it's not all perfection. But still," she sobered, "it's a part of life I'd like to experience for myself. And I've seen how Tyler is around you when you two think I'm not looking. I'll bet if he had any idea you were bawling in the tub for ten minutes, even for *one* minute, he'd be on his knees, wanting to know what he could do to make everything all better for you." She shot her sister a pointed look.

Amber nodded with a rueful smile. "I know. I'm really not complaining. I have it good; I'll admit that."

Liz was quiet. "You've always done things well, you know." She laughed self-consciously. "Makes it hard for a little sister to keep up."

Amber stared at her. "What do you mean?"

"I mean that you've always made Mom and Dad so proud, and you worked so hard in school—everyone was always so impressed with everything you ever did. I never resented you or anything; I just had a hard time trying to follow in your footsteps."

"Liz, there was never a need!" Amber's voice was soft and disbelieving. "You always had your own way about you—how do you think *I* felt every time someone made a comment about how neat and organized you were, and what a slob I was? That happened all the time."

Liz snorted. "That's nothing. Medical school; now *that's* something. Graduating from high school when you're sixteen. That's even *more* something."

Amber shook her head. "I can't believe you've never said anything about this to me! And what's even more amazing is that you've felt this way *at all!* A degree in computer programming is no small thing, either. I've watched you through the years," she continued, frustrated, "becoming more and more like our mother—which makes me totally envious. You even have her name; they didn't name *me* Sigrid. You're organized, practical, and smart, just like she is, and you don't let people push you around. You're more beautiful than a Barbie doll, and you never lose your keys!"

Liz laughed genuinely. "Well, there is that. I can tell people, 'Yes, my sister is a medical doctor, but me? Well, I never lose my keys, I'll tell ya that much!' They'll be so impressed with me."

Amber chuckled. "You know what I mean."

Liz shook her head. "All this time I've been jealous that you were named after Grandma."

Amber smiled. "Too funny," she murmured. She studied her sister intently. "When was the last time you read your patriarchal blessing?"

Liz sighed. "It's been a while, I suppose. The longer it takes for things to transpire, the more I doubt its accuracy."

"That's not wise."

"I know. I'm just impatient. Contrary to everything I've said about what I learned at my job, I really do like men. I'd like to have one to call my own."

Amber smiled in sympathy, remaining silent.

"I find myself wondering what he's doing," Liz continued quietly, "what he looks like, where he is. For all my independence, I'd really like that companionship." A fleeting image grazed the edges of Liz's consciousness: dark hair, eyes a startling cobalt blue. It was gone as soon as it appeared, but she didn't have to wonder who it was her subconscious was trying to conjure.

"Well," Amber finally replied, "all I can say is to try to be patient. Life happens when you least expect it; trust me on that one. I was your age when Tyler and I met. Not only was I happy in my career, I was content being alone. Until I met him, and realized what life would be like without him. Things happened fast after that." She smiled. "And you might want to dig your blessing out of whatever trunk you've locked it in. I read mine all the time."

Liz quirked the corner of her mouth into a smile. "And you think *I'm* the one who turned out like Mom. She's always telling me stuff like that."

"Well, good. I'll take that as a compliment."

* * * * * *

Liz finally left the bathroom, where she'd been soaking in the tub for a good hour with a novel. She padded to the guest room, closing the door behind her with a small sigh. The house was quiet. She slipped into a pair of soft pajamas and crawled between the crisply fresh sheets, leaning back into the mountain of pillows with a moan of pleasure.

She lay in quiet thought for a few moments, staring at one of the pieces of art Amber had chosen for the room. It was a print of Gauguin's *Tahitian Landscape*. Something about the scene seemed so optimistic. The use of bright colors, she supposed, gave the picture a feeling of hope and light. She looked at the man in the painting, walking down the road in the distance, and wondered what he was thinking about. Probably his day, or his duties, maybe his family. Or maybe, she mused, he was just appreciating the fact that he was alive and outside. Maybe he hadn't a care in the world because he chose to look at things in a bright light.

Liz reached for the scriptures she had unpacked and left on the nightstand. Flipping through the four standard works, she glanced at verses she had highlighted at various points in her life. Some made her smile, others made her wonder what she'd been thinking. She turned the pages back toward the front, and stopped on the words in Proverbs 13:12 that she had blocked in completely with a red pencil. *Hope deferred maketh the heart sick.* She read the words twice, and then again.

That was her problem. Her heart was sick because she'd abandoned all hope. Hope of contentment in life, hope of a meaningful relationship with a man, hope of a peaceful existence. Hope was a precious commodity. Apparently, her Heavenly Father wanted her to hang on to it.

She fell asleep reciting the verse over and over in her mind, her body relaxed and her spirit finally allowing itself to rest.

Chapter 7

The chapel was filled to capacity for the missionary farewell. Liz had to smile at the crowd of young girls seated among the throng, staring at the speaker with rapt attention. The young man looked like so many others she'd seen leave before: eager and fresh, ready to take on and convert the world. She knew if he worked hard, he'd return home not only older, but wiser, and full of love for the people he'd met.

She glanced casually around at the congregation. Tyler, Amber, and their family sat to her right, Connor O'Brian on her left. The benches were filled with people, old and young; it seemed a good blend of members—the kind found only in a residential ward. She'd been attending a college ward in Seattle and had missed the wide age span.

A pang of longing assailed her as she observed many of the young parents, wrestling their children into quiet submission, first offering bribes and then threats. Smiling, she reflected that it was a battle she'd like to attempt herself one day. She didn't see herself as the mother of a dozen children, or even *half* a dozen. There were so many women in the Church who effectively gave birth to and raised several children, running their homes with precision and love. She prided herself on her ability to know her limits; she knew she'd do well with a few children. *And I refuse to feel guilty about that fact*, she mused with a wry smile.

She turned her head slightly to her left and cast a surreptitious glance at the man seated next to her. He looked magnificent, and he was dressed to perfection—the white shirt starched and crisp, the dark pants well tailored. He closely resembled many of the other men in the congregation, the one true manifestation of their individual personalities coming forward in their ties. Connor's was trendy and bright, the colors a testimony to the vibrancy of his personality.

The truth of the matter was, she decided, she loved spending time with him. He was funny and charming, and above all else, genuine. His love of people was apparent in his every comment and gesture. She'd watched him chatting with ward members and friends in the transitions between meetings; people loved him because they sensed his genuine interest in their lives. He was the current elders quorum president; how he managed to juggle his career and church obligations was a mystery to her. Throw a family into the mix, and he'd have been really busy.

The sacrament meeting drew to a close, and Liz stretched as the postlude music was played. Eager children bolted from the benches and ran to find friends, or better yet, the door leading to the parking lot. Their parents straggled along behind, scooping up coloring books and baggies partially emptied of their contents, which usually included Cheerios or Froot Loops.

She watched the Young Women president stop to talk with one of her counselors on her way out of the chapel, making notations on a calendar while her young daughter tugged at her dress. Up on the stand, the bishop was besieged by a crowd of people. Liz heard him say, as the amoeba-like group passed by the microphone, "We're doing the Primary settings apart right now in my office."

Liz smiled. An LDS ward was an LDS ward, no matter where in the world it was located. She turned at Connor's chuckle.

"What are you thinking?" he asked, studying her expression.

Her smile deepened. "I'm thinking my bishop in Seattle is probably doing pretty much the same things today as this bishop is."

"Pretty consistent, isn't it." He laughed. "One of the happiest days of my childhood was the day my dad came home from early-morning Sunday meetings to announce he was being released. He'd been bishop for almost six years, and we hadn't seen as much of him as we'd have liked. My mother shouted for joy." He smiled at the memory.

"I can imagine she did."

"Would you believe," he continued, "that the next week in Relief Society, when my mother told everyone how happy she was, one sister told her after the meeting that she ought to be ashamed she was happy about my dad's release, that she should have been in tears that he wouldn't be 'serving the Lord in such a noble capacity anymore.'"

Liz groaned. "There's one of those in every ward. Sometimes more than one."

Connor grinned. "Yeah. But my mom told her exactly what she thought, and where she could take her well-meaning criticism."

Liz laughed. "I'll bet she did." She had met Connor's mother once, and was impressed by the small woman's enormous personality. It had been nearly three years earlier when Amber, Tyler, and Liz all happened to be visiting Liz's parents at the same time, and Connor was home for a visit with his family in Logan, Utah. The two families had met for a large picnic in a park in Logan. Liz had happened to mention to Amber that a woman in their parents' ward had criticized Liz for her single status at the advanced age of twenty-two. Connor's mother had overheard, approached Liz with purpose in her stride, and said, "Young lady, you tell that woman that your life is none of her business, and when you want her inspiration on your behalf, you'll ask her for it." She had winked, patted Liz on the shoulder with surprising gentleness, then turned to help Sigrid Saxton with the food preparations.

Liz laughed at the memory. "I can't imagine what that woman was thinking. I'd never take on your mother!"

Connor's laughter joined hers, warming its way into her heart. "She's the best, isn't she?" He turned to finally exit the pew where they'd been standing, blocking traffic, then turned back. "Um," he said, clearing his throat, "I have a company party tomorrow night, and I'm sadly lacking a date. I know it's late notice, but I wonder if you'd like to come along. You know, make me look less conspicuous than I would standing by myself in a corner."

Liz laughed at the image of Connor standing alone anywhere. It'd never happen. "Well, if it'll save you from being the company wall-flower, sure. I'd love to."

His grin was infectious. "Good. It's a formal deal, so I'll be picking you up in the company limo. Good thing I still have the rented tux. One of these days, I'll break down and actually buy one."

Liz smiled and refrained from mentioning the woman he'd been with the last time she'd seen him wearing said rented tux. "What time should I expect you?"

"Let's say seven. It starts at six, but I figure it's good to show up fashionably late every now and then. Besides," he added with a grimace, "that's one less hour I'll have to tell my boss that everything will be fine and the company will survive the audit."

Liz laughed again. "Okay. Seven it is." An actual date with Connor O'Brian. Well, she figured, it was best not to make too much of it. He was bound to introduce her as "my good friend, Liz" the whole night. *As opposed to what,* an inner voice flatly stated, *the love of his life? You've never even told him you're interested.*

There was never time, she argued back.

There was plenty of time.

Okay. I think you've said enough.

* * * * * *

"Dan, listen to me. You're going to make yourself sick about this. Tyler Montgomery told me himself that they're almost finished with it. All of it. I can see being worried if you had something to hide, but you don't! Just because the company's profits have increased by leaps and bounds doesn't mean you've done anything illegal. Sometimes companies *do* make large amounts of money legitimately, you know." Connor gripped the phone. How many times would he have to repeat the same things over and over?

The sigh on the other end of the line was heavy. "I know. And I appreciate all your hard work, Connor. Call me a pessimist, but something always goes wrong. Just because I have nothing to hide doesn't mean that something can't happen."

Connor massaged his tired eyes. "Something like what?" He impatiently checked his watch.

"I don't know! What if you get sick? What if you're not around to handle the sales details when the time comes?"

Connor suppressed a groan. "Dan, I'm never sick. And I'm not going anywhere. I promised I'd save my vacation time until the audit is over, and I will. Even if I weren't around, the paperwork is all there. The record speaks for itself."

"Yeah, but I like you around to smooth things over."

"And I'll *be* around." Connor resisted a strong urge to run full steam ahead at the opposite wall and ram his head through. "Now, we have a party to get to, and I have a date I'd like to pick up. I'll see you there, okay?"

"Okay. Wait—Connor?"

He ground his teeth. "Yes?"

"Could you print up the last quarter's sales reports for me and bring them with?"

"Dan, that's *this* year. It has nothing to do with the audit."

"I know. I want to be prepared in case this happens again next year."

Argh! "You think you're going to get audited two years in a row?"

His boss sighed. "Well, what if? I'm really sorry to have burdened you so much with all of this. I've never been so stressed out in my life. Creating a multimillion-dollar company seems like nothing compared to the worry of having to explain it all."

Connor closed his eyes. "I'll bring the sales reports with me tonight."

Liz paced the length of the front hall. Where was he? He was late. She hated late. She was never late, and expected that no one else would ever be late, either. Amber looked on in amusement.

"Nervous, Liz?"

Liz stopped pacing. "No, I'm not nervous," she snapped. Just because she'd spent two and a half hours getting ready didn't mean she was nervous. Just because she'd been unable to eat anything of substance all day didn't mean she was nervous, either. It was Connor, for crying out loud. What was there to be nervous about? She'd known him for half a decade. Just because he'd never *formally* asked her out before didn't mean anything. And there was the fact that she was secretly in love with him. She firmly decided to ignore that part and stick to the more manageable facts.

"Then come and sit down," Amber replied, barely suppressing a snicker.

"I don't want to sit down." Liz resumed her pacing.

Amber appraised her sister with a critical eye. Liz was the very epitome of the word beautiful. She was dressed in a black form-fitting dress that fell in straight lines to graze her ankles. The sleeves were short, the neckline scooped, showing off her lightly tanned skin to perfection. The fabric was thin rayon that whispered across her form as she moved. On her feet were simple three-inch black heels, and her hair was styled in an elegant twist at the back of her head. Her makeup enhanced the beauty of her large eyes and full lips. The jewelry she wore was simple: a gold watch, a thin gold rope chain around her neck displaying a one-karat solitaire diamond, and she'd finished the ensemble with simple diamond earrings. She was, in a word, exquisite.

Tyler walked through the door of his study and into the hallway, reading the newspaper he held in his hand. He bumped into Liz, who was still pacing, gave her a quick glance, and turned back to his paper. A few steps later, he stopped dead in his tracks and looked back up at Liz. "Wow," he said after an impossibly long pause, his eyebrows raised sky-high. "You did all that for Connor?" He glanced at Amber. "Is there something I ought to know about?"

Amber regarded her sister, her head tipped speculatively to one side. "I was wondering the same thing myself."

Liz raised her hands in frustration, her bracelet-like watch sliding up her arm as she did so. "There is nothing to know! I am waiting for Connor, who is late. I don't like it when people are late. It makes me very agitated. I don't know why, and I'm sure if we had the time, we could all sit down and try to analyze it. I could tell you all about my childhood, and if we worked *really* hard, I'm sure we could dig up some kind of life-altering incident that I've repressed, but as it stands now . . ."

Her tirade was interrupted by a sharp knock at the door. She whirled at the sound, her hand resting reflexively over her heart. She released a breath and smiled tightly. "Well. Now we don't have to. If you will excuse me," she reached for a small black purse she'd placed on a side table, "I have a date." She opened the door, poised and calm as though she'd been born to someday ascend a throne.

Connor's face broke into a tense smile as Liz opened the door. His smile froze in place as he got a good look at the woman who was to be his date. She was absolutely stunning. Even when dressed for church, he'd never seen her looking so elegant. He was so used to their time together in casual situations that he was completely speechless at her present appearance. "I—I . . ." *I'm an idiot. I can't form complete sentences.* He shook his head. "I'm really sorry for being this late. I had to print some stuff for my paranoid boss."

Liz breathed an inaudible sigh of relief. He'd been speechless. Speechless was good. She allowed herself a smug inner smile. All that worrying had been for naught. *What worrying,* she crossly reminded herself. *I wasn't worried. I just wanted to look nice for his sake; he has a high-profile job, and he needs to be seen in good company . . .* She commanded her chattering inner voice to shut up and smiled at her date. "It's okay. I haven't been waiting long."

* * * * * *

"Hmm. Company limo, huh?" Liz settled back against the black leather interior with a smile.

Connor grinned. "Yeah. I have a new car that I really enjoy, but I figured tonight was a special occasion. It's not every day a man is accompanied by the most beautiful woman in the world—one capable of breaking hearts from one coast to the other."

Liz stiffened inside. She equated the phrase "breaking hearts" with the cheating minions she'd spied on for the past year. Did he consider her to be of the same caliber? "You think I break hearts?" she asked quietly.

Connor grinned at her again. "You break mine every time you come for a visit and then insist on going back home."

She relaxed. Wow. He was better at flirting than she was. "Well, lucky for you I'm staying longer this time," she returned with a comfortable smile. Had it always been like this between them? Good, fun friendship with a hint of flirtation? Yes, she supposed it had. Had she been blind? More likely than not she'd just been naïve. She hadn't recognized the flirtation for what it was. Maybe she should have said something ages ago. The man was devastatingly gorgeous, funny, smart, and compassionate. She softly pursed her lips, wondering if the timing was suddenly right.

Their ride in the limo was a short one; they quickly reached their destination. The hotel hosting Connor's company function was lavish and expensive, brightly yet tastefully lit and teeming with well-dressed people. Connor alighted from the car first, then extended his hand back to Liz. She placed her fingers in his warm palm and moved toward him as though time had suddenly slowed to fractions of moments. She shook herself in bemusement as he drew her to his side and placed her hand through the crook of his arm. *Liz, get hold of yourself!*

Her mental chastisement was rendered useless as he turned the warmth of his smile upon her yet again. "I don't know how this party will rate, as parties go, but I do thank you again for coming along with me at the last minute."

Still struggling for composure, she made an effort to offer a casual smile. "My pleasure."

Liz's first impression upon entering the enormous ballroom was of the apparent wealth of the company Connor worked for. She asked him about it as they made their way further into the room.

Connor nodded at her observation. "Dan Fernatelli started his company about twenty years ago, beginning small with plastics—gloves, supplies, things of that sort. Then about ten years ago, he merged with another company that produced more elaborate medical supplies. The last five years or so have been exceptionally profitable. It's worked well," he shrugged, "and the rest is history."

"A history that the sales division has played no small part in, I'm sure." She nudged him gently.

He cocked his head to the side with a grin. "Well, there is that."

The first hour was a blur of faces and names for Liz. Among the first to approach Connor was his employer, Dan Fernatelli, a man Liz liked instantly. He somewhat sheepishly accepted the file folder Connor handed him. "You're a good man," he said, clapping his employee on the shoulder. He then turned his attention to Liz. "Are you sure we've not met before? You've never been with Connor at any other company functions?"

Liz shook her head with a curious smile. "No, I don't think so."

As Dan moved on, he was replaced by scores of other people, coming to address Connor with comments, work concerns, or just to offer friendly greetings, many of which included the same observation Dan had made—that Liz somehow looked familiar. She noted the proceedings with a certain amount of amusement. She'd presumed they'd be making the rounds, greeting people and socializing as they circulated. Instead, it seemed that every one of the hundreds of employees took his or her turn in coming to Connor; they never moved from the spot they'd first occupied upon entering the ballroom.

The crowd around them eventually thinned. Liz was beginning to think they'd see a moment's reprieve when a young man spied them from across the room and made his way quickly to their corner, a questioning expression on his face. He clasped Connor's hand and said, "Nice to see you made it, O'Brian. I was wondering there for a minute."

Connor turned to Liz with a good-natured grin. "I guess my 'fashionably late' theory wasn't such a good idea . . ." The man who still grasped Connor's hand tugged insistently and pulled Connor off to one side before he could make introductions.

The man spoke in an undertone that was, unfortunately, still loud enough for Liz to overhear. "Hey, man—I thought your fiancée was dead!"

Chapter 8

Connor's face was ashen, his gaze turning from shock at the man's pronouncement to cold anger. "She is!" he hissed. "What are you *talking* about?"

The young man retreated a step, clearly regretting his hasty assumption. "It's just that . . . she looks just like her . . ."

Connor ran a shaky hand through his hair. "She's not Allyson." He turned toward Liz, drawing her hand again through his arm, his jaw clenched. "Allow me to introduce my good friend, Elizabeth Saxton." She proffered her free hand to the uncomfortable young man, who mumbled something inconsequential and turned away, practically fleeing in an attempt to escape his blunder.

Liz remained quiet, intensely aware of Connor's agitation. She had known about Connor's relationship that had begun nearly a year earlier and had ended in his fiancée's death. She'd spoken briefly with Amber about the details at the time, most of which she had forgotten in the face of her own turbulent breakup.

She decided on levity. "Well, you know, they say everyone has a twin somewhere."

Connor closed his eyes. "I'm really sorry about all that." He turned to look at her, regret shining clearly in his gorgeous blue eyes. "That man is notorious for not thinking before he speaks." He shook his head and led her over to a nearby table, set with appetizers and drinks. They sat in the most remote spot Connor could find, away from the crowd. He pulled his chair close to Liz and offered a short laugh, ending on a sigh. "I can't imagine where he came up with that. You are *nothing* like my former fiancée."

Liz raised one eyebrow, wondering if she should be offended. Connor read her face and laughed again, although the sound was decidedly lacking in humor. "No, no. You misunderstand." His expression hardened, then went blank. "Allyson was the most deceitful woman I've ever had the misfortune of being close to. The only reason we were still engaged when she died was because I hadn't told her yet that the whole thing was off."

He sat back and took two glasses of water from the table, handing one to Liz. He took a drink from his, placed it again on the table, then stood and offered her his hand. As good as he looked on the tennis courts, Liz realized, he was magnificent in a tux.

"Would you care to dance?"

Liz blinked. Just like that—would you care to dance? *Okay,* she mused. *So he's not much into sharing details.* She recovered and placed her glass on the table next to his. "Sure."

They moved across the crowded ballroom to the other end, where couples were dancing slowly to music being softly played by the small live orchestra. *This has to be the most bizarre date I've ever been on in my life,* Liz thought as she placed her left hand on Connor's shoulder and allowed him to clasp her right hand with his left. *I'm suddenly seriously considering telling a good friend that I've had feelings for him for years, while HE apparently has unresolved feelings of resentment for a dead woman. Great.*

Connor was stiff and unyielding, moving appropriately to the rhythm of the music but not at all relaxed. One glance at his face told Liz he was still irritated over his colleague's erroneous assumption. She couldn't remember a time she'd seen him less than happy, or at least content.

"We don't have to do this," she finally murmured. "We can go mingle some more if you'd rather, or we can even go if you're done here . . ."

Connor looked at her, apparently startled out of a distant, unpleasant reverie. "No!" he said quietly, looking shocked that she'd even suggested it. He sighed, his shoulders drooping a fraction. "I'm so sorry, Liz," he said softly. "I don't think about Allyson anymore. I don't like to, anyway. I wasn't expecting that guy's comments, and they caught me off guard. No," he said, tightening his arm around her waist and pulling her closer, "this is nice." His smile returned and he relaxed, the difference in his demeanor apparent in the set of his shoulders and the expression on his face.

One number melted into two, and then three. Connor showed no signs of releasing Liz from his hold, and what was worse, she had no desire to ever leave. She was acutely, intensely aware of everything about him from the scent of his cologne to the muscles of his firm physique, hidden beneath the fabric of his tux. She had almost forgotten how devastatingly charming that smile was. She'd squelched the impulse to act on her attraction through the years, probably as a way of avoiding the possibility of rejection. Besides, Connor's friendship had meant too much to her to risk pursuing a more complex relationship that could well have ended in disaster, taking the friendship down with it.

And now? Unfortunately, she'd learned a thing or two about relationships over the past year. She'd discussed marriage with jilted wives, often wondering what had drawn people together in the first place. She knew for a certainty that to attempt a serious relationship with a man who had raw feelings about his past could well lead to messes on both sides. Perhaps he didn't love Allyson anymore, but he was still so unsettled about his former fiancée that the very mention of her elicited an unfavorable response.

Well, that was fine, Liz decided. She was a rational woman with a realistic view of the world. She'd leave things the way they were and see if Connor ever cared to move beyond step one. Should it come to that, she'd be sure his feelings for Allyson were resolved one way or the other before she allowed herself to be caught in a triangle, one corner of which was no longer a reality among the living.

"Liz?"

She shook herself from her musings and looked up into Connor's face. In her heels, she stood with the top of her head just at his chin. He suddenly seemed awfully close.

"Yes?" Her voice was husky and low, even to her own ears.

"Let's go somewhere and get dinner."

She cleared her throat. "I thought dinner was being served here."

"It is. I don't want to be here anymore."

"Oh." She nodded and let him lead her by the hand away from the crowd, feeling the loss of his physical warmth. He made excuses for their departure as they walked through the crowd, laughing with people and accepting good-natured slaps on the back.

* * * * * *

Connor relaxed as he and Liz were shown to a cozy corner table of his favorite Italian restaurant. The view of the city lights was calming, and he sat back with a sigh. "Thanks for indulging me."

Liz smiled and settled comfortably into her own seat. "No problem. I imagine it's nice to get away from the crowd every now and then."

Connor nodded. The waiter approached after they'd had a chance to peruse the menu, and they made small talk while waiting for their food to arrive. He watched Liz over the rim of his water glass. She was absolutely, stunningly beautiful. It wasn't just the physical trappings, either, he mused with a sense of wonder. He'd forgotten how easy it was with her, how comfortable the conversation always was, and how much he appreciated her insights on life.

The last time he'd allowed himself to be seriously drawn in by a woman, he'd nearly made the biggest mistake of his life. To risk his friendship with Liz was unthinkable. Besides, how realistic was the notion of a relationship with her, anyway? She made her home on the opposite coast, despite her extended vacation for the time being. He knew that sooner or later she'd want to go back. She always did. The casual comment he'd made earlier in the car hadn't really been all that casual. She always *did* eventually leave, and he always noted the loss. He curiously considered that fact as their food arrived.

"Are you enjoying your vacation so far?" he asked over a bite of pasta primavera.

Liz nodded, chewing and swallowing a piece of grilled chicken before answering. "I am. I needed this, very much."

"I'd like to get away sometime soon myself. I've thought a lot about going back to England."

"To visit your old mission haunts?"

He nodded, enjoying a bite of well-buttered garlic bread before continuing. "I've missed it through the years."

She'd heard him speak fondly of his mission before. "You had a good experience, didn't you?"

"I did. I was lucky. I had a really good mission president the whole time, and the people were wonderful." He took a drink and smiled. "I wouldn't necessarily call it the *best* two years of my life, but it was definitely the time when I noticed the most growth. And I'm not talking height."

She smiled in return. "I hear that about a lot of people. Almost makes me wish I'd gone on one."

He cocked his head to one side. "Why didn't you?"

She shrugged. "It never fit into my plans, I guess, and it's not a given for a girl to go on a mission. It's more of a choice, and I opted for other things." She chewed her food, a speculative look on her face. "I guess I'll always wonder, but I wouldn't say I have actual regrets about the way I've gone. It's worked for me."

He nodded again. "A mission's not an easy choice, either. Even for a guy who's expected to go. There were times when I was so frustrated I just wanted to come home." He paused, looking at her. "There were some missionaries in my mission who were so concerned about numbers that they would baptize people who still had issues with the Word of Wisdom and weren't sure they wanted to pay a tenth of their income to any church." He shook his head, remembering a time he'd been so frustrated with a companion that he'd kicked a hole in their apartment wall.

"It just didn't make sense to me to baptize people who weren't really converted. What good does it do to go home and say 'I baptized eighty people' if none of them ever go back to church?" He shrugged. "It messes with people's lives. If they're not ready for the gospel, they shouldn't be coerced into making serious commitments they're incapable of keeping."

Liz nodded her agreement. "I know. Makes you wonder what the missionaries are thinking."

"They're not. Or maybe they are, but they're not thinking about anything beyond their own numbers. I don't think it's the norm for missionaries to behave that way. I *know* it isn't. But those few who do . . ." Connor shook his head and continued eating. "I guess the thing that really makes me mad," he said when he swallowed, "is that when Church members, missionaries or not, do and say odd things, it leaves people with a bad impression of the Church. One thing I've learned to hold on to is that the gospel itself is the true part. Sometimes the members do damage that has nothing to do with gospel principles, but people who aren't familiar with it won't know the difference."

"Yeah." Liz squeezed a lemon into her drink and sipped it. "Growing up, I used to hear horror stories about Church members who wouldn't let their kids play with the nonmember kids on the street. I don't think it happened all the time, but enough to really hurt the poor kids who were ostracized." She nodded thoughtfully. "That's why I love my parents so much. They made sure we were good friends to everyone, and Amber and I were both better for it." She paused for a moment. "I'm sure it helped that my mom is a convert herself. She was an only child, and her parents weren't LDS. We loved them so much; we've missed them terribly since they died. They were totally accepting of her choice to join the Church, and she never pressured them in return. She just lived her life, and I think they always respected her for it."

Connor studied his date over the rim of his glass. She was beautiful. And, as he had noted earlier, he was not looking at the body alone. What he noticed specifically, though, as the meal progressed, was that she had a beauty that shone from within. He'd always noticed it. She was special; there was something fantastic about her, and he'd always counted himself lucky to be considered her friend. He realized with a small pang that whoever she finally married would be a lucky man, without a doubt.

"So," she said casually, cutting another small bite of her chicken. "How have you been lately?"

It was a loaded question, and he knew it. Funny, but it didn't bother him the way it would have coming from someone else. "I've been okay," he said. "Things are getting better for me, day by day."

"And you're dealing with, um . . ."

"Allyson?"

She flushed. "I'm not trying to pry, really. Just curious."

He shook his head and smiled. "From you, Liz, it's never prying. And yes," he said with a small sigh, "I'm dealing with it. I don't know how much you know," he said, looking at his food and stirring his pasta around in small circles, "but the whole thing was a huge mistake. I've looked back on it all and felt really stupid."

She shook her head. "Connor, there's no need to feel stupid. Sometimes I think life is like a weeding-out process; you just keep looking until you find the person who's the right fit."

He smiled, glancing up. "You make it easy on me."

"Nah. I make it easy on myself. I'm harboring my own feelings of stupidity. My last boyfriend was so obviously the *wrong* fit, in retrospect, that I'm wondering what I was thinking."

"Do you still love him?" Connor leaned forward, intent on her response.

She sighed and wiped the corner of her mouth with her napkin. "No. I never did. I loved the idea of being with him."

He nodded, as if answering his own question, and settled back in his chair. "Sometimes I've felt guilty that I haven't missed Allyson more."

"Yeah, but you shouldn't." Liz's mouth pursed in speculation. "Didn't you say it was basically over before she died?"

He nodded. "It was. I never got the chance to tell her, though. I think that's part of the problem." He hesitated. "She was cheating on me." He scratched the back of his neck, looking embarrassed and uncomfortable. "With her boss."

Liz stared. "She must not have been very smart, Connor." *Why on earth would any woman in her right mind give him up?*

He shrugged with a half-smile. "It kinda makes you wonder what your problem is when the woman who says she loves you runs around behind your back with another man."

"You thought *you* were the problem?"

He shrugged self-consciously. "It takes two, you know? I just . . ." He rubbed his eyes. "I wanted someone who was active in the Church, and I didn't think I was asking for that much. We had disagreements sometimes, though . . ." His laugh was short and bitter. "Here I am preaching about the evils of missionaries committing people before they're ready, and I was doing the same thing to her. She wasn't ready."

"Ready for . . . ?"

"Any of it." He gestured lamely with his hand. "She hated going to church, which I didn't realize until later, and she never had any intention of staying with it once we were married."

"Where were you planning to be married?"

"We hadn't decided." His voice was low. "I had assumed we'd pick a temple we both agreed on and fly our families in for the ceremony. It never really got that far."

She nodded and twirled her fork around the delicate angel hair pasta situated very aesthetically on her plate. "When did you know?"

"Know what?"

"That it was wrong."

He sighed. "I don't know. Probably right from the start. There was just something about her that seemed familiar, I guess." He shrugged. "I tried, and she tried in her own way, I think. It just didn't work."

"Well, you're one up on me. I didn't know my last boyfriend was all wrong for me until I found him with someone else." *Yes, you did.* The pesky inner voice was back. *You knew it all along.*

She set her fork down and took a drink.

"Do you want to talk about this anymore?" His smile was back.

"No."

"Good. I'm done, too. Let's just enjoy the food. Oh, and make sure you save room for dessert."

Liz groaned. "I've had more dessert since I got off that plane than I've had all year at home."

"Well, good. Dessert makes life worth living." His grin was welcome and infectious.

She lifted her glass in salute. "Here's to dessert."

* * * * * *

"I can't thank you enough for coming with me tonight," Connor said as they made their way out of the restaurant and into the comfort of the waiting limo.

"Really, it was my pleasure. I had a wonderful time." She paused, smiling slightly in self-deprecation. "It's been a long time since I went out on the town with a date of my own instead of following someone's unfaithful husband around."

Connor shook his head with a half-smile. "I can so *not* picture you in that setting."

"Good. I'd rather no one did."

The ride home was altogether too short, Connor decided. He waited until the car came to a smooth stop in front of the Montgomery home, then stepped out and offered his hand to Liz. As she stepped onto the curb, she turned and offered him a small smile. "I'd invite you in, but I'm sure your poor driver would like to be getting home himself."

"Oh." Connor glanced at the man seated inside the car, hidden behind darkly tinted windows. "Yeah." Shouldn't there be more? He watched as Liz made her way to the front door, turning as she opened it, the breeze lightly ruffling her dress as she lifted a hand in parting.

He shook his head. *Leave things the way they are, O'Brian,* he advised himself. *Friendship is irreplaceable.*

"Bye," he whispered as she entered the house and closed the door, leaving him feeling strangely, distinctly alone.

Chapter 9

W ell, fast food probably wouldn't have been my first choice for lunch out, but I didn't want to go home to shower and risk the kids waking up," Amber said to Liz as they chose a corner table in the restaurant. "I'd never get out of the house again if Isabelle saw me."

Liz smiled. "She is a mama's girl, isn't she? Looks just like you, too." She breathed a small sigh as they sat down. "I haven't been this tired in a long time," she admitted. "An hour a day on the treadmill doesn't really compare to hustling on a tennis court."

"That's two weeks in a row now that you and Connor have beaten me and my poor husband. His pride simply will not allow another defeat." She shook her head. "You're still as good as you ever were. I can't believe you don't play anymore."

"Before I came here, I'd become a bit of a hermit," Liz admitted. "I'd work long hours, then go home to surf the Net or read." She paused, reflecting. "I don't think I've played tennis since the last time I was here."

Amber laughed. "Great! That says wonderful things about Tyler and me! We play all the time." She looked up as Tyler and Connor approached the table, carrying trays laden with food. Connor slid into the booth next to Liz and began doling out the items on his tray.

"I hope I have this right: grilled chicken sandwich, small fries and a diet cola," he said as Liz accepted the food.

"Yup. Thanks." She peeled the wrapper partially off her straw and blew the remainder of it across the table at her sister, who swatted at it and made a face.

The table was silent for a moment as the two couples devoured their lunches. When they were nearly finished, Tyler broached the topic he'd been wondering about from the week before, but hadn't had the opportunity to ask.

"So how serious are things between you and your friend, Brenda?" he asked Connor.

"Yes, she seemed very nice," Amber added, and avoided looking at Liz, who was choking on her drink.

Connor smiled. "I know you all too well for that to fly. She's not nice, and you know it." He wiped his mouth with a napkin and leaned back in his seat. "She was my date for one evening because I couldn't get anyone else at the last minute. She's my boss's niece and I hardly know her," he held up his hands to ward off the inevitable queries, "despite the fact that she seemed to think otherwise." He shook his head and shrugged. "I'd have been better off going stag." He turned to Liz with a grin. "Had I known you'd be in town, I'd have picked you up at the airport myself."

Tyler popped a french fry into his mouth. "Well, the way you've been going through women these days, I wasn't surprised to see you with someone new. You haven't dated a woman more than once since . . ." He looked up at Connor, and his face flooded with color. "I'm sorry." He paused, searching for words. "I'm . . . sorry."

Connor waved his hand. "Hey, it's no big deal. Really. Anyone for a refill?" He rose and gestured toward the fountain drinks with his empty cup. Liz nodded and handed him hers.

"Thanks," she murmured as he walked off to refill the drinks. She turned in sympathy to Tyler, knowing he was probably mortified.

Connor returned with the drinks and made a small joke about the evils of caffeine addiction, but Liz noticed the same grim set to his mouth and eyes that she'd witnessed for a short time the evening of his company party.

* * * * * *

Liz entered the kitchen freshly showered, dressed, and blow-dried. She picked up Ian, who was tugging on his mother's shirt. Amber was balancing the phone between her chin and shoulder, trying to feed

Isabelle with one hand and flipping through a calendar with the other.

"Yes, that will be fine. No, our Relief Society meeting isn't until the third week this month." She paused. "No, we had to bump it back because the Young Women needed the cultural hall."

Liz shifted Ian so he lay stomach-down across her arms, and flew him, airplane style, into the living room. The little boy was soon laughing so hard she could barely hold on to him. They flew around the lower level of the house making airplane noises until Liz heard Amber finish her phone call.

"Oh, that woman will be the death of me! Not a week goes by that she doesn't have something earth-shattering to tell me." Amber pressed a hand to her forehead and turned as Ian flew into the kitchen. She took a deep breath and smiled at her son. "Who has you, Ian?"

"Aunt Lizzie! She's flying me like Peter Pan!" Ian laughed as Liz plunked him down on the kitchen counter. Isabelle banged her spoon on her highchair in an effort to add to the general din.

"So this is your life, huh, Amber? Two little cherubs and a crazy woman from Relief Society?" Liz ruffled Isabelle's curls and smiled. "Not bad, actually. I wouldn't mind it myself someday."

Amber sighed. "I wouldn't trade it. I do get tired, though." She smiled and kissed Ian's cheek. "It's a good kind of tired." She glanced through the kitchen windows and spied Tyler in the backyard. "Yay! Daddy's turning on the sprinklers!" She lifted Ian down from his perch on the counter and wiped Isabelle's mouth clean after taking her out of her highchair. Opening the glass door connecting the kitchen and the backyard, she shooed both children outside. "They're all yours!" she called to Tyler and shut the door.

"But they're not even in swimsuits!" Tyler shouted through the closed door.

"They'll be fine!" Amber shouted back. She turned to Liz. "Sometimes you just have to shift the mantle of responsibility. I figure I have a good twenty minutes to get this kitchen clean."

Liz laughed and began putting food into the fridge while Amber wiped down the counters and filled the dishwasher. They worked in companionable silence until Liz could no longer contain her curiosity.

"How bad was it for Connor when his fiancée died?" she finally asked.

Amber stopped her activity and leaned on the counter with a sigh. "I don't know the whole story, but he had asked Allyson to marry him and they were actually engaged for about a month. I started getting a little concerned, because he just wasn't himself. He was really moody and seemed depressed every time he was over here. We only met her twice."

She paused, reflecting. "One night, after they'd been engaged for just over three weeks, he came over to tell us he was going to take her to dinner and break it off. She'd been vacationing in the Rockies or something, and he was supposed to pick her up at the airport. He was deflated, completely dejected—said he'd thought he could make it work, but he realized he couldn't. He left the house, and then came back several hours later when we were already in bed. He said he'd received a call from a hospital in Colorado. She'd been run off the road by a drunk driver and killed."

Liz let out a breath she hadn't realized she'd been holding. "Oh, wow. I can't remember you telling me any of this!"

"I'm sure I did. You were going through your own mess at the time." Amber shrugged. "He's never really talked about it beyond that one night. Tyler's taken him to dinner to do the male bonding thing, but he just says he's fine and wants to forget it."

The women turned at the sound of a short knock at the front door. It opened, and Connor walked down the front hallway and into the kitchen. "Hey," he said in greeting. He stopped short and looked at the two women, who seemed rooted to the spot. "What?"

"Nothing," Amber hastily answered and began shoving the few remaining dirty dishes into the dishwasher.

"Just cleaning up," Liz added, furiously scrubbing an already meticulously clean countertop.

"Uh-huh." Connor grinned. "Why do I get the feeling my ears should be burning?"

Amber closed the dishwasher door with a flourish and stood, her face flushed. "What are you talking about?" She turned. "Oh look, Tyler's running through the sprinklers with the kids. I'm sure they'd love your company." She put her hand on his back and propelled him to the door.

"But I just came to . . ." He broke off as Amber nudged him out the door and into the backyard. She waved at him through the glass and turned around. Connor stood for a moment, looking at the door with a bemused expression on his face before turning at Tyler's greeting.

Liz choked on a horrified laugh. "Couldn't you have been a little less obvious than that?"

"Me? What about you? You looked positively panicked when he walked in!" Amber put her head in her hands and leaned on the counter. "Great. He knows we were talking about him."

"What is this, high school?"

Amber shook her head. "It wouldn't be a big deal if he weren't such a good friend. He doesn't like to talk about her, and I wouldn't want him to think I was gossiping behind his back. Which I was."

Liz patted her hand. "Well, at least when we crash and burn, we do it together. We were pretty pathetic." She laughed. "He must think we're total idiots."

"He wouldn't be far off."

* * * * * *

"What's up with your wife and her sister?" Connor smiled as he dodged Ian and Isabelle, who were flying at his legs like wet missiles.

Tyler shrugged. "You never can tell with those two. They're a pair. A pair of what, I haven't decided yet," he finished with a grin. "So what are you doing here? Going to hang out for a while?"

"I just came by to see if you guys wanted to go to a movie tonight. We could hit a late one after the kids are in bed, if that's better for you."

"Sure, that sounds good." Tyler eyed him speculatively. "Listen, I want to apologize again for this afternoon. The comment I made at lunch . . ."

"Forget it. Really—it's okay." Connor smiled. "It's done. I don't think about it anymore."

Connor made his way back into the house as Tyler resumed his play with the children. He stepped into the kitchen and smiled at the two women, who looked a bit sheepish and flashed small smiles of their own. He told them of their tentative plans for the evening. "I'm going now to buy tickets. Most of the shows are new and will probably be sold out by the time we get there tonight."

"I'd better try to get a baby-sitter then," Amber remarked, reaching for the phone. "Hopefully I can find someone at the last minute." She started muttering to herself as she looked for a phone number. "I have a few errands to run as well . . ." She looked at Liz. "Why don't you go with Connor? I have a lot to do, and Tyler's playing with the kids. I'm sure Connor won't mind." She looked at Connor, who smiled.

"I'd love the company."

Liz watched as Amber ran her finger down an impossibly long to-do list. "Are you sure you don't need any help?"

"Go. I'll be fine . . . Yes, hello, is Charlene home?" Amber turned her back as the phone was answered on the other end.

Connor smiled and gestured toward the door. "After you."

He opened the passenger-side door for Liz, and she eased herself into the car, admiring its interior. As Connor sat in the driver's seat, she fastened her lap belt and relaxed in the simple yet beautiful luxury of the sports car. She'd caught a glimpse of it the week before, then again that morning when he'd driven it to Amber and Tyler's to play tennis, and she'd barely been able to suppress a squeal of admiration.

"This one is different than the car you had last time I was in town," she observed, glancing at his profile.

"Yeah," he grinned. "I got a raise. I tried not to go overboard, but I've always had a thing for cars. I was like a kid with a new toy when I first bought it. I've mellowed a little now, though. I no longer find excuses to sleep in it."

Liz laughed. "Well, it is nice. I think I'd be sleeping in it if it were mine. I wouldn't ever want to be *out* of it." She paused as they rode down the street in silence, feeling the awkward aftermath of being caught discussing someone behind his back. She was too uncomfortable not to address it.

"Amber and I acted like, well, we were pretty stupid when you came in the house just now. And yes, your ears should have been burning." She decided to be brave. After all, they'd shared a perfectly wonderful evening together a few nights ago, and they'd discussed his former fiancée in some detail. It wasn't like she was grubbing around for new information. Her stomach, however, didn't follow her brain's logic, and it clenched in protest.

"I was talking to Amber about your relationship with . . ."

"Allyson?"

Liz couldn't read his tone. *Why did I ever open my big mouth? I'll have to look into having it wired shut.* "Yeah," she mumbled. "Amber didn't tell me much I didn't already know. I just . . ." *Definitely wired shut. The sooner the better.*

Connor smiled at her discomfort. "It's okay; I really don't mind. We've known each other for a long time, and you have every right to be curious." He scratched his nose and cleared his throat. "Actually," he said, "I have something I'd like to ask *you* about."

She sighed with relief at the subject change. "Okay."

"What do you think of Amber and Tyler's story?"

"Story?"

He nodded. "Their *story.* The way they met, and all."

"Oh." She bit her lip. "That story. What have they told you?"

"All of it. My mom sent an old diary and a copy of the Book of Mormon in the mail. I opened the box at Tyler and Amber's, and they freaked out." He shook his head. "They told me everything, and I still don't know what to make of it. I've been thinking about it ever since."

"Do you believe it?"

"Yeah, I do. I don't know why, but I do." He shrugged one shoulder. "I guess it's because I know and trust them, and I felt something when they were giving me all the weird details."

She nodded. "I know. That's how it was for my parents and me when they told us. Had it come from anyone else, I'd have said they were ready for the funny farm."

He nodded. "They're not exactly weird people, you know? The fact that they are who they are gives the story credibility." He paused. "It must have been amazing to see it all firsthand, you know? I mean, no matter how many times you read about something, you can't capture the actual experience."

"I know," she agreed. "And there were so many interesting tidbits they shared with us after we got over our initial shock. My father's a history professor, you know, and he was plenty curious. Their experiences are interesting because, in many ways, they debunk some of the common stereotypes." She paused, searching for the right words.

"It's easy to portray the Union as angelic, and that wasn't always the case, the same way the entire Confederacy wasn't populated with bigots. For example," she continued, "the most evil and bigoted villain in their entire experience was Tyler's ancestor, the general, who was a Yankee. And Claire shared an experience about their friend Ian's aunt ..." At that, Liz's eyes widened. "I guess that would be *your* aunt as well, many times back . . ."

He raised his eyebrows and nodded, muttering, "That's too weird . . ."

"I know, isn't it?" She paused, thinking, then continued. "Anyway, Amber went with Ian to visit his aunt, who was a Southerner, living in a small town that had been completely overrun and destroyed by northern regiments. This woman was living with, supporting, and embracing her widowed daughter and two biracial grandchildren. Her son-in-law had been black and was killed, leaving his wife and children behind; she took them in and loved them. Doesn't quite fit the typical southern stereotype of the time, does it?"

He shook his head. "Not at all."

"I think," Liz continued, tapping her finger against her leg, "that Amber also mentioned a doctor who gave her some grief when they were in D.C. He was a Northerner, and as rotten as they come. And at one point they went on a reconnaissance mission to a Southern camp, and the similarities between that regiment and her own made quite an impact. She said that had the gray uniforms been blue, she'd never have known the difference. Of course, that's common sense— on either side of any issue, especially war, you're dealing with real people who really aren't so different from each other; but it's easy to envision the 'enemy' as monsters. I think we tend to stereotype opposing sides and people in images of good or evil, but the lines get blurred and it's not always as simple as it seems."

"It's not so much different today, is it?"

She shook her head with a smile. "Not much. I guess portions of history repeat themselves."

He sighed. "Well, I still find the whole thing really odd. I'll be thinking about it for a long time, I'm sure."

She scrunched her nose. "It's one of those fanciful things that I've spent my life hoping is possible, so I guess it's really not so hard for me to believe. I like the unexplained, you know?"

He widened his eyes, his head cocked to one side. "I guess. I kind of like the explained, myself."

She laughed. "Oh, come on. Don't you want to believe in UFOs and other dimensions and all that?"

He grinned. "Yeah, in a way I do. But I guess I've always liked easy definitions. It makes life much easier."

"Yes, but much less exciting."

"You sound like Amber, saying something like that."

Liz smiled. "She must be rubbing off on me after all these years."

They arrived at the movie theater, purchased the tickets, and headed back toward home.

"Do you mind if we stop by my house for something?" Connor asked as they sped down the road.

"Not at all. It'll give me more time in this car."

He smiled back and made a quick detour to his townhouse condo. They pulled into his driveway and Liz stared. "Very nice, Mr. O'Brian! You're moving up in the world."

"Yeah, well, trying to, anyway. I'll be just a minute. Do you want to come inside?"

"I'll just wait here, thanks. I was serious about wanting an excuse to stay in this car. I've never seen such beautiful leather."

"All right! A woman with a good eye!" Connor laughed and jogged to his front door. She watched him as he stopped and stared at the lock. He pushed the door open with two fingers and stepped cautiously inside; she heard the roar of outrage mere seconds later. Opening her car door, she ran toward the house, bumping into him as he stood on the threshold of his living room. The house had been turned upside down.

Chapter 10

"Not again!" Connor shouted as he moved to survey the damage. "I can't believe this!"

Liz stood openmouthed. "What happened?"

Connor grabbed his head and sank down on the couch with a groan. "This is the third time!" he groaned. He leaned against the couch cushions, which had been brutally slashed, and closed his eyes.

Liz picked her way across the mess and sat gingerly next to him. She said nothing, merely waited for him to speak. And waited. He was silent for a full minute before he finally opened his eyes.

"This has happened twice before. Once," he stopped, counting mentally, "a few weeks ago, I guess, and the first time about five months ago. The cops didn't know what to make of it. No fingerprints, no evidence left behind, nothing. And mine was the only house in the neighborhood they hit."

"Was anything taken?"

"No. Just destroyed, as if someone was looking for something he couldn't find. Kind of like this." He gestured to the mess and dropped his arms at his sides. "Only this time it's worse," he muttered as he viewed the battered furniture and the artwork and photographs that had been slashed and broken.

"I'm so sorry," she murmured. "Do you want me to get the phone so you can call the police?"

He rubbed a hand across his eyes. "Yes, please. It's in the kitchen. If there's still a kitchen to be found. Let's not touch anything else, though. Let the cops deal with it when they get here."

Liz nodded and found her way to the kitchen, which had been summarily trashed. She picked up the cordless phone and carried it to Connor, who still sat motionless on the couch. She handed it to him and watched as he listlessly dialed 911.

Fifteen minutes later, the condo was being thoroughly inspected by a few police officers. She had to agree with a sentiment she heard expressed by one of them; there was definitely a pattern evolving. The house had been meticulously dismantled in the same manner as it had been during the first two break-ins, and nothing appeared to be missing, just destroyed in the haste of an apparent search.

"For what, though?" Connor was asking himself as an officer wrote his comments on a notepad. "I don't have anything that anyone would want!"

Liz stood next to him, hoping to offer some kind of moral support. She rubbed a comforting hand along his arm; his muscles were bunched and tense. He placed a hand over hers in appreciation.

"I'm going to call Tyler." She moved off to find the phone as he nodded his agreement.

By the time Tyler arrived, the preliminary police work was nearly finished and the house was emptying of people. His eyes widened as he viewed the mess, and he approached Connor, laying a hand on his shoulder. "You okay, buddy?"

Connor nodded with a sigh. "Yeah. I guess I'll start cleaning up. Again."

"I can't believe this! It looks just like the last time. Only worse." Tyler surveyed the damage, his eyes narrowing. "It's a little too coincidental, isn't it?"

"Yes. Entirely. I don't get it." Connor kicked aside a broken lamp and stifled a curse. "My insurance company's going to love this."

"Amber's at home. She said she'd come over later when the kids are down and the baby-sitter gets there. I think we can kiss the movie good-bye."

Connor shook his head. "You three can still go. I'll just stay here and make use of the trash cans."

"Are you kidding?" Liz interjected. "We're staying right here."

Tyler nodded and moved to pick up the slashed front cover of what had formerly been a state-of-the-art speaker. "We'll make a night of it." He smiled grimly. "It'll be fun."

Amber arrived after the children were in bed. The trio had made a certain amount of headway in cleaning the mess, but the damage was still evident in every corner of the house. She put her hand over her eyes and groaned. "Unbelievable," she murmured to herself. Her concern grew by leaps and bounds as she remembered the last two times they had helped Connor clean. Tyler entered the living room, saw her, and motioned to the mess.

"Can you believe this?" he asked quietly.

"No, I can't. And I'm getting scared for him. Someone's after something specific. I don't buy the vandalism theory anymore. Does he have any idea what's going on?"

Tyler shook his head.

"Where is he?"

"In the study with Liz. You can come and help me in the kitchen if you want."

Amber viewed the damage with dismay. All the dishes had been swept from the shelves, as though someone was looking for something and didn't have the time or inclination to be gentle about it.

* * * * * *

Liz sifted through a stack of papers and set them carefully on the computer desk. She watched quietly as Connor attempted to salvage what he could from the mess. He suddenly stopped and began searching desperately through the piles on the floor.

"What is it?" she queried.

"My disks. They're gone." Connor lifted books and papers, shoving them aside and growing more frantic by the minute.

"What disks?" she asked, getting on her hands and knees in an attempt to help him search.

"All of them. Every single floppy I own!" He sank to the floor and closed his eyes, pinching the bridge of his nose between his thumb and forefinger. "I think I'm going to have a stroke," he muttered.

Liz stood, biting her lip, and surveyed the damage done to his computer. The outer casing to the central processing unit had been ripped off and the computer chips inside torn out. "Your hard drive is gone, too, Connor," she said quietly. "Did you have more than one?"

He nodded and leapt to his feet to join her at the desk. "I had two." He peered inside the computer, his brows drawn in frustrated panic.

"They're both gone," she murmured.

He sank again to the floor and put his head in his hands. "I had all my work files on the hard drives. Only some of the duplicate floppies are at my office. The rest were here."

Liz sat down next to him on the floor and ran her hand across his back. "Could someone from work be behind this?"

He raised his head and looked bleakly at his computer. "I don't know who. I never have time at work to do computer stuff; I'm always in meetings or out of the office. I did all my office work here, on this computer."

Liz's eyes narrowed in concentration. "Did this happen the last two times? Were your disks stolen? I thought you said nothing was ever taken."

He looked at her. "Nothing ever was taken." He paused to think. "The first time, I was in New Orleans at Allyson's funeral. I had to go on a business trip straight from the funeral, so I had all my work disks with me. The only ones here were CDs, and they were clearly labeled as software for the computer and the modem. They weren't stolen, just dumped on the floor. The computer wasn't here; I had a new one on order and had given the old one to a friend."

He paused again, reflecting. "I came home from the business trip, found the house trashed, called the cops, and then cleaned everything up. The second time was a few weeks ago. I was at work, and when I came home, the same thing had happened. Nothing taken, just messed up. There wasn't a computer here that time, either. The new one had come, and I'd taken it to my friend's house. He loaded some things on for me that I didn't have time to do myself. I picked it up from him yesterday. He lives clear across town and had no idea I'd been robbed. Either time."

"Everything okay in here?" Tyler asked from the doorway.

"Not really," Liz answered for Connor. "His computer stuff is gone. His disks, the hard drives, everything."

Amber pushed past Tyler and entered the room. She sat down on the floor next to Connor and threw an arm across his shoulders. He smiled grimly at her. "When did you get here?"

"A few minutes ago. Looks just like it did the last time. Except for the missing computer stuff."

Connor nodded and the group was silent, each lost in his or her own thoughts. Tyler finally turned and headed down the hallway. "Don't you have an attic, Connor?" he asked over his shoulder as he walked. "In the bedroom, isn't it?"

"Yes," Connor answered, coming to his feet and picking his way across the mess and into the hallway. He followed Tyler's voice into his bedroom. "It's in the closet, but it's hard to detect." The ceilings in the bedroom and closet were sectioned into large squares bordered by long pieces of oak molding, the same used on all the door frames and molding throughout the condo.

"Right there." Connor pointed to the center square in the closet and reached for a chair. He stood on it and pushed against one end of the section. The square gave way to reveal a trapdoor leading to the attic. An attached ladder folded down from the door, giving easy access to the recess above.

"The attic wasn't discovered the other two times, was it?" Tyler asked as he pulled down on the ladder.

"No." Connor crossed the room to find a flashlight that had been ripped from one of his nightstand drawers. He switched it on and preceded Tyler up the ladder. The two men reached the dark enclosure and visually followed the narrow beam of light as it bounced off boxes and bags of stored items.

"I haven't been up here for ages—since Allyson helped me move some boxes up here that my mom had sent." His jaw clenched. "About a week before she went to Colorado."

Tyler looked at his friend in sympathy. "We don't need to stay up here. I was just wondering if anything had been disturbed."

"No. At least one room left intact. I should be grateful for small favors."

"You can bet if they knew this was up here, they'd have gone through it as well."

Connor nodded, and was just turning to descend when the flashlight's beam caught a box at the very edge of the attic opening. He walked down a few steps until his face was level with the box in question. He shined the light across its front, which clearly stated his name in large block letters.

"What is it?" Tyler asked, moving closer.

"I don't know, but it's Allyson's handwriting. I don't remember her putting this up here." He lifted the box, which was not even a foot square, and carried it down the ladder.

He exited the closet to find Amber and Liz trying to make sense of the chaos in his bedroom. They were hefting the mattress back onto the bed when Liz turned and noticed him carrying the box.

"What's that?"

"I don't know. It feels like nothing." Connor turned, and using the pocketknife attached to Tyler's keys, began slicing the tape that bound the box. Lifting the lid, he found the package full of Styrofoam peanuts. He tossed the packaging heedlessly to the floor, unconcerned about adding to the garbage already present, and raised his hand from the box to reveal a floppy disk. There was nothing on the label save his name. He raised his eyes to his friends. "I have no idea what this is. Furthermore, I have no way to find out what this is. This is Allyson's handwriting, though, and I can't remember her putting it in the attic."

"Let's take it home. You can use our computer." Amber motioned toward the door and the other three followed, stepping over papers, books, and ruined accessories as they exited the condo.

Chapter 11

S o what do you think?" Liz glanced at Connor, who was seated next to her, staring at the computer monitor.

"I don't know." He scrolled down the screen, the expression on his face as bemused as was Liz's. Whatever Allyson had left on the disk was not easily discernable. There was a list of several foreign countries with dates and numbers next to each, and a simple spreadsheet containing city abbreviations and what appeared to be names, presumably of individuals. There were also listings of dates and certain numbers, some in long series.

"Let's print it out," Tyler finally said. "I want to look at all of it together."

Even gathered around the kitchen island with the papers spread over every square inch of space, the mystery behind the disk remained just that. Liz picked up the list of foreign countries and studied it. There was a pattern, a connection among the countries that she couldn't quite place.

"Where did you say she worked?" she asked Connor.

"Allyson?" At Liz's nod, he continued. "She worked for Frasier Pharmaceutical. I don't know a lot about the company, just that they emerged on the scene about five years ago and have been growing by leaps and bounds ever since."

Liz nodded. She had seen a newsmagazine article on the company not long ago. In addition to prescription drug production, they had developed a research branch that was making amazing progress with cancer research and effective treatments.

"Well," she sighed, "I don't get it. A few explanations along with the disk would have been helpful."

Amber nodded slowly. "Unless it was something she didn't want just anyone knowing about."

Tyler shrugged. "Maybe it's just bookkeeping stuff she was doing as part of her job."

Liz raised one eyebrow. "Why would she hide her bookkeeping in a box in someone's attic?"

Tyler grinned. "She was a very conscientious worker?"

Amber snorted in derision and smacked his shoulder with the back of her hand. "You're a geek."

Connor smiled at the moment of comic relief. "You guys are good for me," he said with a yawn, and began gathering the papers. "It's late. Let's sleep on it, and I'll decide tomorrow what I'm going to do with the disk."

Tyler nodded. "Leave the disk and papers here. I think it's pretty obvious why your house was trashed. Someone must want that disk. Why else would she have hidden it?"

"I can't ask that of you. The same thing could happen here, if that's the case."

"I insist. You probably ought to stay here tonight, too."

Connor shook his head. "I'm not staying away from my own home. I'm not going to be intimidated by whoever's doing this."

Amber scowled. "Oh, don't be such a man! You don't even have a lock on your front door anymore, and 'they' must be frustrated by now. Three times, for heaven's sake! What makes you think they won't come back when you're home next time?"

Connor clenched his jaw. He paced the length of the kitchen, running his hands through his hair in frustration. "Well, I'll have to at least go home and get my church clothes for tomorrow." He stopped pacing and faced his friends. "I hate this."

Liz moved around from her spot behind the island and headed toward the front door. "Come on," she said. "I'll go with you."

Amber tossed her keys to Connor. "Take the Jeep. It's in the driveway."

Connor reflexively caught the keys and made his way to the door behind Liz, who was already venturing outside. She climbed into the passenger seat of Amber's Jeep Grand Cherokee and looked expectantly at Connor, who was hovering near the doorway with Tyler and

Amber. He finally turned toward the vehicle with a muttered curse and climbed into the driver's seat.

Liz pushed the power button controlling her window as Connor turned the key. "We'll be right back," she said to Amber, who had moved onto the front lawn.

Amber nodded. "Be careful. How about some leftover Chinese for a late-night snack?" she called as the car backed out of the driveway.

Liz grinned. "Sounds great. If you can find it." Amber elbowed Tyler in the ribs as he laughed at Liz's obvious reference to the unsightly state of their fridge.

Liz closed the window and glanced at Connor's grim profile. "It'll be okay," she said quietly. "I'll help you figure this out. Espionage is right up my alley, you know."

Connor pursed his lips, not wanting to appear rude by asking her how experience at catching cheating husbands would be of any use to him.

Liz smiled as though reading his thoughts. "I *am* actually a PI, you know. Licensed and everything. I have experience under my belt aside from mere home wrecking."

Connor grunted in surprise, momentarily distracted from his troubles. "I thought you had to be a cop first."

"Only in some states. Washington isn't one of them. Believe it or not, my training extended beyond staking out the extracurricular activities of cads and degenerates." She paused. "Are you going to give the disk to the police?"

Connor's eyebrows drew together in thought as she pinpointed one of the questions that had been bothering him. "Well, Allyson *did* leave the disk for me, right? And there's nothing on that disk to indicate it should be turned over to the police, right?"

Liz smiled at his dismissal of the voice of reason. She was certain the disk was the reason for the burglaries, and she knew he was aware of that fact as well. There were answers on that disk, however, that could explain things about his relationship with his former fiancée. Answers that might give him some peace. "Why bother the law with something so trivial?" she finally said.

"That's right. Until I figure out what it means, I'll just hang on to it."

They covered the remainder of the distance to Connor's neighborhood in silence. As he pulled into the driveway, his eyes were immediately drawn to a shadowy figure standing on his front porch. "What the . . ." His question trailed off as he cut the engine. He was out of the car in a flash, with Liz close on his heels.

The man smiled and extended his hand as Connor and Liz approached. "Are you Connor O'Brian?" he asked.

Connor eyed the man warily. He took in the expensive cut of the slacks, the crisp white shirt and conservative tie, the jacket slung casually over the shoulder. "Can I help you with something?"

The man reached into his pants pocket and extracted a badge. "My name is Phillip Malone. I'm with the FBI. Can I come in and talk to you for a minute?"

Connor paused. "Sure," he said, and pushed the front door open. He pulled Liz in behind him and flipped on the overhead light. Tyler had disposed of most of the refuse on the floor before they had left, but the disturbing reminders of the break-in still remained in the ruined furnishings.

Connor and Liz sat on what was left of the couch, and Phillip Malone sat gingerly across from them on a cushionless chair.

"I'll come right to the point," Malone said. "I understand you've had three break-ins over the past few months, is that correct?" At Connor's nod, he continued. "We think they might be tied to your late fiancée, Allyson Shapiro."

Connor stared at the man. *How would he know?* He glanced at Liz, who was looking intently at the FBI agent. He cleared his throat. "What makes you say that?"

"Well, she was an undercover FBI agent, for starters." He paused. "You seem surprised. You should be, actually . . ."

"You do realize we were engaged," Connor broke in. "I knew her quite well."

"Yes, sir, I understand that. I'm not suggesting you didn't. She simply wasn't allowed to disclose that information to anyone, even someone she may have been personally involved with."

Liz stared long and hard. Something wasn't right. She couldn't put her finger on it, but something about the man didn't fit. She'd seen enough men who had something to hide, and she recognized the signs. She watched him closely as he continued to talk.

"Did she ever give you anything, or tell you anything about the company she worked for? Anything at all that might be a reason for your home to be burglarized?"

Liz broke in before Connor could reply. "We've searched the entire house, and nothing seems to be missing," she said as she tossed her hair over her shoulder and cocked her head with a small smile. She offered a tiny, helpless shrug. "We can't think of any reason someone would want to do this," she said, gesturing to the ruined room. She laid her hand softly on Connor's leg. "We're very distraught."

Malone narrowed his eyes and smiled at her. "I'm sorry . . . I didn't catch your name."

"Sharon."

"And you are?"

"Connor's girlfriend." She gazed at Connor with huge, adoring eyes before she turned back to Malone. "I'm so *horribly* frightened for him," she murmured, allowing her eyes to become liquid as she spoke. "I don't want him to get hurt."

Connor did his best to keep his jaw from dropping in amazement. If he didn't know better, *he'd* have believed her story. He looked down at her hand and responded to the gentle pressure she exerted on his thigh by covering her hand with his own and leaning over to kiss her cheek.

"I'll be fine, honey," he said and turned back to Malone. If he hadn't been so leery of the FBI agent, he might have noticed that his heart had been pounding out of his chest from the moment she'd put her hand on his leg.

"Allyson never gave me anything that I can recall being of interest to the FBI," he answered truthfully. "If I come up with anything, I'll let you know."

Malone looked at him quietly for a moment before he smiled and came to his feet. He extracted a card from his jacket and scribbled something on the back. "This is the number at the hotel where I'm staying. I'll be in town for a few more days if you think of anything you might need to tell me."

Connor rose and accepted the card Malone handed to him. "You can reach me anytime, day or night," Malone said as he made his way to the door. "It really is very important."

"I'm sure it is," Connor replied, thinking of the disk. He draped a casual arm across Liz's shoulder as they stood in the doorway and watched Malone climb into a sand-colored sedan parked across the street.

"Nice duds," Liz muttered under her breath.

"Easy," Connor said quietly as Malone pulled slowly away from the curb. "He's still looking."

Liz rested her head against Connor's chest and sighed, hoping to give Malone one last, good eyeful of true love—a committed if slightly air-headed woman who was more than willing to speak for her boyfriend.

"Well," she said with narrowed eyes as Malone rounded the corner, "that ought to give him something to think about." She turned and entered the house.

Connor stared after her and slowly followed behind. *That ought to give ME something to think about*, he mused. He quietly closed the door and watched her as she stood in his living room, hands on her hips, restlessly tapping one foot.

"He was up to no good," Liz said, staring at the chair Malone had occupied. "He may be FBI, but there was something . . . something . . ." She was silent for a long moment before finally turning toward Connor. "I'm really sorry for speaking up like I did, and that whole charade thing," she said, waving a hand absently at the couch where they'd sat together. "I just didn't trust him, and I didn't want you telling him about the disk."

"It was a good call. I didn't trust him, either." Connor turned toward his bedroom and motioned for her to follow him. Liz walked with him to his closet and stood at the doorway while he ventured inside and began rummaging through his clothing. Most of it had been torn from the hangers and trampled, some of it cut to ribbons, presumably having been considered possible hiding places for the disk.

He dropped a pair of dress slacks to the floor and shook his head in resignation. "There's nothing here suitable for church," he muttered. "I'll have to borrow something from Tyler."

He exited the closet with a noise of disgust and moved to the bed, where he sat down and glanced up at Liz apologetically. "I'm really sorry you got caught up in all this."

She sat next to him and patted his leg. "It's okay. Really. I can help you figure this out if you'll let me."

A short, humorless laugh erupted from his throat. "I'm sure that's just what you wanted to do on your vacation."

She smiled. "My only aim for this vacation was to find a change of pace. Trust me, this is much more exciting than what I was doing before." She paused. "Do you think Allyson was really an FBI agent?"

Connor released a frustrated sigh. "I don't have a clue," he stated flatly. "It wouldn't surprise me. Nothing about that woman was what it appeared."

The silence lengthened. Connor finally rose, turned toward Liz, and offered her his hand. They left the house and silently climbed into the Jeep. Neither spoke a word until they were five minutes away from Tyler and Amber's home.

Connor broke the stillness with a low murmur. "He's following us."

Chapter 12

Liz whirled about in her seat, immediately regretting the quick movement as her head spun and her stomach lurched in protest. She groaned. Motion sickness was the bane of her existence. It was no respecter of persons and plagued her relentlessly, regardless of her choice of transportation. "Are you sure?" she managed to squeak.

"Yes. Same car, same guy. I caught a glimpse of his blonde hair when he passed under the last street light." Connor was angry. For a man who liked his life well ordered and under control, the day was beginning to wear on his patience.

"Well, apparently Mr. Malone doesn't want to sit around and wait for your phone call." Liz stared straight ahead, trying to decide how much of a threat the FBI agent actually posed. "Maybe we should just give him the disk," she mused aloud. "No," she said before Connor could answer. "We can't. Something about that man is all wrong."

Connor shook his head. "I wasn't going to give it to him before, and I'm definitely not going to now."

"Okay, think . . . think . . ." Liz tapped her finger against her forehead, her brows drawn in fierce concentration. "We can't lead him back to Amber's. Next thing you know, their house will be trashed from top to bottom."

Connor ran a hand anxiously through his hair. She was right. If anything happened to his friends or their kids, he'd never be able to live with himself. He glanced at Liz, who was staring intently at the road ahead. He could almost see her mind working, selecting and discarding solutions to their dilemma. It was evident in the narrow focus of her eyes and the small, nearly imperceptible shake of her head as she thought. She was, he realized, without a doubt one of the most clever, insightful, intelligent people he knew. She was also achingly beautiful and had a delightfully sharp sense of humor. He enjoyed her company and valued her friendship. And he couldn't run the risk of endangering her, any more than he could imagine placing Tyler and his family in jeopardy.

"I'm going to find a way to shake this guy, and then I'll get you back to Tyler's house," he told her grimly.

She looked at him in surprise. "And where will you go?" she asked, her eyes huge.

"I'll figure out something."

She laughed, and he glanced at her in irritation. "What?" he barked.

"Are you serious?" she asked, torn between mirth and incredulity. "You need my help, buddy, so you can abandon any preconceived notions of chivalry."

"This has nothing to do with chivalry. It's called simple responsibility and human decency." He cranked the wheel harshly to the right and screamed around a corner onto a dark side street.

"Oh, that's a good one!" she shot back furiously and scrambled to right herself in the seat. "You need my help; you wouldn't last two minutes by yourself."

He shot her a dark look and snorted. "You apparently don't know me very well."

"Oh, for crying out loud," she rejoined impatiently. "I'm not trying to insult your superior masculine abilities." She took a deep breath to calm herself. "I wouldn't last two minutes by myself, either. But as it happens, I have a good friend who has an amazing network of contacts spanning the globe. We need to get to him and have him dig into Allyson's background, for starters. Then, I'm thinking a perusal through Frasier Pharmaceutical's history wouldn't be a bad idea."

Connor eyed her speculatively while maneuvering through a maze of quiet subdivisions in Amber's Jeep without the use of headlights. She glared back at him, silently daring him to challenge her wisdom.

"Where, exactly, is this friend?"

"Seattle."

He was silent, thinking. "Okay. I guess it's not a bad idea for me to disappear for a while. I have some vacation time coming." He sighed and rubbed his eyes. When he'd wished for a change the day he was beaned in the head with that racquetball, the current situation wasn't exactly what he'd had in mind. "My boss is going to freak."

"I can go to Seattle for you. In fact, I could just call my friend from here, and he can go to work on Allyson's background check." She paused. "The only problem is Malone, I guess, and whoever's behind the break-ins at your house. They're not going to leave you alone as long as they're convinced she gave you the disk."

"Well, Malone had a good long look at you," he said irritably. "He's not going to leave you alone, either. If he figures out where Tyler and Amber live, he'll hunt you down to get to me. Let's just go to Seattle together and lie low for a few days."

Liz nodded and turned to look out the back window. "I think you lost him," she said, picking up the car phone and dialing Amber's number. "We've got to get that disk. And my purse. I'll need my credit cards."

Connor shook his head as Liz put the phone to her ear. "I'll be footing the bill. You won't be paying for this."

"I have plenty of money, Connor."

He shot her a wry glance. "So do I, Liz. Or haven't you seen my car?"

"I've seen your car, and I'm sure, driving a machine like that, you can't possibly have any money left over to buy anything but the bare necessities. Like a loaf of bread and a gallon of milk." She stopped talking as Amber picked up the phone.

"You'd be surprised," he murmured, but she was talking and didn't hear. That was fine. Let her assume he was on a budget. It'd be the first time in recent history he'd be spending time with a woman who wasn't after his money. The thought was a novel one, and he might have smiled in anticipation if he hadn't been so tense.

"So anyway," Liz was saying, "meet me at the front door with my purse and the disk. Better give me the papers we printed out, too." She paused. "No, we're flying to Seattle tonight. We'll stay with Bump. Yes, I'm sure. We'll be fine."

"Liz, give me the phone," Connor interrupted tersely.

She glanced at Connor in surprise.

"Please," he capitulated.

She dubiously handed the phone to Connor and listened to the evidence of his uncharacteristic stress. "Let me talk to Tyler, Amber," he said into the phone without preamble. He paused, then resumed speaking as Tyler picked up the other end. "Something's going on with that disk. We've got to get out of here for a while." Liz listened while he explained their purpose in going to Seattle and assured him they'd be back as soon as they could formulate some kind of plan. "I wonder if you'd also call my first counselor for me. We have elders quorum activities coming up that he'll have to take over. I also need this month's home teaching numbers . . ." He closed his eyes in frustration. "Will you just tell him I'll get with him when I can? He knows what needs to be done. Thanks, I appreciate it." He disconnected the call after offering a curt "I will," and slammed the phone back into place.

"What is *wrong* with you?" Liz asked, knowing why he was upset but unable to reconcile the easy-going man she usually knew with the one who currently sat beside her, scowling and clenching his jaw. The answers to the dilemma seemed fairly uncomplicated, in her estimation.

"Do you really have to ask me that? I don't like this, Liz, at all! I don't like you being in this position. I've been feeling uneasy ever since we saw Malone on my porch, and the feeling isn't going away." He turned a corner, pulled to a stop in front of the Montgomery home, and rolled down his window as Tyler and Amber ran outside. Tyler handed Liz's purse through the window, having placed the disk and papers inside. "Be careful," was all he managed to say as Connor pulled away from the curb.

"I'll leave your car in long-term parking," Connor called out the window as they sped off. He hadn't seen Malone's headlights for several miles, and hoped he'd been able to lose him for good. The prospect of the FBI agent locating Tyler and Amber's house was unthinkable. If the agent found the house, those responsible for the burglaries could find it as well. He gripped the wheel.

"Okay, Connor. You've got to calm down a little."

He looked at Liz as though she were deranged. "My home was invaded for the third time in less than six months. Every stick of furniture, every dish, every article of clothing dismantled or destroyed. I just found out that a woman to whom I was once quite close was a government agent, and she left a mysterious disk in my attic that has international intrigue written all over it."

He paused, then continued dramatically. "Now I'm being trailed by a man with an evil look in his eye who says he's with the FBI, and I'm facing the very real possibility that I have placed my best friends in the *world* in danger. You want to tell me again to calm down?"

She narrowed her eyes. "I've known you for a good five years, Connor. I may not know you as well as Amber does, but I think we're good enough friends that I can speak my mind. Let's try to put things into perspective here, shall we?" She spoke the last through clenched teeth. "Your home is insured, so your furniture can be replaced. You lost the guy tailing us, so Tyler and Amber are safe. You finally know why your house was broken into before, and you have me to help you solve the mystery behind it." She paused. "There's only one real problem here."

He eyed her cautiously. "What's that?"

"I'm going to throw up." She searched frantically in her purse for her ever-present stash of motion-sickness pills, and finding it, gripped the package tightly. "How close are we to the airport?"

"About fifteen minutes. Why didn't you tell me you were sick?" he asked, cranking up the air conditioning and turning all the vents on Liz. How could he have forgotten? Every time she came to visit, she popped those pills like candy if she was going to be in a car for long periods of time.

"It was all that twisting and screeching around corners," she managed as she took deep, even breaths.

Connor smacked his forehead and thumped his skull against the headrest. The one and only thing in the world that made him sick was witnessing someone else being sick. If she lost it, he would too. "Try to think happy thoughts or something," he told her, eyeing her anxiously. "I'll drive really carefully."

Happy thoughts. That would have been funny if she'd dared to laugh. There were no happy thoughts for someone who was carsick. Only a deep, burgeoning desire for a quick and painless death. She held on, to her credit, as they made their way through the airport parking, and was out of the Jeep like a shot when Connor finally brought it to a halt. She took several gulping breaths and started walking slowly. Extracting a motion-sickness pill from the package, she gulped it down, grimacing at having done so without the benefit of water, and hoping desperately it would have time to take effect before their plane took off.

Connor stashed Amber's keys under the front bumper and mentally crossed his fingers that no one would find them. He took one look at Liz's pale face, placed his hand under her elbow, and propelled her gently toward the airport terminals. "Are you okay?" he asked as they walked.

"Yes, I think so. I'll be fine in a minute."

They approached the gates of their chosen airline and Connor pulled his wallet from his pocket, taking out a credit card and asking about the next available flight to Seattle.

"Wait!" Liz pulled on his arm. "Use my card." She smiled at the woman behind the desk and pulled Connor down so her lips brushed his ear. "They can trace your card because they know your name. I didn't tell Malone my real name."

He gritted his teeth and reluctantly conceded the point. She pulled her wallet out of her purse and purchased two tickets for a flight leaving in an hour. Connor felt waves of guilt as she put her wallet back into her purse. "I'll pay you back," he murmured. "I can't believe I didn't think of that."

Liz shrugged. "It's okay. Really. You just get that car paid for." She gave him a smug smile, and patting his arm, turned away from the desk.

"I take it you're feeling better," he muttered as he followed her to their gate. He was tempted to whip out his ATM card and make use of the nearest cash machine by bringing up his checking and savings account balances, just to set her back a bit. "I have news for you, Ms. Saxton," he said as they sat to wait for their boarding call. "The car *is* paid for."

He took a huge amount of satisfaction at the look of shock that covered her face. That ought to keep her quiet for a while.

* * * * * *

Across town, a sand-colored sedan pulled to a stop in front of Connor's townhouse condo. Phillip Malone cut the ignition and sat for a full minute, looking at the front door, before extracting his cell phone from his jacket and punching in a series of numbers.

"It's Malone," he said to the voice at the other end. "Send reinforcements; we're looking for O'Brian. Give everyone his description. He's with a woman named Sharon. She has straight blonde hair that hangs approximately halfway down her back, and green eyes. I mean *green*. You can't miss her." He nodded at the question posed from the other end. "Yes. Check his office, the bus terminals, and the airport. Call me when you find something."

He disconnected the call and dialed another number. "It's me," Malone said when the call was answered. "I talked to O'Brian earlier tonight."

"And?"

"And I think he has it. He wouldn't tell me, though. And his girlfriend seemed more than happy to speak for him."

"He doesn't have a girlfriend."

"I know."

"Well, who is she, then?"

Malone rubbed his eyes in frustration. "I don't know. I followed them for a while, but—"

"But what?"

He hesitated. "I lost them."

The pause on the other end of the line was palpable. "Find them."

* * * * * *

Charles Frasier ended the call and returned his cell phone to the inner pocket of his dinner jacket. He walked the length of the hallway leading to his spacious living room, his feet beating a firm staccato rhythm on the elegant marble tile. He stood for a moment at his living room window, which actually spanned the length and height of his entire wall, and looked out over a nighttime view of the intracoastal waterway. He had paid handsomely for the breathtaking Miami Beach view, and he intended to keep it in his possession.

He flicked a speck of dust from its unwelcome perch on his sleeve and reflected on his current status as one of the world's leading philanthropists. His donations to charities around the world were becoming legendary. That his pharmaceutical company was making impressive strides in the war against cancer only polished his halo further. Perhaps the time was right to add AIDS research to his list of wonders.

"Mr. Frasier?" He turned at the voice of a servant behind him.

"Yes?"

"The car is ready."

"Fine." He turned to leave the room, and as he did so his gaze fell upon a sideboard bearing a small picture. He walked slowly to the photograph, picked it up, and studied it carefully. Allyson. Proof of his own vulnerability. He kept the picture as a constant reminder of past mistakes. He'd been foolish to lower his guard for even a moment; the treachery of her betrayal had been painful, if a man of his stature could admit to such frailty.

Allyson had been a weakness that had nearly toppled his empire. She had come highly recommended as a candidate for his executive assistant; he'd taken one look at her and hired her on the spot. That she'd been a quick learner had been an added bonus. Had she not, he'd have kept her around for other purposes; as it was, she was able to fulfill her duties as his assistant, and performed them well. When he had learned of her true purpose behind their association, he'd taken quick and decisive action. He was not a man to wallow in regrets.

Once the loose ends were tied up on O'Brian's end, the entire episode would be concluded and he could comfortably move on with his life. He ran a finger along the top of the picture frame, which was dust free, as always, and replaced it on the sideboard. No visible emotions played across his face as he studied the picture for one moment longer before turning and exiting the room, his step only slightly less determined than it had been upon entering.

Chapter 13

Connor glanced at his sleeping companion with a wry smile. She'd stayed awake long enough for the plane to take off, mere moments after she'd happily proclaimed that she no longer felt at all carsick, and didn't anticipate being sick on the plane, as she'd taken her medicine in plenty of time. She had also gone on to sing the praises of this new, less-drowsy medicine she'd discovered which didn't make her nearly as tired as did her former pills. "In fact," she'd said as they'd found their seats, "I'll probably be awake this whole flight."

Connor settled back into the roomy seat with a shake of his head. She'd actually bought first-class tickets. He again resolved to pay her back as soon as possible, and stole another glance at her sleeping form. He brushed away some stray hair that had fallen across her cheek, and observed her face as she took deep, even breaths. Her lashes lay like miniature fans across her skin, and her complexion was soft and lightly tanned, a testament to her enjoyment of outdoor activity. Or maybe, he mused with a gentle smirk, it was a testament to her use of a tanning bed—Seattle wasn't known for its consistently sunny weather.

His hand reached up of its own accord, and he lightly brushed his knuckles across her cheek. He drew his eyebrows together as he watched her face, so still in sleep. Why hadn't he noticed before how much she resembled his former fiancée? Allyson had also had thick, straight blonde hair and green eyes. Her eyes had been substantially lighter, he reflected—more of a watered-down green. It was too bad, really, that in his estimation, Allyson had never measured up to Liz.

He pulled his hand from her face as though she had burned him, and stared. All the time he'd been engaged to Allyson, he'd been comparing her to Liz. The realization made him sick. Not only had he wanted the woman to change, he'd wanted her to be someone else altogether. It was probably why he'd been attracted to her in the first place.

Allyson had reminded him of Liz.

He fumbled with his seatbelt and made his way to the cramped lavatory. Once there, he flipped the lock on the door and sank onto the closed toilet lid. He stared straight ahead at the door and murmured, "No." Was it really possible that he'd thought he was in love with Allyson because she resembled Liz?

He closed his eyes as his mind sorted its way to the truth. It would certainly explain some things. The way he'd felt like he was seeing an old friend the first time he'd laid eyes on Allyson. The reason he was so willing to overlook the evidence pointing to the fact that she'd been seeing someone else during their relationship, although she'd said she wasn't.

He groaned and leaned forward, resting his elbows on his knees, his head gripped tightly in his hands. Why? Why had he pursued Allyson when she had been merely a stand-in for someone else? The answers came swiftly as he allowed himself to closely examine his motives. Allyson had lived close by. Liz lived across the country. Allyson had pushed intimacy from the first date. Liz had never pursued anything beyond friendship. Allyson was available. Liz always seemed to have a boyfriend.

The reasons seemed pathetic when he considered the fact that he'd very nearly shackled himself for eternity to someone he was interested in merely because she happened to remind him of someone else. To be grateful for Allyson's death would be beyond morbid; besides which, he'd decided to end the relationship before she had died. He had to give himself some credit; his judgment hadn't been totally skewed, just a little off. Also, in retrospect, he had to admit that he'd formed some nice memories with Allyson. Unfortunately, he reflected grimly, the pleasant memories stemmed from occasions when Allyson had seemed most like Liz. The easy smile, the laugh—why had he never seen it?

He rose and splashed cold water on his face, wanting to punish himself. For what? For wanting a woman simply because she reminded him of another? For ruining her life because he'd expected her to be someone she wasn't? No. She had been well on her way to ruining her own life; she hadn't needed his help for that. He had, however, been dishonest with himself emotionally, and with her as well. It was no wonder he'd been so unhappy. She must have sensed it. She hadn't been happy either; that much had been evident.

"You're a coward," he said aloud to his reflection in the mirror as he patted his face dry with a paper towel. *You went after the wrong woman and didn't even realize it.* He thought of Liz, sleeping peacefully outside the walls of the small rest room, and felt a momentary rush of panic. Now what was he supposed to do? He couldn't very well wake her up and say, "Hey, I just figured out I'm a total idiot. Do you think you could ever develop any real feelings for me?"

He groaned and leaned forward, his forehead resting on the mirror, and closed his eyes. Is that what he wanted with her? He knew the answer as quickly as the question formed. He'd been attracted to her from the moment they'd met. Unconscious Connor had been in love with conscious Liz. Unfortunately, that realization was new to him, and he had no idea if she would even entertain the notion of a serious relationship with him.

"Okay," he said, lifting his head and opening his eyes. "You're going to leave her alone. You're not going to destroy a great friendship by professing your undying love." She'd never buy it anyway. She saw him only as a friend, after all.

* * * * * *

Liz managed to force her eyelids open despite the fact that they felt like lead. The plane was making its descent into SeaTac airport, and she rubbed her temples, hoping to convince her brain to function. She had to call someone. Who was it?

She turned her bleary gaze to Connor, who looked into her eyes and then quickly glanced down to fumble with his seatbelt. "We're landing," he mumbled needlessly, avoiding further eye contact with her.

Liz squinted at him. Of course they were landing. He looked extremely uncomfortable. What was wrong with him? She shook her head. She had more important things to worry about. Like clearing the cobwebs from her brain. "I'm supposed to call someone, aren't I?"

Connor looked up in surprise. What was wrong with her? "Yes," he said slowly. "Your friend, Lump, or Slump, or something. Mr. International Contacts."

"Bump!" Her memory assailed her in waves, and all was suddenly clear again, much to her relief. The medicine must have knocked her flat. "Okay." She leaned over to retrieve her purse from underneath the seat in front of her and pulled out her cell phone. "As soon as we get off, I'll call him. We can rent a car and drive to his apartment."

Connor stood with her as the plane stopped at its gate and they moved into the aisle. "Are you sure he won't mind any of this?" he murmured in her ear as they made their way into the airport.

"Of course he won't mind. He's a really good friend. Besides, he owes me a few. I helped make him a rich man." Liz looked casually around at their surroundings before choosing a relatively secluded corner from which to make her call.

Connor stood close by, glancing over his shoulder, suddenly suspicious of the world and expecting Malone to materialize out of thin air. He watched as Liz turned on her phone, punched in her security code, paused, and then hit two more buttons. She lifted the phone to her ear, waiting for the call to be answered. *So,* he mused silently, *she has this man's number programmed into her phone.* He raised his eyebrows at the casual manner in which she addressed her "friend" when the call was answered.

"Bump? It's me." Pause. "Yeah, I know. I'm in town with a friend and we, uh, well, we need your help." Another pause. "Okay, we're on our way."

Hmm. They were good enough friends that he recognized her voice unidentified on the phone. Connor clamped down on an irrational spurt of jealousy. Liz had said the man was a computer genius. Probably some tall, gangly type who never remembered to shower and couldn't fight his way out of a wet paper bag. He consoled himself with that thought and took Liz's arm as they made their way to the rental car counter.

"Don't be stupid, Connor," Liz stated flatly as she marched ahead of him to the rental car, key in hand. "I know my way around this city with my eyes closed. You've never even been here." Her eyes widened in surprise as Connor overtook her and pinned her against the car. Drat. She'd seen him play rugby, and had forgotten how fast he could move. They had been debating who should drive for a good five minutes, ever since she had snatched the key at the rental counter and made her way to the car. Now back on her own turf, she felt a certain sense of empowerment at being in a city that had been her home for several years. She wanted to be behind the wheel, where she'd feel she was finally controlling things for the first time in several hours.

Connor's breath was warm on her ear. "I appreciate what you're doing, Liz, you know I do. But there's no way I'm letting you drive. You're still tired from that medicine you took—you can't even walk in a straight line. Besides, I *have* been here before. Many times. On business."

Liz blinked. Maybe she was still a bit tired. She glanced down at the top of the car, to which her face was precariously close. She felt the warmth of Connor's chest and torso seeping into her back, and found it excessively . . . nice. The Seattle weather was doing its best to live up to its soggy reputation, and she found herself wanting to twist herself around in the cage he'd made with his arms and wrap her own arms around his waist underneath his jacket. She blinked again. What was she thinking?

"Here," she said quickly. "Take the keys, then."

Connor raised his eyebrows in surprise. Just like that? She'd fought him all the way to the car. Why the sudden turnaround? He released her and took the keys she dropped into his hand. As she walked around to the passenger side of the car, he got a good look at her flushed face and cursed himself for ten times a fool. He followed her around, opening and closing his mouth several times while trying to think of something to say.

He unlocked her door, saw her safely inside, closed the door, and smacked his forehead with his palm as he made his way to the driver's side. *Nice one, O'Brian,* he thought in disgust. *Body-slam her into the side of a car. Great way to impress a girl.* Was he so desperate to touch her, now that he realized he was attracted to her, that he'd turned into a total Neanderthal? He was reminded of the definition of Freud's

"Id"—the kind of person who had no social conscience; someone who saw what he wanted and took it. A caveman who clubbed the screaming woman upside the head and dragged her to his cave.

Liz was quiet as they drove through the streets of Seattle. Other than offering directions to her friend's house, she didn't say much. Connor wasn't surprised. In all the years they'd known each other, the closest physical contact they'd ever shared were hugs at greeting and parting. Except for the dancing the night of his company party. That had been nice.

But that had been *dancing*. What was she supposed to think when all of a sudden he'd pinned her against the side of a car because he'd been frustrated that she wouldn't stop and listen while he explained all the logical reasons why he should be the one to drive? He thought of the sophisticated social creature he'd become since graduating from college, and nearly laughed out loud. He must be losing his touch, to take such a twelve-year-old-boy approach to winning an argument. Maybe he *had* just wanted an excuse to touch her.

Liz stared straight ahead at the city lights and tried not to be so intensely aware of the man driving the car. A casual gesture of physical aggressiveness on his part was just that. Casual. A ploy to get her to hand over the keys. She was obviously reading too much into it, the way her heart was pounding. Poor man. He was preoccupied with the fact that his home had again been burglarized, his former fiancée had possibly been a government agent, and they were being followed by an FBI guy who wanted a mysterious computer disk that they probably had no business keeping from him. All she could think about was how to get him to pin her up against the car again. The damp weather must have addled her brain.

"His apartment is on the twenty-third floor," Liz stated when she and Connor parked the car in Bump's underground garage and made their way into the lobby. She was altogether too aware of his nearness; she tried not to fidget as the elevator climbed, and she managed not to breathe an audible sigh of relief as the doors opened.

It was with no small amount of curiosity that Connor waited for the multi-talented "Bump" to open the door. "Ooh," Liz suddenly murmured, "I hope he's not, um, entertaining anyone tonight. I didn't think of that."

Connor looked at her, his expression flat, and opened his mouth to respond when their knock was answered. On the other side was a man who stood two inches above Connor's height and matched his width through the shoulders and arms. So much for his "scrawny computer guy" theory. He was contemplating offering the man his hand when Liz beat him to the punch. She leaned forward to give him an affectionate, comfortable hug, followed by a quick kiss on the cheek. "Hi, Bump," she said with a weary smile.

"Back already, huh? I knew you couldn't stay away from me." Bump released Liz and offered his hand to Connor. "You must be the friend," he said.

Liz nodded. "Bump, this is Connor O'Brian. Connor, Bump St. James. I don't know his real first name because he won't tell anyone what it is."

Connor returned the handshake with the same amount of pressure that was exerted on his own hand. Bump apparently wanted to send a message. Connor respected that. Liz was worth protecting.

Chapter 14

Connor sat in Bump's study, watching Liz's friend as he scanned the contents of Allyson's disk on his computer. Liz had disappeared after breakfast at Bump's suggestion that she visit her old place of work and go through the "costuming department," whatever that meant. "All of your stuff is still there," Bump had told her. "Paperwork and everything. We need to find a few things for Captain Marvel, here, too," he'd stated, inclining his head toward Connor.

Connor watched as Bump shook his head at the computer monitor. "Not sure what these lists are," he said, his voice distracted. "Give me a minute, though. I'll figure it out."

Connor bit back a sarcastic reply, and, taking a deep breath, closed his eyes. The man had an extremely high opinion of himself. He could stomach it, Connor supposed, provided the ego produced some results.

"This is interesting," Bump murmured to himself.

"What's that?"

"These names listed here next to the cities—I think they're street names." He ran his finger down the list, pausing at one spot in particular. "In fact, I'm sure of it." He glanced up. "You know—street names. Names people pick up from their associates . . ."

"Hmm. On the streets, maybe?" Being treated like a child was not a feeling Connor was accustomed to, nor was it one he particularly enjoyed.

Bump sighed and sat back in his chair. "So she never mentioned any of this to you?" He gestured toward the monitor and took off his glasses.

"No. She never talked about work." Connor shook his head. "She never gave me any indication that she wanted me to look after the disk. It's pretty obvious that she was hiding it."

Bump's eyes narrowed. "Who would she have been hiding it from?"

Connor looked at the man before him, unblinking, before finally bothering to reply. "I don't know," he stated succinctly. "Presumably, if she *was* working undercover for the government, she may have been gathering information on the company. I might hazard a guess that she didn't want anyone at Frasier Pharmaceutical finding out about it."

The corner of Bump's mouth twitched. "Hazard a guess, huh?"

Connor raised one eyebrow. "If you don't follow me, I can use simpler phrases."

Bump held his hands up in a placating gesture. "I understand your stress, really I do," he said. "And since you're a friend of Liz's, I'll see what I can do. Speaking of Liz," Bump made a show of casually aligning his mouse pad with the edge of the desk, "how well do you know her?"

"I know her very well. We've been friends for several years." Connor's reply was serious, without a trace of malice or flippancy. He'd been anticipating this discussion since Bump had opened the door the night before and enveloped Liz in a thoroughly protective gaze. "I think very highly of her and consider her a good friend."

"I'm glad to hear that, because I think highly of her, too." Bump met Connor's expression with an equally serious gaze and nodded. "Just so we understand each other."

"I'm sure we do."

"Good."

The men were silent as they perused the contents of the disk, Bump using his computer and Connor shuffling through the hard copies he and Liz had printed from Amber's computer.

Connor looked up as Bump shifted in his chair and began jotting some notes on a piece of paper. "I'll start with your fiancée's background and then see what I can dig up on Frasier Pharmaceutical."

"And how is it that you plan to access government files?"

Bump smiled. "There's no such thing as an impenetrable system, especially when one has friends on the inside."

Connor studied Bump with his mouth drawn in a half-smirk, and finally gave in to his curiosity. "Didn't you get the stink beat out of you as a kid with a name like Bump?"

Bump rubbed his chin and smiled. "Actually, I got the stink beat out of me because of my given name. I came up with the nickname as a means of self-defense. My dad called me Bump when I was little because I was forever banging into stuff with my head."

Connor bit back a snicker. *That would explain a few things.* "Must be quite the name. Your given one, I mean."

"I don't like to think about it. My mother, bless her heart, is British, and she wasn't too concerned about searching the annals of England's history to find a masculine name for me. She just chose the most beautiful-sounding one she could think of."

Before Connor had a chance to mull over this possible clue, they were interrupted by a soft knock on the open door to the study. Both men turned to see a woman with short dark hair and trendy, wire-framed glasses enter the room. She was wearing a tan tweed skirt that grazed the tops of her knees, with a matching blazer and cream-colored blouse. She carried an attaché case and appeared every inch the business professional. Connor's manners prompted him to rise, and he waited for Bump to introduce him to the woman.

Bump grinned. "I thought you said you knew her well," he said.

Connor's gaze widened as he regarded the cool, beautiful woman. She offered him her hand. "Ellen Deveraux," she said, smiling. Eyes that should have been green were now dark brown, and hair that should have been long and blonde was now black, cut blunt at the jawline with a fringe of bangs on the forehead.

"Liz?" Connor's grip on her hand held of its own accord, and he stared. He cleared his throat. She looked so . . . not like Liz. "What did you do?"

She winked at him. "I transformed."

He tilted his head to one side and squinted. "And you're British?"

She nodded and pulled her hand from his grasp, moving to open her attaché case. She extracted several documents for his inspection. He sifted through them: a birth certificate for one Ellen Deveraux, a driver's license with a picture of Liz looking exactly as she did now, a passport with a similar picture, and a handful of credit cards.

"My name is Ellen Deveraux, and I'm an advertising executive from London."

He thought of his mission to England. "I've heard that accent a time or two, you know."

She nodded. "How do I sound?"

He grinned. "Good. Really good, in fact. I'm impressed."

"Why, thank you. I actually took a class to learn a few accents."

Bump settled back in his chair and crossed one ankle over his other knee. "Liz can effectively speak English while sounding British, Irish, Italian, Hispanic, and Russian."

"Well, well. Hidden talents I knew nothing about."

Liz laughed and sank down into an overstuffed chair. "Something like that." She turned her attention to Bump. "So where do we go?"

"I've been thinking it wouldn't be a bad idea to start in New Orleans." He turned to Connor. "Did you know your fiancée's family at all?"

"I didn't ever meet them until the funeral. She has a mother and a sister. They didn't say much; they were obviously upset."

"Do you think they'd talk to you if you dropped by for a visit?"

Connor thought for a moment. "They might."

Bump tossed his pen onto the desk and tipped back on his chair. "If you could get a feel from them about Allyson's job—anything she might have mentioned, even in passing—it would help."

Connor nodded.

Liz eyed him speculatively. "Are you up to this?"

"Yeah. But it's weird."

"I know. We'll just make a quick trip down south and get it over with."

* * * * * *

"Okay," Liz said as she shuffled papers. "Follow 1-10 east to the New Orleans Business District exit."

Connor glanced at Liz, the corner of his mouth turned up in a half-smile. "I know how to get there. I've been here before. Besides, I was the one who made the arrangements. Who do you think printed out those instructions?" He maneuvered the car carefully, not wanting to make her sick.

Liz chewed absently on her lower lip as she flipped through the pages printed from an Internet web site. "I thought Bump did it."

"Well, I guess Bump isn't the only one who's handy with a computer, now is he?"

Liz looked up in surprise. "I never said he was," she remarked. "I just, well, I just thought he took care of everything."

"While you were busy packing all your fake IDs, I made our travel arrangements."

Liz nodded. She had been so busy trying to get her clothes and wigs in order that she had been occupied while the men finalized the details of the trip to New Orleans. Connor had insisted that Bump provide him with a false ID so he could charge his and Liz's expenses with credit cards he would pay off when they were done with their charades. A manly code of honor or something, Liz assumed. Connor hadn't been happy when she'd paid their airfare to Seattle, and she had decided not to press the matter further when the threesome had discussed financial details. Let him pay, she decided. Chivalry was a lost art anyway, and could use some revival. At any rate, she and Bump had decided Connor might need more than one disguise, should their trip become more involved than they'd planned.

The sky was black overhead, and threatening rain. It had taken all day in Seattle to make arrangements for the trip and secure an alter-identity for Connor. Bump had delved into his bag of magic tricks and worked miracles, as usual, and Connor stepped onto the plane leaving Seattle for New Orleans with his wallet full of credit cards and a driver's license issued to one "Brad Edwards." He had gratefully clasped Bump's hand at the gate and expressed his thanks. Bump merely inclined his head toward Liz and murmured, "Be good to her."

Connor drove into the heart of New Orleans with mixed feelings. The last time he had been in the city was for Allyson's funeral. He had stayed at the same hotel where his and Liz's reservations were, and was hoping to exorcise some ghosts.

Liz sensed his somber mood and tried to decide whether or not to ask him about it. Her curiosity finally made the decision. "What are you thinking?"

Connor cleared his throat. "I don't know, a bunch of things. The last time I was here was for a depressing reason. I had decided to break it off with her, and then she died so suddenly—I really had no sense of closure, I guess." He gave a short, humorless laugh. "Psychobabble."

Liz smiled softly. "No it's not. It's all very real, you know. All that emotional stuff that men never want to talk about." She glanced at his profile and felt her heart give a small leap. He was so devastatingly handsome. Impossibly enough, he got better looking every day. She shook her head and stared straight ahead at the city lights. He needed time and space. Her own needs were going to have to take a backseat. She wondered if they'd ever come to the forefront.

She sighed.

Connor glanced at Liz. "Tired? We're almost there." He paused. "I can't tell you how much it means to me that you're helping me with all this. I wouldn't want to be trying to do it by myself."

Liz smiled and patted his shoulder. A friend in time of need, that's what she'd have to be. There was a chance that he'd never see her as anything else. "I don't mind a bit, Connor. This is actually more meaningful than anything I've done in a long time."

* * * * * *

The hotel was magnificent. Connor had booked a suite of rooms at the Royal Sonesta Hotel New Orleans, which was situated in the French Quarter on Bourbon Street. "Depending on how things go with Allyson's family, we may have some time to do some sightseeing. I didn't do much when I was here last, and I'd like to," he said to Liz as they deposited their luggage in the suite.

Liz nodded. "I'd like that, too. I've never been here." She glanced uncomfortably at Connor, then motioned toward the two small bedrooms situated off the main living area. "Which one do you want?"

He shrugged. "Whichever one you don't." He grinned. "I've been told by various family members all my life that I snore, so I hope I don't keep you awake."

"You won't. I'm so tired I think I could sleep through a natural disaster." *Unless, of course, I'm awake because I'm entirely too aware of you sleeping in the next room,* she thought ruefully. "I think I'll take a shower and then get some sleep."

Connor watched her as she picked through her overnight case, sighed, and hefted the whole thing into the bathroom. He was coming to realize the true meaning of torture, he mused as he considered his situation—having something he wanted very badly just within reach, and yet too far away to grasp. It was going to be a long night.

Chapter 15

Connor stepped forward and knocked on the door of the old house. The paint was cracking and the windows were smudged. A front-porch swing hung by one chain and dragged pitifully against the wooden boards that creaked underfoot. Connor glanced at Liz, who had once again donned her Ellen Deveraux disguise. He had suggested she wear it. When she'd wondered why, he had thought to himself, *Because you look like my dead fiancée. I'd hate to freak out her family.*

He hadn't actually told her that—instead had said something along the "we don't want anyone remembering what you looked like in case Malone shows up and asks questions" line of logic. She'd accepted it without argument, saying she'd already planned on dressing in disguise. But the look on her face suggested she was wondering what he was thinking.

He looked again at the closed door. "I don't know if anyone's home," he said quietly. "We really should have called first."

Liz nodded. "Yes, but sometimes it's easier when you catch people by surprise. This isn't exactly a social call."

She stopped speaking as the front door creaked on its hinges.

A face appeared.

Connor cleared his throat and stepped forward. "Excuse me—Angelica, is it?"

"Yeah?" The door opened wider, revealing a teenager, probably around eighteen or nineteen, Liz mused. The girl looked as though she'd been awakened from sleep. Her hair was mussed, and dark traces of mascara left over from the day before showed under her eyes.

She squinted at Connor. "Don't I know you?"

"Yes, I was engaged to Allyson. We met at her funeral."

The girl's expression cleared. "Oh, yeah."

Connor placed his hand under Liz's elbow. "This is my friend, Ellen. We're here because we were wondering if we could ask you some things about Allyson."

The expression became shuttered, guarded. "What kind of things?"

"Can we come in for a minute?"

Angelica glanced behind her into the darkened house. "I have somebody over and he's still asleep. I'll come out here."

Connor nodded, and the three moved to sit on the front porch steps, Angelica in the middle with Liz and Connor on either side and down a step. Connor attempted to put the girl at ease. "How's your mother doing?"

Angelica's jaw clenched. "She's dead."

Connor stared for a moment before collecting his thoughts and replying. "I'm sorry to hear that. When did it happen?"

"She kicked it about two months ago. Finally drank herself to death."

"How are you doing?" Liz interjected. "Do you need help with anything?"

"What are you, a social worker?"

Liz smiled, her eyes narrowing. "No, I'm not a social worker. Sometimes people have a hard time when they lose loved ones, and it's nice to have someone to help out."

"Trust me, lady, my life is better now that she's gone. I have the house to myself, and no one screaming at me when she's had one too many."

"Angelica, I wonder if you can tell me some things about your sister." Connor resumed control.

"Yeah, you said that. What kind of things?"

"Well, did you know much about her job?"

The answering expression was blank. "Her job? You mean with that drug company?"

"Yes. Did she ever talk about it, or leave anything here when she was home visiting the last time? Papers or computer disks or anything at all?"

Angelica snorted. "She hardly ever came home. When she did, she didn't stay for long, and she never left anything."

"Do you have any of her old things still here at the house? In boxes or anything?"

"Yeah, I think there's a trunk full of stuff in the closet of her old bedroom. Why do you want it?"

Connor hesitated. "Things have been happening lately that I think may have something to do with her old job. My house has been broken into a few times, and it might be related to Allyson."

Angelica looked impressed. "Hmm. Well, you can look through the trunk if you want, but I think it's mostly old stuff."

"It would help, if you don't mind."

"I think it's too heavy for me to carry out here. You can come inside if you're really quiet."

Connor and Liz ventured cautiously into the house behind Angelica. The lights were turned off, the drapes drawn. The air inside was still and smelled of stale cigarette smoke. They followed Angelica into a bedroom off the living room. She opened the closet door and pointed to a trunk on the floor under a heap of old clothes. "That's it," she muttered quietly. "You can look, but keep the noise down."

"So you have a friend visiting?" Liz asked the woman.

"Yeah. A friend." Angelica smirked and left the room.

Liz turned to Connor with one eyebrow cocked. He held up his hands in a gesture of resignation. "Allyson was nothing like that," he said in his own defense. "I'd never have guessed she came from such . . . humble beginnings." *It shouldn't surprise you,* a little voice whispered inside his head. *You didn't know nearly enough about her.* Connor mentally told the voice to shut up and reached into the dark interior of the closet, shoving the pile of clothes to the floor and dragging the trunk out into the middle of the room. He and Liz both tensed at the resulting racket the object made as it protested the movement, but as Angelica didn't come bursting into the room brandishing weapons, they relaxed and lifted the lid.

The trunk was full of old ribbons, certificates of achievement for cheerleading competitions, and photographs. Liz plucked a picture from the middle of a fist full of papers she had grabbed. Within seconds, she realized she was staring at a version of herself.

Connor watched her through lowered lashes. What to say? Liz studied the photograph for a moment before setting it aside. He cleared his throat. "That picture was probably taken a good five years before I met her. She hadn't changed much, though." He glanced at the picture. "Her hair was a little bit different and her face a bit more mature, but pretty much the same."

Liz nodded. She sorted through certificates, old school papers and newspaper clippings. Pictures of Allyson cheering at football games and participating in competitions. Snapshots of her with friends at school and parties. She felt odd pawing through a dead woman's belongings. "She seemed to enjoy her high school social life," she mused aloud, wanting to break the eerie silence.

Connor nodded. "I guess she did. She never talked about her past or things she'd done. Never, ever talked about her family," he finished in a subdued tone.

Liz turned her attention from the papers in her lap and looked at his face. "I don't get it," she said. "It seems so out of character for you to almost marry someone you knew nothing about."

Connor gazed at her pensively for a while before replying. "She reminded me of someone," he finally said. "When she said she was trying to get active in the Church again and seemed so interested in my life, I suppose I just jumped into the relationship because I was lonely and ready for that stage. We were actually engaged for only a month before I realized it wasn't working. I'd known her for six months at that point." He stopped for a moment, thinking. "You're right. It is completely out of character for me. Proposing to her was the most impulsive thing I'd ever done, and I've lived to regret it."

Liz nodded in sympathy and patted his knee. "We all do things we regret. It's a part of life." She turned back to the papers in her lap, quickly perused them, and reached back into the trunk for more. They worked in silence for several minutes before Liz finally spoke again. "I don't think we're going to find anything in here. This is all stuff from high school. Did she go to college?"

"No, I don't think so. I went through the things in her apartment and sent her clothes to her mother. She didn't have any books, journals, or anything personal, really, except for knickknacks and a few pictures of herself. If she went to college, she didn't save anything.

Not like she did with this high school stuff, anyway. She never talked about a degree, or working toward one."

Liz glanced up, her expression puzzled yet sincere. "There seem to be a lot of things she never mentioned. What did you two talk about?"

Connor shook his head. "Not much, apparently. We talked about my family, and she asked about my work a lot—mostly surface subjects. I guess I always figured we'd get to the deep stuff later."

"Connor, the deep stuff is what convinces you that you love someone."

Connor was silent for a moment. "I guess that pretty much sums it up, then, doesn't it? I never loved her."

The words hung in the silence between them, heavy and palpable. He looked extremely uncomfortable. "You must think I'm really stupid."

"How could I think you're stupid when I made the same mistake myself? I very nearly married a man who didn't really love me, and I know in retrospect that I didn't love him. It happens all the time. We ought to be grateful that nothing came of our bad relationships. We'd be miserable people right about now." She leaned over and kissed his cheek, wanting to linger, feeling a thrill at the scent of his skin. Drawing back, she rubbed her finger on the smudge of lipstick she'd left on his face. A soft smile played about her lips, and she winked. "Life, huh? Just when we think we have it figured out, something wacky happens."

Breathe, he ordered himself. Life, indeed. Wacky didn't begin to describe his state of affairs over the past few days. And it was getting wackier by the minute. What Liz had considered a simple gesture had sent his heart rate into orbit. He glanced down at a picture of his former fiancée he held in his hand. It was time to bury some ghosts.

He shoved all the papers and medals back into the trunk, lowering the lid and shoving it back into its lair. He closed the closet door and offered his hand to Liz. "Let's go. There's nothing here."

They had made their way to the front door unimpeded when they started at a voice behind them, coming from the dark interior of the living room. "Find everything you needed?" Angelica asked through a haze of cigarette smoke.

Connor stepped toward her, pulling Liz along and offering Angelica his free hand. "Yes, thanks," he said.

She stared at his hand for a moment before she took it and shook awkwardly. Then she nodded toward Liz and said, "You got yourself a good one there. Allyson always said she'd snag herself a rich man, and when she called to say she was engaged, that was the first thing she told my mom. 'He's a rich one.' Like she was shoving it in the old lady's face or something." She took another deep drag on her cigarette and blew the smoke from her mouth in a long, drawn-out motion. "That was Allyson's main ambition in life. To marry well."

Liz forced a smile. "She sounds lovely."

"She was a beast."

"Indeed."

"Let's go." Connor yanked on Liz's hand and pulled her out the front door, throwing another murmur of gratitude at Angelica over his shoulder as they made their exit.

He was silent as they drove away from the old neighborhood. Liz sat awkwardly in the passenger seat, wanting to say something witty but unable to come up with anything that didn't sound insulting. She couldn't reconcile the man sitting beside her with the man who had apparently wanted a relationship with a woman who was superficial and shallow. She knew him to be a man of substance. It didn't make sense. How could he have been taken in by such a scheming woman? She could feel the fury radiating from him as he maneuvered the car through several subdivisions, onto a main thoroughfare, and finally through the gates of a cemetery. *Ah, closure,* she thought. *May you find it, my friend.*

Connor cut the ignition and sat for a moment in silence. He rested his head on the steering wheel and closed his eyes. His money. It always came down to the money. She'd wanted him for his money, just as he'd wanted her because he thought she was like Liz. They'd used each other for their own respective ends, and they'd made each other miserable in the process.

He raised his head and looked at Liz. "I need to say a few things to her."

Liz nodded. "I'll wait here."

Connor made his way to Allyson's gravesite and stood in silence for a moment, staring down at the headstone. "Allyson Maria

Shapiro—Beloved daughter and sister." He mentally scoffed at the last sentiment. It seemed to him, in light of the past hour, that Allyson and Angelica's mother had treated them abominably, and had raised daughters that learned to behave in like fashion. For that he pitied her.

I'm sorry, Allyson, that I wasn't honest with either of us. I could have saved myself some heartache and you some valuable husband-hunting time if I'd known what I was looking for. He didn't feel the need to speak the words aloud; he knew they were more for his peace of mind than hers. His thoughts turned back to the dingy house, to a trunk full of memories belonging to a girl who hadn't had much of a head start, and who seemed to feel that her most important accomplishments in life had occurred before she had graduated from high school. The surge of pity overpowered the anger, and his soul felt a measure of peace. And if she had indeed uncovered something big at Frasier Pharmaceutical, he mused, then she had accomplished a great deal.

"Good-bye, Allyson." With one last, long look at the headstone, he turned away from the grave and made his way back to the car. He sat next to Liz, who offered him a sympathetic smile.

"Better?" she asked.

"Better."

Chapter 16

Liz and Connor shared a table at an outdoor café situated in the heart of the French Quarter. With a sigh of satisfaction, Liz leaned back in her chair and regarded the remains of their dinner, a delectable blending of Cajun and Creole cooking that would have her mouth watering in memory for weeks to come. She eyed the one last shrimp sitting on her plate and resisted the impulse to gobble it down, hoping her stomach, full of spicy jambalaya, wouldn't know the difference. "That was divine," she remarked, closing her eyes.

Connor had to agree. The meal had topped off a day spent in leisure exploration of the French Quarter. The French Market, the Flea Market—countless shops had kept the couple busy from the time they had returned from the cemetery.

"Someday," Liz said quietly, her eyes still closed, "I'd like to come back here when we have more time to spend. Something about this place is so exotic."

Connor wondered if Liz had noticed she'd said "we," not "I." Maybe, just maybe, if he played his cards right he could make it happen.

Liz reluctantly opened her eyes to find Connor's gaze riveted intently on her face. His expression was unreadable; the only aspect of his countenance that betrayed anything specific was his eyes. Normally a beautifully cool blue, they seemed to burn with an intensity she'd glimpsed earlier in the day at Allyson's house. Her heart stopped functioning altogether, it seemed, and then suddenly resumed its rhythm with such speed that she felt it would beat its way out of her chest. She held her breath, finally releasing it when Connor broke the spell by shoving his chair back and tossing his napkin on the table.

"We need to get back and check in with Bump," he said, placing his hand on the back of her chair.

Liz nodded and cleared her throat. "Okay."

They made their way to the hotel in silence.

* * * * * *

Liz felt blissfully refreshed, having doffed her "Ellen Deveraux" disguise and showered. She sat in her bedroom, combing her fingers through her damp hair, and waited until she heard the shower running before she went to the living room area, picked up the phone, and dialed Bump's number.

"Well, the fiancée was definitely working for the government," Bump said without preamble when Liz reached him. "She was on their payroll with her actual name, although the details of her assignment were vague. There aren't any other agents, undercover or otherwise, currently assigned to Frasier Pharmaceutical."

Liz was silent for a moment. "Then who is Phillip Malone?"

"That I don't know. But I'm working on it."

"Hey," Liz lowered her voice and glanced at the bathroom door, "how would I go about getting a look at Allyson's autopsy report?"

"Why?"

"Well, she didn't exactly have a close relationship with her mother and sister, and Connor said the weekend she died, she was at a family reunion in Colorado. That doesn't make sense to me."

"Colorado, huh?" Bump was silent for a moment, presumably jotting down notes. "I can take care of that. What you two may want to do next is hop a plane for London."

"London? Why?"

"I've done some . . . research . . . on Frasier Pharmaceutical, and have discovered a few things of interest."

"Like what?" Liz smiled. She could almost see the predatory gleam Bump surely had in his eye. Uncovering secrets was what he did best.

"Well, for starters, while the D.C.-based office receives a lot of correspondence from their worldwide contacts, the London office is the only one that receives any electronic input from a business in Greece."

"And you find this suspicious because . . . ?"

"Don't know, exactly. Call it a hunch. What I'd suggest is that you pull the same kind of deal we did with the Shoreline Insurance Company here. Do you remember?"

Liz nodded. "I do. I suppose we'd be safe enough—provided no one from Frasier knows Connor. I've never asked if he met the people Allyson worked with."

"Well, she was the executive assistant for the president of the company. If he *had* ever met her boss, we might be in trouble, as it's his offices you'll be checking out. He's supposed to be headed for Greece, where he'll be for the next two weeks, so it should be a fairly easy procedure."

Liz closed her mouth, which had dropped open of its own accord. It was the first part of Bump's statement that had her floored. "Allyson never even went to college, and her high school grades weren't that good. I should know; I've seen the evidence myself. She'd only been out of high school for five years or so when she got that job. What I'd like to know is how she got it!"

Bump laughed. "Honey, the government could have made her look as good as they needed her to be. It's not hard to fabricate a good resume, and if she had enough charm to go with it she was probably set, no questions asked."

Liz pursed her lips. "I don't know that 'charm' is the word I'd use."

"Was she pretty?"

Liz thought of the photos she'd seen that morning. Virtual images of herself. "I suppose so," she admitted guilelessly. "She resembled me."

Bump paused. "Well, there you go," he said quietly.

Liz heard the water turn off in the shower. "I'll keep you posted on our travel plans," she said. "Let me know what you find out with that autopsy, okay? And don't mention it to Connor just yet. I don't want him to know, in case I'm wrong."

"Will do. Be careful."

* * * * * *

When Connor finished his shower and exited the bathroom wearing jeans and a white T-shirt, he found Liz in her bedroom with the door open, studying a wide array of wigs and clothes that she had spread liberally across her bed.

"What's all this?" he asked as he entered, rubbing a towel across his wet hair.

She took a good, long look at him before she reluctantly tore her gaze away from the appealing image of large, freshly washed male and mentally recited the Young Women's Theme. Finding that unproductive, she focused instead on her pile of paraphernalia on the bed.

"Well, we have to go to London, and I'm trying to decide who to be." She took a deep, shaky breath and tried to ignore the scent that was so uniquely Connor. Closing her eyes, she rubbed a hand along her forehead. Focus on work. Work was safe. "Had I known we'd be headed for England, I might have saved Ellen for later."

Liz recounted the details she'd obtained from Bump. "What we did with the Shoreline Insurance Company in Seattle was study the patterns of the cleaning crew that went through the offices each night, and I got a temporary job with them under an assumed identity. Then I was able to get the information we needed from the executive offices, and we brought down the company."

Connor squinted at her. "You broke in, basically, and toppled an entire business?"

"It wasn't really 'breaking in,' per se, and when the story broke, it just looked as though an innocent little cleaning lady had stumbled across some illegal dealings." She grinned. "Okay, so it's a little murky on the moral side, but I'd say the ends justified the means. That insurance company was robbing people blind."

Connor glanced at the piles of clothes, hair, and documents on the bed. "So how many people am I traveling with?"

"Six, including me." She held up a long-haired, curly red wig. "With this one I'm Maggie O'Scanlon, Irish watercolor artist." She exchanged the red wig for one with medium-length black curls. "With this wig I'm Anna Mendoza, Spanish elementary school teacher. I also use it to be Maria Scarlotta, Italian cosmetics model. I even have my own portfolio."

"I'll bet you do," Connor murmured.

Liz dropped the wig on the bed and fished through a pile of documents. "With my own hair curled like this and blue contacts," she said, holding a passport in front of Connor's face for his inspection, "I'm Nina Petrov, Russian would-be actress extraordinaire. I'm not Nina very often. Her accent is the hardest for me. She's also more risky because I use my own hair, and even though I style it differently, it's still the same color. Now, my dilemma is this: I've already been Ellen Deveraux, so I need to switch in case someone is following us. It would have been handy, however, to be Ellen in London. She is British, after all."

Connor looked a bit dazed. "How do you keep all these people straight?"

Liz shrugged. "I've studied each persona inside and out so I don't make mistakes or slip up. And I've used each one several times, so I know my stuff. The names themselves are very stereotypic for the cultures I'm trying to mimic, but I find that people believe what they expect to see and hear." She dropped the passport back onto the "Nina Petrov" pile and glanced up, swallowing audibly at the expression on Connor's face.

"I like you as you," he murmured.

"I like being me, too." She motioned toward the piles on the bed. "It was just a job."

He nodded, his expression guarded. "One you were good at."

She arched an eyebrow. "Meaning?"

"Meaning I've always known you as such a sincere person. I never would have imagined you to be such a good actor."

"A person can be sincere in real life and still be a convincing actor. Besides, I've never acted around you. When I spent time with you, I was also with Amber and Tyler, two of the few people in the world I can be myself around." She gritted her teeth. "You've never seen me as anyone but myself, Connor. I did what I had to do to perform well at my job, because it made good money and I didn't have some man around to support me." Her eyes flashed. "I don't appreciate your judgment or your censure."

She attempted to stem the flow of anger and refrained from saying anything further. Beneath the anger was pain. She didn't want disappointment from him. There was nothing dishonorable about the things she'd done while working for Bump; she'd pretended to be someone she wasn't in order to catch people who were doing things they shouldn't.

Connor raised his hand to brush the backs of his fingers across her cheek. He leaned toward her, his eyes holding hers. "I'm not judging you," he murmured. "I would hate to think the person I care for so much isn't real."

Liz very nearly allowed her arms the freedom they desired to reach up around his neck and pull his lips to hers. She stopped herself as she remembered the events of the day—his former fiancée's home, her pictures, her life. He was very likely confusing old feelings for Allyson, negative or otherwise, with Liz's proximity. "I need some air," she whispered, walking out of the bedroom and toward the balcony overlooking Bourbon Street, closing the French doors behind her.

Once outside, she took a deep breath and closed her eyes. It would be too easy to allow it, she mused—to let him to use her as an outlet for the emotions he'd most likely been experiencing all day. Except that he'd said he'd never loved Allyson. *So what must he think when he looks at me?* she wondered. He couldn't help but remember *her.* She couldn't let him confuse his feelings for another woman with the fact that she was there with him, and willing. A girl had her pride.

She leaned forward, bracing her arms on the balcony railing, and looked down into the city lights. And sighed.

Connor stared at Liz through the closed French doors and muttered an unintelligible curse. What was he thinking? He was going to ruin their entire friendship if he couldn't get a grip on his feelings for her. With Liz at his side, going through Allyson's belongings had been like comparing something one loved and cherished above all else with something that was beautiful but represented no lasting signifi-cance. If there had been any lingering doubts about his feelings for Liz, they had vanished in an instant when he had watched her sift through Allyson's things. Even in her "Ellen Deveraux" disguise, his memories of Allyson paled in pathetic comparison to the reality of Liz.

And how had he made manifest his newfound enlightenment? He'd actually had the audacity to insult her by questioning whether or not she was authentic—whether her relationship with him, spanning five enjoyable years, was all an act. By suggesting that her former job somehow said something significant about her personality; something less than flattering and more than a little insulting.

He paced the length of the room, shaking his head slightly at his own stupidity and wanting to pound the wall with his fist. For a man who knew people inside and out, and how to deal effectively with those he was close to, he was botching it, and in an extremely big way.

Running a hand impatiently through his wet hair, Connor turned toward the phone. He'd had something on his mind, and since he'd pretty much ruined the evening for both of them anyway, now was as good a time as any. He reached into his wallet and pulled out a piece of paper, punching the numbers written on it into the phone. Holding his breath, he hoped to complete the call before Liz decided she'd had enough of the balcony.

He was relieved to hear the voice he was anticipating pick up the other end. "Bump?" he said.

"Yeah?"

"It's Connor O'Brian. I can't talk long, but I'm wondering if you can look into something for me."

"Where's Liz?"

"Outside. I wonder if there's a way we can get a copy of Allyson's autopsy report."

Silence greeted his request. "What is it you're looking for, exactly?" Bump finally asked.

"Well, now that I know more about her family, I'm convinced she wasn't in Colorado for a family reunion. I don't want to mention it to Liz, because, well, this could get dangerous if what I'm thinking is true." He paused. "I think someone killed Allyson."

"Liz is pretty tough, actually. Your suspicions probably wouldn't shock her feminine sensibilities, you know."

Connor tensed as he watched Liz shift her position outside and move toward the doors. "Just leave that to me. I don't want to frighten her unless it's absolutely necessary. Can you get the report?"

"Yeah, I can get the report. Check in with me when you get to London."

Bump hung up the phone and laughed out loud. Liz and her sidekick were running a three-ring circus and didn't have a clue. He wondered how long it would be before they finally gave in to the chemistry that was so palpable between the two of them. He'd noticed it within minutes of watching them together.

They probably wouldn't end up in the same bed; he knew Mormons had a thing about that. He wouldn't be surprised, though, to see a wedding announcement sometime in the near future. He shook his head at the oddities of organized religion and turned to look out his spacious windows at the darkened Seattle skyline. Reflected in the glass he saw his expensively furnished living room, full of things but void of people. He clamped down on an uncustomary surge of loneliness and made his way to the sidebar for a drink.

* * * * * *

Liz was carefully packing away her disguises when Connor approached her, determined to lighten the somber mood that permeated the room. "You never did tell me what this pile is for," he said, gesturing toward a short blonde wig and several hats.

"That's yours," Liz said, offering him an oddly quirked smile as she continued her packing process.

"Mine?" Connor furrowed his brows. He had listened with only half an ear when Liz had given him several different "outfits" to pack in a large suitcase Bump had provided.

"Yes. I've decided to be Maggie O'Scanlon, Irish watercolor artist, when we go to London. You'll be Zach Williamson, my tennis-playing American boyfriend."

"It won't be very convincing, given that I don't even have a racket with me."

With a flourish, Liz unzipped the lining in the bottom of her suitcase and produced a tennis racket, followed by a nylon tennis racket carrying case that had been folded and stashed with the racket.

"Voilá," she grinned, relieved that the tension in the room had dissipated. "And you'll wear this." She reached across the bed and retrieved the shoulder-length blonde wig that Connor had noticed.

"Yeah, you think," he retorted, eyeing the thing with disdain.

"Yeah, I think! What good does it do to have me in disguise if you're the same no matter where we go? Why do you think Bump gave you more than one set of IDs?"

"I've been thinking about that. The other IDs are useless without my picture on them in disguise."

"Oh, that's no problem," Liz said, dropping the wig back on the bed and pawing through her carry-on case. "I have this little camera here. If you'll notice, on all your fake IDs, everything's good to go but the picture. So we just slap the wig on your head, I snap the picture, and bingo!"

"I'm not wearing a wig."

"Then we'll have to bleach your hair."

He stared at her in silence. "I won't let you leave the room to buy the hair dye," he finally said triumphantly.

She grinned wickedly. "You won't have to." With one hand, she reached into her carry-on and pulled out a box of hair color.

At his sulky silence, Liz decided the time had come to smooth things over. She smiled. "Come on, Connor. It's no big deal. You might even enjoy acting for a while." She sobered. "Besides, it really is necessary. I'm not lugging all this stuff around just for fun."

He ran a hand over tired eyes. "I know, and I do appreciate it. But I don't like the idea of you getting caught in the middle of all this."

She waved a hand. "Not that again. We've both agreed that I'm here of my own free will."

Connor was silent for a moment before venturing another reply. When he finally did, his voice was low and husky, gentle and apologetic in its tone. "Liz, I'm so sorry for making you feel uncomfortable, for even suggesting that . . ."

Liz cut him off with a soft, pained smile. "It's okay, really. I know you didn't mean it. I just . . ." She faltered. "I have so many of my own issues connected with what I did for a living this past while—I don't know how to explain it, but I can't handle criticism from you. I really . . . You're really . . ." *What? You mean the world to me? You always have?* She looked down and ran her fingertip across the top of the box of hair color she still held in her hand, tracing a pattern along the edge while her brows furrowed in a light frown.

Connor closed his eyes, hating himself for putting her in a vulnerable position. "I'm sorry," he murmured again, extending his hand toward her and cradling her cheek in his palm. "I'm sorry."

She leaned against his hand, closing her eyes, wishing. Then she smiled and opened her eyes, deciding the time had come to again lighten the mood. If she didn't, she'd dissolve into a puddle of pathetic tears and pour out her heart to him, confessing everything she'd ever felt for him in the years since they'd met.

The phone rang, startling her and interrupting anything she might have said. She moved away from Connor and picked up the receiver curiously. It was well past midnight.

"Liz?" It was Bump. "You two have to go to London *now.*"

"What?"

"One Phillip Malone was on a plane from Virginia to Seattle this morning, and two hours ago he boarded a plane for New Orleans."

Liz's heart raced. "How did he know?"

"It was only a matter of time—all he had to do was flash his badge and offer your descriptions to the airline workers. Plus, he's probably got people working with him, so it won't take long to track you down."

Bump sighed with disgust. "So now, presumably, he's looking for 'Brad Edwards,' a man who resembles Connor's description, because I was stupid enough to think you were really the only one who needed to be in disguise. And, of course, he'll be looking for one 'Ellen Deveraux.' I've been checking passenger lists, and sure enough, he's on to you."

Liz released a pent-up breath. "Okay. We're leaving. We'll try to get on standby, and I'll call you when we get to London."

She hung up the phone, closed her eyes for a fleeting moment, then flew into a flurry of activity, packing her bags and relaying the contents of the phone conversation to Connor over her shoulder as she moved. "Put on the long, baggy blue shorts and the oversized white T-shirt with the Slick Rock mountain-biking logo on it," she ordered as she pulled together pieces of her own disguise. "We have to check *out* as the same people we were when we checked *in.* Can you fit your Brad Edwards clothes on top of the baggy Zach stuff?"

Had the situation been even a bit less dire, he'd have laughed. This conversation was ridiculous. He nodded. "If you can be two people, so can I."

She gave him a halfhearted smile as she hurried to the bathroom with an armload of clothes and her makeup bag. "We need to be out of here as soon as possible. I'll be ready in a minute."

Grateful her hair was still damp from the shower, Liz pinned it close to her head and positioned the short dark wig in place. She stepped into her suit for the second time in twenty-four hours, then inserted the dark-brown contacts. Hastily applying some light makeup, she quickly finished and scooped up the clothes she had discarded. She raced out of the bathroom and stuffed the clothes into her suitcase with the same grimace one might display while thrusting an arm into a pile of worms. To say that it bothered her to leave things sloppy and disorganized would have been the understatement of all millennia combined, but she gritted her teeth and zipped the suitcase shut, fighting off a physical shudder as she did so.

She glanced at Connor, who had changed as she had instructed and was adjusting his long khaki pants over the baggy shorts. "Come with me," she said as she grabbed the shoulder-length blonde wig and her small camera.

He followed her into the bathroom, his eyebrows raised.

"Stand against the wall," she instructed.

He felt as though he were facing a firing squad. "Might I have one last request?" he quipped.

"What?" She was busily adjusting the camera.

"Nothing. Is that like an instant camera or something?"

"Yes," she said, positioning his head squarely in the middle of one large tile, grateful the wall was a stark white. "Now," she said as she fit the wig snugly on his head and tucked the sides of his new hair behind his ears, "give me a tennis player kind of smile."

"And just how does one manage that?"

She snapped the picture in mid-sentence.

* * * * * *

"I look like I'm high on something," Zach Williamson muttered as he examined his new driver's license and passport ID pictures.

"Well, since you're not a well-known tennis player, I'm sure it won't be a problem," Maggie O'Scanlon told him in a lilting Irish accent.

The couple sat at the airport, hoping to board a plane that was looking frighteningly overbooked. They had checked out of their hotel, driven to the airport, and turned in the rental car. Then they had retired to the rest rooms to change identities.

Liz reached up to tuck "Zach's" hair behind his ear.

Connor ducked his head. "Why do you keep doing that?" he snapped in annoyance.

She leaned forward, smiling as though she was about to whisper something sweet in his ear. "Because it looks dorky hanging down by your face, that's why."

"It looks dorky behind my ears, too!" he hissed. "And it itches!"

"You played rugby in college."

He eyed her warily. "So?"

"You can handle having your face ground into the turf as a means of recreation, but you can't manage a wig for a mere day or two?"

"A day or two?" His voice squeaked in an effort to keep the volume down.

"You're pathetic."

Chapter 17

To a casual observer, the man walking down the dusk-enshrouded Chicago street seemed large, powerful, and oblivious to all around him. Only the man himself knew better. He was large; that much was accurate. He also knew that power was in the eye of the beholder, and he had learned at an early age to walk as though he were king. The world merely assumed he was in charge because he acted as though it was true. Bump fought back a smirk. If only his mother had seen fit to give him a tough-sounding name, his image would have been nicely completed.

The street he traveled was witnessing the shift from those who inhabited its space during the daylight hours to those who possessed it at night. Bump's stance of oblivion was a front. He was keenly aware of the people he passed: those lurking in quiet corners, those who tried to blend into the shadows, and those who wished to command a presence.

He approached the appointed meeting place without pause and entered the small family-owned restaurant. Selecting a corner booth that afforded him a view of the room, he sat, his back to the wall, and began the wait. Patience was a virtue, he'd heard, and he supposed it to be true. He possessed it in huge amounts, and it was a quality that had served him well. It wasn't put to the test this time, however.

By the time he finished the soft drink he'd ordered, the front door opened and Bump observed the object of his wait as a man sauntered casually toward him. "The Doctor." That was the man's street name. Bump assumed that at some point the guy had probably gone by a more conventional and socially acceptable name. But given the fact that Bump's own handle of choice bore no resemblance to his birth name, he allowed the man some space and never pressed the issue.

He assumed "The Doctor" had acquired his moniker due to his handiness with a hypodermic syringe, but what the man did on his own time was none of Bump's business. The important thing was that he was a font of knowledge that never ran dry. He'd been a treasure trove of information that had proved invaluable through recent years. Bump had squelched the conscience-driven impulses to avoid looking the other way for so long that it had become second nature. What's in a name, anyway? Maybe the man had aspirations leaning toward med school. Mmm. And the last time Bump had seen monkeys fly, he'd been extremely impressed.

The painful part, he reflected, was that he'd met The Doctor when the young man had been fourteen years of age. He'd seen the boy move from an innocent bystander to a street-wise kid who was frighteningly knowledgeable. And no matter how hard Bump had tried, the boy had avoided help like a plague. He had been an exceptionally good-looking young kid, a problem that had plagued him relentlessly on the streets, and had evolved into an extremely attractive young man, when he managed to get himself cleaned up. On those occasions, he always reminded Bump of a blonde male model.

"Hey Doc," Bump said, offering his hand for a quick clasp as the young man took a seat opposite him. "How've ya been?"

"Can't complain." Doc's eyes held the dull, flat look of one coming off a recent hit, yet his demeanor seemed lucid enough. His hair, ragged and unruly, was matted in some places, and Bump supposed it had been a while since the younger man had found his way into a shower. "What brings you around this time?"

"I'm not sure, exactly. I've come across some interesting information—something I'm thinking you can help me with." Bump withdrew a piece of paper from his pocket and unfolded it methodically, laying it on the table and smoothing the creases before turning it so his companion could read it.

Doc scanned the contents, his flat expression giving away nothing. He shrugged. "So? A bunch of cities. What's the big deal?"

"You wanna tell me why your name's on this list?"

Doc's eyes scanned the sheet one more time, picking up the detail he'd missed on his first cursory glance. He shrugged again, the only alteration of his expression being a light flush that crept up from his neck. "What do I know?"

Bump turned the sheet of paper toward himself and made a show of studying it carefully. "That's what *I'd* like to know," he said without lifting his eyes from the paper. "Here I was, thinking you've been straight with me all this time, and now I see your name on someone's list. A list with names, dates, and something that looks to me like bar codes or serial numbers."

He finally looked up and pinned the man with a direct gaze. "You never told me you were one of the big boys. You expecting a shipment of something, Doc?"

"What I do is really none of your business, man. I don't owe you anything."

Bump's smile was feral. "Oh, but you do, my friend." His tone was quiet, lethal, to the point. "I have enough dirt on you to put you away for a long, long time."

Doc squirmed uncomfortably in his seat, averting his gaze by looking out the window at the darkening street. "I don't know exactly what it is," he finally said, and looked at Bump. "When Lucas got busted a month ago, his business started falling into my hands. I get this call one night, someone asking for Lucas. I told the guy that Lucas wasn't around and I didn't know when he would be. He asked me who was taking care of things in the meantime, and I told him I guess I was. He got my name and told me to expect something on that date there." Doc motioned to the paper still positioned innocently on the table in front of Bump.

Bump's eyes narrowed a fraction. "Did he leave you a number to contact him if there was a change of plans?"

Doc swallowed and nodded reluctantly.

"I need it."

"Oh, come on, man! You're asking too much here! It's my life we're talking about!"

"You shouldn't whine, Doc. People might think you're not all that mean." Bump leaned back in his seat and regarded the young man before him. He'd be lucky to live out the year. If the drugs he continually took didn't kill him, the people he associated with eventually would. It would be sad indeed to see a life ended, wasted, at twenty-four years of age. "You're in way over your head here, you know that?"

Doc scowled. "I know what I'm doing."

"No, you really don't. Give me the number the guy on the phone gave you, and I just might be able to save your sorry hide."

"No."

Bump leaned forward, his elbows on the table. He gazed into the younger man's eyes, determined that the poor fool would feel his intensity, even if he didn't comprehend the words. "You give me that number now, and I'll get you out of here when everything hits the fan. I'll create a new life for you where no one will ever find you."

Doc's face took on a stubborn expression. "I don't want a new life."

"Then this one will come crashing down around your ears, and you'll wonder how you're going to live through it. And I won't lift a finger to help you." Bump nodded at the man's uncertainty. "You know I can do this. I can make or break your life."

Doc's jaw clenched as he flagged a passing waitress and borrowed a pencil from her. He hastily scrawled the phone number he'd committed to memory onto a napkin and thrust it at Bump. "You'd better hope," Doc said as he stood to leave, "that you get to them before they get to you. And if you bail on me—well, just remember that I have some pretty powerful friends of my own."

Bump grinned. "Are you threatening me, Doc?" The grin faded into nothing but cold speculation, and Doc eventually squirmed under his focused scrutiny. Bump St. James had eyes that glowed like a tiger's. Doc shuddered and made his way out the door and onto the streets where he felt safe.

* * * * * *

Connor and Liz stared upward at the enormous clock tower, their necks becoming stiff with the effort.

"He's a big sucker, isn't he," Liz finally said.

"That he is. It's been a while since I last saw him. When I finished my mission, my family flew over to pick me up and we took the long way home. We spent two weeks in England, a week in Ireland, and a week in Scotland. We had a really good time."

Liz smiled. "I'll bet your sisters loved it."

Connor chuckled. "Claire wanted to hit all the sites of archaeological interest, and Paige hunted out all the art museums. They knew their callings early in life."

They walked in companionable silence away from Big Ben. "What are your sisters doing these days?" Liz asked as they strolled slowly down the street.

"Claire's now a Ph.D. in archaeology. Let's see," he mused, the pride in his voice evident, "she's twenty-five now, almost twenty-six. Paige is twenty-three. She's at Stanford doing her MBA."

"And her bachelor's was in what?"

"Art," he smiled. "They're funny. My sisters together remind me of you and Amber. They're really good friends."

Liz grinned. "Sisters are a good thing when they get along. Amber and I had our share of battles growing up."

He raised his eyebrows in surprise. "You fought?"

"Like rabid dogs. Once I clawed Amber's arm so hard, I think I left scars." She laughed. "It was never over anything major. We were always friends again within an hour or so."

"Actually, I remember Claire and Paige going the rounds, too. Usually over whose turn it was to wear the red sweater, or who had borrowed the white tennis shoes without asking."

Liz sighed. "Ah, yes. Those were the days." She paused as her stomach rumbled.

"Hungry?"

She nodded with a grin. "Let's find some quaint little pub. I'd like to be able to say I've experienced some local culture."

Connor observed Liz surreptitiously as they walked down the street. Her movements were always fluid and soft; he'd wager his last stock option that she had no idea she was so effortlessly graceful. He smiled when she pointed at something quirky in a shop window, distracted by her close proximity, and certain that whatever he murmured in response was probably inane, at best.

He loved the way she made eye contact with and smiled at the people they passed as they walked the streets of London. He relished watching her eyes light up when she spoke of funny memories with Amber. Her laugh was contagious, and spending time with her reminded him of times his family took vacations high in the Rockies—she was a breath of fresh air, and while part of his brain mocked him as hokey for making the comparison, he knew it was true. She was his long-needed breath of fresh air.

That he had only just realized it, he figured, made him a fool. She'd been right in front of him for years. A fool indeed. The worst kind.

"The worst kind of what?"

He stared at Liz blankly. Had he actually spoken the thought aloud? "Oh, uh, you know . . ." The worst kind of *what*? "This wind here." He cleared his throat. "Sometimes it can be the worst kind."

"London wind?"

He nodded lamely. "It keeps blowing your hair around."

She studied him closely. "Are you tired?"

"Yeah, a little." *Actually, I'm more of a dork than anything. That's something sleep won't cure.* "And hungry. Let's eat here." He steered her into the next pub they passed and tried not to look at her bemused face.

Liz watched Connor over her plate of fish and chips, munching thoughtfully. If the opportunity to express her feelings for him never presented itself, she'd just have to deal with it. So what that she'd loved him forever? So what that he had no clue? That was life. Sometimes things were meant to be, and sometimes they weren't. *Maybe he's really not all that great after all. I'm a good person. I'm fun, I'm likable, and I'm smart. He's never noticed all that, so maybe he can just go take a flying leap.*

She lifted her glass and took a drink, examining Connor over the rim. *Yeah, right.* If he ever took a flying leap off *anything*, she'd be right behind him throwing him a rope, and she knew it. *Be honest, Liz. You've never even pretended to feel more than affectionate friendship for him. How's he supposed to know?*

And then there was the issue of Allyson.

"What are you thinking?" he asked over a mouthful of food. "You look confused."

"I, um . . . well . . ." Pathetic. She'd mutated from an urbane, witty, Seattle socialite into an idiot. "Nothing, really."

What was she supposed to say? *Hey, I really love you, and always have. I realize I closely resemble your dead fiancée, but do you think you could look past that fact?* She couldn't suppress the sudden stab of anger she felt when she thought of Allyson, and it surprised her. What had he been thinking? If he was into blonde-haired, green-eyed women, why hadn't he ever pursued *her*, instead of someone who made promises she couldn't keep and who didn't begin to match him in substance?

She scowled at the voice of reason that intruded itself upon her thoughts and directed her toward the obvious. She and Connor had never lived anywhere near each other, had never spent more than a few days or weeks at a time in each other's company, and she had never implied that she was interested in him as anything more than a friend. She sighed.

"Are you angry?" He finally put down his fork and looked at her in concern. "Did I do something wrong?"

Yeah, you did something wrong. You didn't give up your wonderful job on the East Coast and come to Seattle to profess your undying love for me. She managed a rueful smile. "No. I'm just really tired—I think that notorious jet lag is finally catching up with me, and we're nowhere near bedtime yet. Not to mention the fact that we have to stake out a certain pharmaceutical building tonight." She rubbed her eyes. She was thinking irrational thoughts. It always happened when she was tired. Everything always seemed wrong when she was tired.

She needed a distraction. "Tell me some more about your mission," she said.

He raised his eyebrows. "Are you sure you're okay?" At her nod, he began regaling her with tales of his favorite people in England.

* * * * * *

"So how long do we have to keep walking up and down the same streets?" Connor asked, yawning. The London sky was dark, as was much of the street he and Liz were repeatedly traversing. They had been haunting the section of the city that housed the majority of the region's banks and large businesses, most of them now closed and locked up for the night. Frasier Pharmaceutical was situated amidst some of the city's older buildings that had survived barrages of World War II bombings. It seemed odd—a structure of steel and glass alongside the more stately and mature buildings.

"We have to wait for the cleaning company vans to show up," Liz explained. "Hopefully, Frasier has hired an outside company to come in and clean every night, and they should be here sometime soon." If the cleaning was done by Frasier employees, and the supplies were already housed inside the building, they'd have to try a different tactic. She tried valiantly to stifle a yawn of her own.

Connor was considering complaining about his wig again, just to pass the time, when they noticed a white van pulling up alongside the Frasier Pharmaceutical building.

"Oh, no," Liz moaned in frustration. Fatigue had made her morose. "There's no logo or company name on the van. We need to know who they are so you can get a job!"

Connor watched silently as several workers piled out of the van, each carrying cleaning supplies. They wore identification around their necks, flashing their pictures through the glass wall at a security guard seated near the front doors. One lone straggler trailed behind the group, a young woman who struggled with an armload of cleaning supplies. "Bingo," Connor said with a grin.

Liz faded into the shadows as Connor approached the young woman. "Can I help you with that stuff?" he asked.

She looked up in surprise. "Yes, I'd appreciate it." Her breath caught as she looked into eyes that were bluer than the Mediterranean.

Connor smiled. "My name is Zach, and actually, I've been watching you all get out of this van. I'm looking for a job, and I have some experience cleaning . . . things." He did his best not to wince at the lame excuse.

"You're an American, aren't you?"

"Yes. I play tennis, and I'm hoping to train with some coaches here. I need a job in the meantime, though. Can you tell me who I might talk to about that, Karin?" he asked, reading the name on her identification tag.

My, but those eyes were blue. Karin's heart did a thump. With a face and body like that, the man should forget tennis and take up modeling. "I don't know if my boss is looking for anyone, but I can give you our phone number at the office."

"Wow, thanks. I'd really appreciate it." Another flash of the grin. Maybe he hadn't lost his touch. His recent experiences with Liz had made him wonder. He waited while Karin groped around in the van for a piece of paper and a pen.

"Here it is," she said, offering him the paper. "Maybe I'll see you later, then."

"I hope so." He helped her carry her supplies to the door and watched her walk inside.

"Psst!" The sound came from the shadows. Connor turned toward the noise and approached Liz, who had been hiding around the corner.

"Nicely done," she said. "A few more choice words, and that girl would've married you."

"She's sweet."

"Really."

He raised his eyebrows. "Is something wrong?"

Liz scowled. "No, nothing's wrong. I just didn't know what you were doing, that's all. You should never have just walked off without telling me what you were up to. I might not have approved, and for all you know, it could have ruined everything."

Methinks the lady doth protest too much. Connor smiled. Hope. Maybe there was hope after all. Time to test the theory.

"She was really cute, didn't you think? And that accent just kills me," he sighed as they walked back to their hotel.

"It's not that hard to do a British accent, you know. I did it for a whole day in New Orleans. You didn't seem too charmed by it then." Her mood blackened with each step.

"Careful," he whispered with barely suppressed glee. "You're not sounding very Irish."

Liz stopped walking, appalled at herself. She had never, ever slipped out of character on a job. She was losing her focus, and making a fool of herself in the process. She closed her eyes. "I'm just tired," she mumbled. "Let's get to our rooms."

He might have pitied her if he hadn't felt so darned euphoric. She was jealous. Had he known she would be, he'd have tried that angle long before. Petty, yes. But effective. He smiled. "I'm tired too," he said, throwing an arm around her shoulders. "Let's get some sleep. Tomorrow, I have to get myself a job."

* * * * * *

"We're not really looking to hire anyone right now, Mr. Williamson." The man regarded Connor wearily.

"I understand, sir. I really need some money right now, though—just enough to buy food every day. I'll work for less than you usually pay your new employees. I work very hard," he finished hopefully.

Connor's prospective employer eyed him for a few seconds. If he thought it odd that a clean-cut man in his thirties was sporting a teenage haircut and looking for a low-paying cleaning job, he was kind enough not to mention it. "I suppose I could use you for a while. I assume you'll want to start immediately?"

Connor nodded gratefully. "Yes, sir. I'd love to start today, if I could."

* * * * * *

"Okay," Liz said. She and Connor were seated at the small round table situated in the corner of his room. "Here's the deal. If Frasier Pharmaceutical is like most multi-level buildings, there should be a wire closet next to the stairwell or elevator shaft. Most buildings have the d-mark, which is where the telephone system connects to the phone company, at ground level, and then the wires go up to the offices. The network hub, or at least one of them, will most likely be in this same wire closet."

Connor nodded. "So what's the plan when you get into the closet?"

"Well, there's the first trick. We have to get into the closet; I'm sure it's security protected. We go through the digital lock, using these little thingies." Liz motioned to an electronic credit card key she had hooked to a notebook computer. "Once we're in, we plug the notebook into the network hub to gain access to the system, which *hopefully* should be UNIX®, the same kind I broke into at Shoreline Insurance."

Connor nodded.

"Once we're in, I'll connect to the system and try to break the password for Mr. Frasier's computer. If his password can be found in a dictionary, then I'll know it in a matter of seconds. If it's a random combination of letters, I could be sitting in the closet for up to twenty-four hours. If it's a combination of numbers and letters, the process can take as long as a week. Hopefully not. I'm planning on the twenty-four-hour deal. Think positive thoughts."

He stared. "Okay." How in the name of heaven was he going to stay calm with her locked in a closet for twenty-four hours? "Maybe you should bring along a book or something."

She laughed. "I think I'll go shopping a little later for a good magazine. As for right now, I'm going to get all my equipment organized so we'll be ready for tonight. You know what to do on your end, right?"

He nodded. "I clean the dang building while you're marooned in a dark closet. Are you sure this is a good idea?"

"It's the only one we've got that'll work. Quit griping; someday you'll have a wife who will appreciate the fact that you've cleaned professionally. You'll be great around the house."

He groaned. "Right." He looked at the equipment arranged on the table before them. "How long do you think it'll take you to have everything ready?"

She shrugged. "Give me thirty minutes."

He nodded. "When you're finished, there's somewhere I'd like to take you."

Chapter 18

Connor looked out the bus window as the countryside sped past. The ache in his throat was unmistakable. He'd missed his two-year "home" so much it hurt. He turned as Liz placed a light hand on his arm.

"Are you okay?"

He nodded. "I couldn't be this close without saying hello to some people I met." He cleared his throat and willed his emotions to stay in check. Apparently Liz wasn't the only one who'd been suffering the ill effects of sleep deprivation. He wasn't usually the weepy sort.

"I met this couple the last month I served here," he continued, "and they were so good to me. We baptized them right before I went home."

Connor stood and pulled Liz behind him by the hand as the bus slowed near their stop. She swallowed a knot of disappointment as they exited and he released her hand. "We need to walk a little bit this way," he said, motioning with his head.

She fell into step beside him and listened as he explained a bit more about the couple he'd mentioned. "They first learned about the Church from their grandson, who was baptized while going to school in London. He's my age, and was in college at the time; he met some kids who were members, and it didn't take long before he started asking questions." Connor smiled. "Those kids were such good people. They made sure he knew they'd still like him even if he decided he didn't want anything to do with the Church. It's the kind of situation you dream about." He kicked a small rock off to the side of the road.

"Anyway," Connor continued as they walked, "he used to come home on the weekends and stay with his grandparents. He told them what he was doing, and they were loving enough to trust his judgment. He was baptized not long after he'd met his friends, and shortly after that, I was transferred into the area." He smiled at the memory. "The grandparents wanted to know what it was all about, and I was lucky enough to be here for it."

"What are their names?"

"Robert and Emily Holmes."

They rounded a corner and Liz stopped short, catching her breath as Connor gestured toward a house. "This is it," he said.

"Oh!" She put her hand to her heart. "It's just like a Thomas Kinkade painting!"

"I know. Isn't it great?" He moved to approach the front door, but turned back when she didn't follow him. "Are you coming?"

"No," she breathed. "Just give me a minute." She stood, staring at the cozy cottage, wishing for all she was worth that it was hers. *Covet, shmovet,* she thought. *I'll have to repent for this one.*

He smiled. "They're going to come outside and wonder why you're staring like that."

She sighed, then followed him up the small walkway to the front door and waited while he knocked. The door was opened a moment later, and she couldn't help but smile. The little woman who answered looked just as Liz had imagined she would. Small, white hair, a gentle smile.

"Yes?" the woman asked.

"Sister Holmes," Connor said and offered his hand. "Do you remember me?"

The older woman scrutinized him carefully for a moment before her eyes widened behind her glasses. "Oh, Elder O'Brian!" She clasped his hand, and he moved closer at her gentle tug to envelop her in a warm embrace. When he pulled back, tears sparkled in the woman's eyes.

"What are you doing here?" she asked, pulling a lace-edged handkerchief from her pocket and sniffling.

"I . . ." He glanced at Liz. "We're here on business," he said and gestured to Liz, placing an arm around her shoulders. "This is my good friend, Elizabeth Saxton."

Liz mentally gritted her teeth. If he introduced her one more time as his "good friend," she'd have to stomp on his instep. She smiled at the small woman and offered her hand. "It's so good to meet you," she said. "Your home is just breathtaking," she added, and looked again at the small house and yard.

"Why, thank you, dear." Sister Holmes motioned for the couple to enter the house. They followed her into a charmingly decorated parlor, where she sat opposite them.

"I can hardly believe you're here," she said to Connor. "You've not written for a while," she added with a small shake of her finger. She softened the reproach with a smile.

Connor had the grace to flush. "I'm sorry," he said. "It's inexcusable."

Sister Holmes waved her hand, dismissing his apology. "I know you're a busy young man," she said. "Now, tell me again what you're doing in England."

Connor glanced at Liz. "We're here for some business meetings," he said, hating that he was lying to one of the sweetest women on earth.

"And this is your friend?" Sister Holmes smiled and regarded Liz with a speculative gleam in her eye.

Liz nodded. "We met several years ago," she said. "I'm helping Connor with some computer work."

"Well, it's a pleasure to meet you."

Connor leaned forward, resting his elbows on his knees. "Where's Brother Holmes these days? You two haven't written to me for a while either, you know."

The older woman's brow wrinkled softly. "I know," she murmured. "Brother Holmes is . . . he isn't well."

Connor frowned. "He's sick?"

Sister Holmes nodded. "I'm afraid so. His cancer was in remission when you were here on your mission, but it's returned."

Connor was silent for a moment. "Is he . . . can I see him, or would it be awkward for him?"

Sister Holmes opened her mouth to reply, but was interrupted by a soft knock at the door. She rose as a young man entered, and her face broke into a smile. Beckoning to him with her hand, she turned back to Connor. "You remember Ben, don't you?"

Connor stood, his grin spreading from ear to ear. He moved forward to embrace the young man, who appeared to recognize him on sight.

The two slapped each other on the back as men are wont to do, and Ben pulled back to examine Connor's face more closely. "Elder O'Brian," he said with a smile. "You don't look much different. Maybe a few more lines about the eyes, but other than that, you're the same."

Connor laughed. "Thanks for pointing that out."

Sister Holmes watched the scene unfolding with a smile of her own. She took her seat, motioning for the men to sit as well. "Connor's here with a friend," she indicated to Ben.

"Oh, yes." Ben rose from his seat and approached Liz with his hand outstretched. "I'm sorry," he said. "I was caught up in the moment."

Liz smiled and stood to take the hand he offered. She shook it briefly and smiled.

Connor made the proper introductions. "Liz Saxton, this is Sister Holmes' grandson, Ben Holmes."

"It's a pleasure," Liz said as she sat back down. "Has anyone ever told you that you're a dead ringer for Gabriel Byrne?"

Ben laughed. "Gabriel Byrne, the actor?"

She nodded with a grin. "It's true. You look like a slightly younger version."

"Well, thank you for that, I think. I'll choose to take it as a compliment."

"Oh, it was."

Connor glanced sharply at Liz. She missed his expression, but Sister Holmes caught it. The older woman covered a small laugh with a cough, unwittingly turning the attention back to her.

"Oh, I'm sorry," Connor apologized. He turned to Ben. "We were discussing your grandfather when you arrived."

Ben's own light expressions faded. "He's not doing very well," he stated, shaking his head. "I try to come by every day for a visit, and it seems he's worse each time."

"I asked Ben to come by and give him a blessing today," Sister Holmes interjected. "I think he needs one."

"In fact," Ben said, "I had asked a ward member to come with me and help, but he was unable to at the last minute. Since you're here . . ." He left the question hanging.

"Of course," Connor murmured. "I'd be honored."

Ben turned to his grandmother. "Is now a good time?"

Nodding, she rose to lead the way and turned back to make sure they all followed. Liz was hanging back uncertainly, not wanting to intrude.

"You're welcome to come with us, dear," Sister Holmes told her.

Liz smiled and followed the group out of the parlor and down a small hallway to a bedroom at the back of the house. The room was small and charmingly furnished, with crisp white doilies adorning the nightstands. On the bed, asleep, lay an older man, frightfully thin, with a shock of white hair on the top of his head. He wore a pair of comfortable-looking flannel pajamas, and the homemade quilt on the bed covered him and rested snugly under his arms. Sister Holmes approached the bed and sat gently at his side. "Robert," she said softly and rubbed his arm. He awoke slowly, his eyes opening a fraction and apparently attempting to focus on his wife's face.

"Ben is here," she said. "And someone else is here to see you, too." She gestured toward Connor, who approached the man's side.

Connor watched as the older man studied his face and knew the moment Brother Holmes recognized him. The elderly gentleman's face broke into a weary smile. "Well, well," he said. He reached his hand up, and Connor clasped it firmly between both of his. "My missionary finally returns."

Connor's chest constricted, and he fought the annoying sting in his eyes. "I did," he said, clearing the lump from his throat. "I've missed you."

Brother Holmes nodded softly against the pillow. "And we've missed you, young man." He looked toward Liz, who hovered near the door. "Who's this you've brought with you?"

Connor turned and stretched out his hand to Liz, who approached the bed and slipped her arm through his. "This is my dear friend, Elizabeth Saxton," Connor told the old man.

"Dear" friend, Liz thought to herself. *At least I've moved beyond "good."*

"It's a pleasure to meet you," she said softly, wondering if the sweet man was suffering much pain.

"Likewise," Brother Holmes replied. "I only wish I were in a better position to entertain."

Ben stepped forward next to Liz. "We'd like to give you a blessing, Papa, if you're willing."

The old man smiled softly. "I certainly am."

Liz stepped back to stand next to Sister Holmes, who slipped an arm through hers. Liz looked at the wrinkled hand, now placed on her arm, and patted it gently. She looked into the older woman's face and gave her arm a little squeeze. Sister Holmes winked at her, then turned to look at her ailing husband. She sighed, her brows furrowing into a light frown.

Ben, meanwhile, had walked to the other side of the bed after offering Connor a small vial of consecrated oil. She watched as Connor placed a drop of oil on the older man's crown, and closed her eyes as Connor and Ben leaned forward and placed their hands on Brother Holmes' head.

She listened carefully, allowing the troubles of the past few days to dissolve as a gentle spirit filled the room. She heard Connor seal the anointing, and listened as Ben began blessing his grandfather, wondering what he'd find in his heart to say. As the blessing progressed, she felt the pressure of tears behind her closed eyelids.

Ben told his grandfather that he'd lived a good, full life and that he'd been a blessing to his family and to all he'd known. Then, after pausing for an impossibly long time, he finally told his grandfather, with tears in his voice, that he was now free to leave his life of pain, that his family wouldn't attempt to hold him back through prayer or other medical means. Ben blessed him that his soul would be at peace and his heart would find rest.

Liz rubbed the hand of the woman at her side, squeezing gently as the older woman sniffed repeatedly and leaned on her for support. Tears escaped her eyes and ran down her cheeks. *He will be missed,* she thought. *He'll be at peace, but he'll be missed. It's always harder for those left behind.*

The blessing came to a close and she opened her eyes, while Connor lifted his hands from the old man's head and wiped at his own tears. She bit her lip as Ben leaned down to place his face next to his grandfather's. Brother Holmes placed his hand on the back of his grandson's head and murmured, "Thank you, dear boy."

Ben's shoulders shook as he returned the embrace. He pulled back to look into his grandfather's face. "That wasn't what I'd planned on saying," he whispered through his tears.

Brother Holmes gave a weak laugh. "It doesn't always work the way we think it should, does it?" He looked at his Ben with such love that Liz felt her heart constrict. "I can't tell you how proud I am," he said quietly, his throat sounding thick with tears of his own, "that I have such a grandson. You do well and work hard," he said. "I'll be waiting for you on the other side." At this, he looked at his wife, a solitary tear rolling down his cheek. Sister Holmes left Liz and moved to his side, sitting next to him on the bed as Ben rose to give her his place.

Liz turned to exit the room and leave the family in peace. Connor murmured a few words to the couple on the bed, who clasped his hands firmly, then he accompanied her. Liz heard Ben excusing himself from his grandparents for a moment, and he followed the couple to the front door of the small home.

Ben wiped at his eyes and chuckled self-consciously. "Quite the visit, eh?" he said as he patted Connor on the shoulder. "Aren't you glad you came today?"

"I am," Connor replied seriously. "I can't thank you enough for letting us be a part of that." He drew Liz close and gave her shoulder a squeeze. "I had no idea he was ill." He shook his head. "I should have kept in better contact with them."

Ben shook his head. "Don't beat yourself up over it. You've been living your life; we all do. We get busy. You were here for this, and I think they both appreciate it."

"Will you keep in touch? Let me know how they're doing?"

Ben nodded. "When will you be going home?"

Connor looked at Liz. "We're not sure. I'll call you when I can and let you know."

Ben nodded. "Take care. It was nice to meet you," he said, extending his hand again toward Liz.

She clasped it between both of her own. "The blessing was just lovely," she said. She reached up and kissed his cheek. "Thank you for letting me be here for it."

His eyes misted over again, and he quirked his mouth into a small smile. "Maybe next time we meet, we won't all be crying." He laughed a little and turned to embrace Connor. "Thank you for being here," he murmured. "We'll keep in touch."

Connor nodded. "I'll call you as soon as I can."

* * * * * *

"Are you going to be okay?" Liz regarded Connor with some concern. The ride back to the hotel had been an understandably quiet one. "Maybe we can wait until tomorrow night to do this."

Connor shook his head. He sat on the couch in their suite and rubbed a hand across the back of his neck. "We don't have much of a choice," he said. "Malone could show up any minute, and then we'd be sunk." He paused, rubbing at his temple with restless fingers. "I'm just kind of shocked, you know?"

Liz nodded. "They're sweet people, Connor. You didn't even know he was sick—it's no wonder you're feeling this way."

He leaned forward and rested his head in his hands. "Sometimes even knowing how life fits into the big scheme of things doesn't make it any easier to say good-bye to someone." His voice sounded muffled.

"I know." What to say? There wasn't much to say, really. She sat opposite him in a chair and studied him quietly, leaving him to his thoughts.

He finally raised his head and rubbed his eyes. "I'll be fine. In fact, I'm actually glad I have something to keep me busy. Maybe I won't think about them too much."

Liz smiled. "You'll have plenty of time to think about them when this is all over. And I'm sure Sister Holmes would appreciate more frequent visits from you."

He nodded, and then looked at Liz as though he'd just noticed she was sitting there. "Liz," he began, "you're getting caught up in so much stuff here . . ."

She held up a hand. "Not that again. What would I be doing at home, Connor? Leading unsuspecting men right into divorce court?"

"No, you'd be relaxing with Amber and Tyler."

"Amber and Tyler will be there when I get back. I want to be here." *Emotional baggage and all, I want to be here.*

He sighed. "Well, for my sake, I'm glad. I feel selfish."

She laughed and rose to change her clothes. "I'll make you pay me back someday." She disappeared into her bedroom and closed the door.

Connor stared at the door for several long moments. Little did she know he'd gladly pay her back for the rest of her life, if she'd let him. He groaned and buried his head in his hands again, taking stock of his life. His former fiancée had not only been unfaithful, she'd been a secret government agent who'd wanted him for his money. Her associates were now hell-bent on seeing him driven into the ground, and he wondered if he and Liz would make it home in one piece. Not to mention the fact that one of the sweetest, most gentle people he knew was dying of cancer, and he wasn't going to be around long enough to offer the family any support.

He sighed, rubbing his hair. And then there was Liz. He felt himself falling more deeply in love with her every day, and was mentally kicking himself left and right that he hadn't acted on his feelings sooner. Like five years sooner. Maybe, if he'd pursued things earlier on, they both could have avoided a lot of pain. Or maybe she wasn't interested at all, never would have been, and never would be.

He looked bleakly into the fireplace. "I am so stupid," he said to the log sitting innocently in the grate. *Well,* he finally mused when the log didn't offer any support or useful advice, *at least I've got something to keep me busy.*

Nothing like a little international intrigue to keep one's mind off one's troubles.

Chapter 19

Zach Williamson entered the Frasier Pharmaceutical building ready for his first night on the job. He paid studious and diligent attention to his coworker, Karin, as she explained his duties. An hour after arriving at work, he approached the guard sitting at the front desk. "I left the laundry out in the van," he explained. "I'll be right back in with the basket."

The guard nodded and turned back to his monitors. He barely noticed a subtle blink on the monitor to his far right. It was the one showing an image of the stairwell and elevator on the main level. He yawned and rubbed his eyes. Probably nothing. He tapped the screen, exhausting the extent of his technological expertise. Nothing appeared to be out of the ordinary. Probably just a small glitch in the system. He'd mention it in the morning to the tech guy.

Zach reentered the building pushing a large laundry basket full of fresh linens to be deposited in the luxury suites many of the larger offices boasted. The guard nodded as he walked past.

Anna Mendoza deftly climbed out of the laundry basket, her black curly hair pulled into a ponytail at the nape of her neck, her trim body clad in a black cat suit of sorts. She carried a black nylon bag containing a notebook computer and various electronic paraphernalia completely foreign to anyone who'd never worked with such equipment. With swift, sure movements she inserted a credit card-sized piece of plastic into the appropriate slot of the door handle around the corner and out of view of the front security desk, and punched a key on her notebook.

The door clicked, she grinned, and on impulse, turned and waved at the security camera behind her shoulder, knowing full well it wasn't seeing her. She turned with a smirk to Zach Williamson, and they entered the small closet.

* * * * * *

The airline worker at the New Orleans terminal for United Kingdom Air arrivals and departures glanced with annoyance at the agitated man before him. He placed his pen deliberately next to the computer keyboard on his countertop and sighed. "I've told you, sir, I don't recall anyone matching those descriptions ever leaving through these gates. If they did, it must have been when I wasn't here." He'd checked his records twice for the insistent FBI agent. He had the arrival dates and times for Brad Edwards and Ellen Deveraux, but no evidence at all of their departure.

Phillip Malone gritted his teeth. He'd been scouring New Orleans for two days, and couldn't turn up a thing on O'Brian and his mystery woman beyond the fact that they'd left their hotel in their disguises, turned in their rental car, and disappeared. He was at his wits' end and ready to explode when he caught the eye of a woman working alongside the man he'd been interrogating. She smiled tentatively, unsure of his mood.

He smiled in return. "I'm very tired. I'm on official business with the FBI, and I need some information. Do you remember, at all, any couples that stand out in your memory, for any reason?" He was grasping at straws and he knew it. The woman wouldn't know any more than the man did. Whoever O'Brian had hooked up with was very, very good.

"Actually, I do remember an Irish woman and her boyfriend," the woman said. "They were so cute together, I couldn't help but notice. They kept whispering to each other, and she was playing with his hair. He kept looking at his passport and was annoyed that she couldn't keep her hands to herself. He complained about looking silly, too, I think. Her accent was just charming; I remember that, too."

Phillip Malone regarded the woman with raised eyebrows. "Really?" he asked, his heart giving one deliberate *thump*. "I think I'll need to check the passenger manifest for that flight."

* * * * * *

Bump dialed the 800 number Doc had given him and waited patiently for someone to answer.

"ID number, please."

Bump rolled his eyes heavenward before slowly closing them and counting to ten. Doc had omitted the fact that one needed an ID number to accomplish anything with this phone number. "Uh," he said, doing his best imitation of Doc, "I can't remember it. I just need to talk to someone about the shipment coming in to Chicago."

"I'm sorry, sir," came the reply. "I can't direct your call without your ID number." The line went dead.

Bump sighed and pushed the "stop" button on his recording equipment. Apparently another visit to Doc was in order.

* * * * * *

"Well, that was easy," Liz said with a smile as she finished stuffing a towel in front of the crack in the door. She shone her flashlight around the small confines of the closet and examined the interior. "Looks like we're in the right place. Keep your fingers crossed that I'll be out of here in a few hours."

Connor nodded. "How soon do you want me to go back out?"

"You're good in here for a few minutes. The security camera will show the guard that still shot until someone fixes it. Unless he's really observant, he won't notice it for a long time."

"You'll be okay, then? I hate to leave you in here." Connor studied her face, still hers despite the dark hair and brown eyes. She'd supplied him with a cell phone so she could contact him when she broke the password for Mr. Frasier's files and downloaded the information they needed.

She nodded and took a shaky breath. "I'm fine, really. There's nowhere for me to go, and if this stretches on into tomorrow I have other clothes to change into. I should be able to bluff my way out of the building." She shook her head slightly. "This really has to work tonight. I can't stay in here for a week, obviously, and if I'm still trying to break into the system tomorrow morning, someone could detect it. I hate to sound trite, but it's now or never."

"You're beautiful, Anna Mendoza," he murmured. He leaned forward and placed a soft kiss on her forehead. "Keep me posted, huh?"

She nodded and grinned. "This is no big deal," she lied.

Connor nodded and turned the doorknob. He didn't delude himself for a moment into thinking she wasn't endangering herself. The fact that she was doing it for his sake made his stomach clench. He collected his wits enough to glance out into the hallway before venturing from their hiding place. "See ya," he whispered and closed the door.

* * * * * *

"Fifty-five bottles of beer on the wall, fifty-five bottles of beer. If one of those bottles should happen to fall, fifty-four bottles of beer on the wall." Flipping through a newsmagazine, Liz whispered the litany of a song she'd learned on a first-grade field trip bus. One thing about her had remained consistent from the day she'd first learned that song: she'd yet to actually taste a beer. Maybe that was why, through the years, she'd never substituted the word "pop" as so many of her acquaintances did. The sheer absurdity of the song had always amused her.

It served her well as she entered the fourth hour of her confinement in the small closet at Frasier Pharmaceutical. The machine at her side whirred away as it searched for the password needed to break into the system of the man who owned and ran the company. She was determined to remain optimistic that the code would be found before sunrise. There were some high-tech companies whose executives' passwords changed every thirty seconds. The execs were in possession of small credit-card-like gadgets with LCD readouts that displayed the new eight-digit password every half-minute. Such changes would also be available in the network Liz was trying to break, but if this company employed such a method, she'd need one of the executive's password equipment. She mentally crossed her fingers that their plight wouldn't be further extended by such a complication.

The manipulation of the security camera had gone off without a hitch. She had accessed the camera image remotely and frozen the shot on one frame. If the rest of the evening went off as smoothly as the first part had, she'd consider the operation a success.

* * * * * *

Connor sat at a small café one block away from the Frasier Pharmaceutical building. He sipped a drink and flipped lazily through the pages of a magazine, grateful to have found a twenty-four-hour café so close to Liz. His stomach was in knots; it took every ounce of concentration he possessed to maintain a calm, bored façade.

Just when he thought he'd probably spontaneously combust from the pressure, he chanced upon an article about countries on the U.S. embargo list. The gist of the article outlined the reasons for several of the embargoes, and the duration of their enforcement. As he read through the article, something in the back of his mind clicked; there was an aspect of the information that seemed hauntingly familiar. It was the countries themselves. There wasn't one country in the article that wasn't also on Allyson's disk. Her mysterious list of countries was nothing more than the current U.S. embargo lineup.

Blood roared in Connor's ears as he tried to refrain from leaping out of his chair. That had to be it! Frasier Pharmaceutical must be engaged in supplying countries under U.S. embargo with drugs. Their black-market value was more than likely outrageous; Mr. Frasier was making a monetary killing. It still didn't explain the odd angle with Greece, however. Bump had mentioned his unexplainable suspicions concerning the correspondence coming from an office near Athens. Connor stared at the newsmagazine article, euphoric at having solved a portion of the odd puzzle. He'd have to leave the Greece angle up to Liz.

* * * * * *

Oh, yes! It was all she could do to contain the mental shout. She was in. Hurriedly shoving a disk into her notebook, she began downloading the files she had accessed, copying them onto both her hard drive and the floppy. Five minutes later, she was dialing Connor's cell number.

"I've got it," she said when he answered.

"Okay, just stay put," he said before she could elaborate. "I had an idea before I left. I'll be there for you in a few minutes."

"Wait . . . ," was all she got out before the line clicked.

Chapter 20

The security guard looked up in surprise as one of the cleaning crew approached the front doors of the building. That was odd; they'd been gone for hours. He opened the door at the man's gesture and waited.

"I'm so sorry—this was my first night on the job, and I kept forgetting things. I left one of the laundry baskets upstairs. Is it okay if I get it now so I don't get in trouble with my boss tomorrow?"

The guard nodded. "Be quick about it, though. You're not supposed to be here after everyone else leaves."

"I know, and I really appreciate it. Really."

Connor hurried to the elevators directly across from the security desk and punched the "up" button. He threw another smile of gratitude over his shoulder at the guard and entered the elevator. The security guard shook his head and resumed his seat at his station, radioing to his coworker as the elevator light stopped on the sixteenth floor, telling him to expect one of the cleaning crew shortly.

Connor made his way along the hallway to the office where he'd left the laundry basket. He nodded to the security guard, who had apparently been apprised of his presence, and wheeled the basket toward the set of elevators on the other side of the floor. Minutes later, he was knocking softly on the door of the wire closet.

* * * * * *

The security guard stared as the cleaning worker wheeled the forgotten laundry basket through the lobby with a jaunty wave. "See you tomorrow," he said, and then amended, "or I guess it's tonight." He laughed, glancing at his watch.

"Where did you come from?" the guard asked, looking confused.

Connor motioned with his hand. "From those elevators over there, around the corner. They were closer to where the basket was."

The guard scratched his head. That was odd. He hadn't seen the man coming off the elevator on his monitor. He blinked and rubbed his eyes; he was awfully tired. He walked around the corner to the elevators in question and gazed up at the security camera. Shrugging, he made a mental note to mention it when the executives arrived in several hours. He made his way back to his station and settled into his chair.

* * * * * *

The sleepy Colorado town of Alpine Ridge was just opening its doors for the morning. The City-County Building was coming alive on Main Street, its employees setting up for the day. One young woman sat at the front desk, organizing her supplies and chatting happily to the woman seated at a desk behind her.

She glanced up in surprise as a man entered and approached her desk. He was huge. The only other place she'd ever seen shoulders that wide was when her boyfriend watched Broncos games on TV. The man wore khaki pants and a white T-shirt tucked into a narrow waist. On his feet were white sneakers, and his long dark hair was pulled back into a sedate ponytail. His eyes glowed like gold. He reminded her of a tiger.

He smiled. "Hi, there! Nice morning, isn't it?"

The woman nodded and returned the smile. Alpine Ridge didn't often get infusions of new blood in the off-season; maybe this man was going to be a permanent fixture. One could only hope. "Can I help you with something?"

The man extracted his wallet and showed her his ID. "Julie," he said, reading the nameplate on the countertop, "I'm a private detective, and I'm looking for some information on a woman who died here in this area about six months ago." He leaned on the high counter with his elbows. "What I need is her autopsy report."

Definitely a tiger. A tiger with golden eyes and very white teeth. She couldn't help but ask. "Are you going to be in town for a while?"

He smiled. "I was thinking of staying for a day or two."

"Let me see what I can do about that report."

* * * * * *

Liz and Connor sat in their hotel suite, staring at the notebook monitor. "I think you're right," Liz said. "I *know* you're right. He's shipping prescription drugs to all these countries currently under embargo." Sure enough, the evidence was on the screen. Each country was listed along with cities, specific locations, dates, times, and shipment details.

Liz tapped a few keys, trying to find specific information on Greece. Patience won out, and she eventually found files of old correspondence from an address in that country. She scanned the contents of one e-mail dated two weeks earlier. "Greek shipper, Althena, departing September 26ᵗʰ," she read aloud. "That's in four days."

Connor peered over her shoulder, noting the absence of any particular destination. "I wonder where it's going."

Liz shrugged. "I don't know that, but I *do* know that we have, in our possession, one very physical street address in Greece."

Connor raised one corner of his mouth into an amused half-smile. "And since we have said address, you're thinking we should pay it a visit."

"We might as well. We don't know where the shipper is going or what it's carrying for Frasier, unless it's shipping black-market drugs to those countries on the embargo list. If that's the case, then we'll have enough evidence to finally turn over to someone. Besides," she added with a tired smile, "I've never been to Greece, and I've always wanted to see it."

"Good enough for me. I'd like to see it myself. So what's our plan of attack?"

"First, we bleach your hair."

He paused. "I thought we'd already dealt with that."

"We did. Unfortunately, we had no idea we'd be doing such extensive globe-hopping before this thing was over, and you can't leave this country now as Zach Williamson." She smiled. "I have no more wigs for you."

He groaned. "Fine. Let's just do it and get it over with. How soon do we leave?"

"I need to call Bump. I'll tell him what we're doing and then book flights for Greece." She glanced at her watch. "Why don't we sleep for a few hours and then fly out tonight. I'm beat."

Connor looked at her in sympathy, rubbing his hand gently down the length of her arm. "You were great," he said.

She smiled past the hitch in her breath at his touch. "You weren't so bad yourself."

* * * * * *

The secretary winced at the shouting behind the closed office door. It wasn't often that Mr. Malone visited; he was usually occupied in the D.C. office. She dialed a phone number yet again, hoping this time it would be answered before the wrath of Frasier Pharmaceutical's head of security came down upon her. She sighed with relief as the call was answered. Mr. Malone had said he wanted to speak to the head security guard who had been on duty the night before, and he'd hunt him down himself if he had to.

"Mr. Barnaby," she said. "You must come down to the office right away."

* * * * * *

"So you're telling me you saw the screen blink, and you didn't think to call anyone?" Phillip Malone was calm. Too calm. The man standing before him did his best to maintain his dignity.

"No sir, it didn't seem to be a problem at the time. I still saw the image of the elevator and stairwell just fine."

"Didn't it strike you as a bit odd that for the rest of the evening, you didn't see anyone coming or going on that elevator?"

Silence. The answer was obvious.

Malone rubbed his eyes testily. He couldn't remember the last time he'd slept. Someone's head would roll for that; preferably O'Brian's.

"Now, tell me again. The new man, the American working for the cleaning company, came back several hours later saying he'd forgotten a laundry basket and didn't want to get in trouble with his boss?"

"Yes, sir."

"Okay, now tell me this: Was the laundry basket big enough to hide a person in?"

Barnaby stammered a minute before finally venturing a reply. "I suppose so, sir." He paused. "Was there someone in it?"

"Yes, Barnaby, I suspect there was. That'll be all. I'll call for you if I need anything else. And Barnaby, don't bother coming in for work tonight."

* * * * * *

"Bump's still not home," Liz said, puzzled. "He may be in Colorado, I suppose. I thought he'd be done by now."

Connor's eyes whipped to her face from across the room, where he was searching through his suitcase for the right clothes. "How did you know he was going to Colorado?"

"What do you mean, how did I know? I asked him."

"You asked him—*I* asked him!"

"When did you ask him? *Why* did you ask him?"

Connor crossed the room and took her hand. "Sit down with me for a minute. I didn't want to tell you this, but . . ." He took a deep breath as they sat on one of the beds. "I think someone killed Allyson deliberately." He searched her face for signs of surprise or fear.

She laughed.

"Connor, you're too funny. I was speculating the same thing after we went to her house. I called Bump while you were in the shower and asked him to get a copy of her autopsy report for us. I didn't want to tell you until I knew for sure, because I didn't want you to grieve unnecessarily."

He stared at her. "Well, we were way off on that one, weren't we? All this time I thought I was sparing your feelings and keeping you from being scared."

She patted his hand. "I'm not scared. Not too scared, anyway. We've made it this far; we'll be fine. And incidentally," she said, glancing back at him over her shoulder with a grin as she moved to secure her computer equipment, "you make a wonderful blonde."

* * * * * *

A very tired Maria Scarlotta, Italian cosmetics model, and her blonde American boyfriend, Stephen Davis, photographer, climbed out of their cab, paid the driver, and lugged their bags into the Athens hotel. They found their rooms, dropped their bags, fell on their beds, and slept for a solid twelve hours without stirring.

Chapter 21

Connor entered the hotel suite in Athens to find Liz still sleeping, her bedroom door open. He wasn't surprised. She'd had to take her motion-sickness medicine when leaving England, and that, coupled with stress, he presumed, had left her exhausted. They'd reached their hotel suite the night before; once there she'd slept like a rock, as had he, and she had barely roused in the morning when he'd interrupted her sleep to tell her he was going out for a quick jog.

He entered her room and sat on a chair opposite her bed, having cooled down from his run, rubbing a hand through his hair and looking at Liz as she slept. She was lying on her side, dressed in a simple T-shirt and shorts, her thick, soft hair spread behind her on the pillow like gold. His throat constricted. It wasn't just her appearance; he had been engaged to beauty that was nearly identical to hers in the flesh, but was nothing like hers in spirit. He felt as though he'd loved her forever.

Connor knelt at her bed and gathered one of her hands into his own. He curled her fingers around his thumb and rubbed her knuckles across his lips, closing his eyes against the sweet agony of restraint. His eyes remained closed as he continued to brush her hand against his lips, gently as a feather, and he missed seeing her eyelids flutter.

Liz had never experienced such an intense dream. Surely she was dreaming; reality could never be so poignant. When Connor finally opened his eyes and locked his gaze with hers, she forgot to breathe. He gazed at her, his expression unchanging, his face inches away from hers.

"Sleep well?" he whispered against her hand.

She did her best to nod, then tightened her grip on his hand when he shifted to rise. "Don't leave," she murmured.

Connor stifled a groan and slowly leaned forward to press a soft kiss to the back of her hand, then turned it over and brushed his lips across her palm. He lingered for a moment, hesitating, finally bestowing a last, tender kiss upon her cheek before releasing her hand and pushing himself off the floor.

He made his way to the bathroom, not trusting himself to spare her another glance. Once inside, he closed the door and leaned against it, wondering how he was going to survive the rest of their "vacation" without compromising Liz and vows of his own that he'd made with his Maker. Even in his wildest teenage adventures he'd never encountered such a challenge. With a sigh of resignation, he turned the shower full-blast on cold and stepped in, fully dressed.

* * * * * *

Liz sat on her bed, her eyes huge and unblinking, staring out the window at the Greek sky. What had just happened? One minute she'd been dreaming about him, and the next he'd actually been there, kissing her hand like it was the most amazing thing he'd ever seen in his life. Then he'd paid homage to her cheek with those soft lips in a way that had far surpassed her every dream, only to bolt for the bathroom before she could gather her wits about her. She grabbed a glass of water she'd left sitting on the nightstand the evening before and gulped it down. Now what?

She turned as the bathroom door creaked open a fraction of an inch. "Liz?"

She stood. "Yes?"

"Could you hand me my suitcase?"

"Sure." She retrieved his suitcase from his bedroom. The bathroom door opened a bit wider, enough to accommodate the bag; the only part of Connor that was visible was his hand, snaking around the door to grab the suitcase. The door closed.

Liz blinked. There was no steam pouring from the bathroom. No rush of warm, humid air. She felt her face grow hot, and she pressed her palm against her forehead, knowing full well that she could have used a cold shower herself.

Connor emerged from the bathroom wearing a fresh pair of jeans and a T-shirt. He sat in a chair across from Liz, toweling his hair dry.

"Can I ask you something?" she ventured.

Connor nodded, unsure of her mood. There had to be no doubt in her mind, now, of his feelings for her. He held his breath, wondering if he'd just made the biggest mistake of his life.

"When you look at me, do you see Allyson?" There. It was out; she'd said it. That notion had been bothering her since their foray through Allyson's trunk full of belongings.

Connor stared. Whatever it was he thought she *might* be thinking, that wasn't it. The very nature of the question was ludicrous. How could she possibly even suggest such a thing? Of course, she had no way of knowing. Well, maybe it was time she did.

He cleared his throat. "No," he said, jumping in with both feet and hoping for the best. "I used to see you when I looked at her."

It was Liz's turn to stare. She said nothing.

"It's true," he continued softly. "I've been attracted to you forever. Ever since we met. I never pursued it because, well, we were just friends, and I didn't want to ruin that. Plus, you were always involved with someone, and I suppose . . ." He shook his head. "It's pathetic. I'm pathetic. You may not believe this, but I got involved with her hoping she'd be like you. Hoping she'd *be* you." He rubbed his chin, wishing she'd say something. "I only just realized it myself. I never knew what I was looking for with Allyson, until I saw you again at Tyler and Amber's. Suddenly, it all made sense." He paused. "I don't see her when I look at you. I've always seen only you."

The tears welled in Liz's eyes, making the green more intense, more vibrant. "Are you kidding me?" she finally whispered. "Are you *kidding* me?" Her voice rose a notch. "You don't know how hard it's been for me!" She stared him full in the face as the tears dripped down her cheeks, her anger mounting by the minute. "You're a jerk, you know that? I've loved you forever!" She choked on a sob and clenched her teeth, barely aware of her own fury.

He stared, stunned. As her words finally penetrated, he closed his eyes, filled with remorse. He sat next to her on the couch and tried to gather her unyielding form close with his arms. She relented at last, collapsing and resting her head on his shoulder. "I'm sorry," he finally said. "I could have saved us both a lot of time if I'd acted on my first impulse."

Her breath caught on another sob. "Which was?"

"To take you out of the banquet hall where we were eating Tyler and Amber's sealing breakfast and go sit with you somewhere in a parked car."

She laughed and wiped at her face with her palms, then sat back and looked into his grinning face. "And do what, pray tell?"

His grin faded and he sobered. "I think we'd have figured it out," he murmured.

She nodded and briefly closed her eyes. "I'm sure we would have. We may yet." She cleared her throat. "But we have a lot to do here, and it's just as well; I think we're better off keeping ourselves busy."

He nodded his agreement. "Yeah. I don't know how many more stone-cold showers I can stand."

She flushed. Her supposition had been right, after all. "Well, then," she said, rising from the couch, wanting to put some distance between them, "why don't we get busy so you don't have to suffer from hypothermia." She didn't mention the fact that she could have benefited from a sub-arctic swim herself. She wasn't accustomed to blushing, and found she didn't like it a bit.

* * * * * *

The sun shone hot on the beautiful ruins of the Acropolis. Liz turned her face toward the sky, relishing the feel of its warmth on her face. The hand that held hers, fingers entwined, tugged gently. She turned her face toward Connor and smiled.

"What are you thinking?" was his quiet question.

"I'm thinking I'm happy. Let's just stay here. Let's never go home—we can live here in Athens forever." The last time she had experienced such complete feelings of contentment had been when she and Amber were young teenagers, traveling with their parents. There was something to be said for experiencing the world with loved ones.

Connor grinned. "You know, that's not a bad idea. I'm sure my boss has all but written me off by now. When we do eventually go home, I may be unemployed."

They stood atop the ruins that had existed for centuries, looking out over the great city. Liz took a deep breath. "This is just fantastic," she murmured. "There aren't even words to describe it." She shook her head in awe. "We have to come back here often. Promise me."

He'd have promised her the moon if she'd asked for it. They had left their hotel room several hours earlier, upon finding that the Stanopoulis Shipping offices, located approximately twelve kilometers from Athens, were closed. They had decided their options were to either sit in their hotel suite and flirt with temptation, or do some sightseeing. The latter had seemed the safer option.

They were completely enjoying the sights and sounds of Athens. The people were warm and gracious, the food beyond excellent, and the ancient sights were tremendous. They had been walking along, enjoying the beauty of the National Gardens, casually holding hands and testing the waters of their newfound romance. They cautiously circled each other emotionally, as if trying to determine whether or not their present situation was based on reality or some vague dream. Connor cursed himself for not having confessed his feelings for her earlier. Five years earlier.

He nodded at her request. "One of the bellboys at the hotel was telling me there are some amazing spots to the north and out on the islands as well. I'm thinking we could spend a lot of time in this country and still not see it all."

"So don't you think there is something to all this?" she asked, motioning toward the ancient ruins.

"Meaning?"

She tugged on his hand, and they wandered toward the ruins of the temple of Nike. "Well, this whole god thing," she continued as they circled the temple, looking out toward the city through its stone pillars.

"Well, yeah, I think there is something to that whole 'God thing.'" His mouth quirked into a smile.

She nudged him with her shoulder. "Not that way," she snorted. "I mean the old Greek stories—the mythology. It all comes from somewhere, you know?" Her brows drew together in thought. "I was watching Disney's *Hercules* with Ian the first night I got to Amber's, before she put the kids to bed. Some things stood out in my mind: this, for instance. Hercules goes to see his father, Zeus, the main god, when he learns of his true identity. His father tells him that only gods can reside on Mount Olympus, and that Hercules has to prove himself a hero before he can come home."

"Yes?"

"Doesn't that sound familiar?"

"I suppose . . ."

"And then," Liz continued, "at the end of the movie, Hercules transcends death to save someone, and in so doing, finally achieves his godlike status."

Connor nodded. "I'm sure it all ties back to the same source. There are similarities in so many different theologies and religions—it has to come from somewhere, I guess. I never thought Disney would tap into it, though." He grinned. "Sounds like I need to watch *Hercules* with Ian and Isabelle when we get home."

Liz sniffed. "Mock me if you must; I'm just telling you what I know."

Connor swung an arm around her back and pulled her close. "I'm not mocking. If I ever did, I'd only be mocking myself, because I think you're the smarter of the two of us."

She brushed the tip of her nose across his. "Okay. I'll give you that one."

His grin faded as he considered the proximity of her mouth in relation to his own. He closed his eyes at her next words, coupled with the husky tone of her voice.

"You've never kissed me, you know."

He took in their surroundings, well aware that despite the crowd of tourists milling about the site, they were, miraculously, alone behind the pillars adorning the side of the temple of Nike, overlooking the majestic city of Athens.

"I suppose this would be a good time," he suggested, his eyes the color of the Mediterranean that lay a few miles beyond.

She nodded softly. "Yes, this would be a good time."

* * * * * *

"Hold the flashlight over here. I can't see what I'm doing."

Connor adjusted the light to better serve Liz's attempts to access the Stanopoulis Shipping Company's files. "Once again," he observed, "we're doing something we could get arrested for. I find it a little disconcerting that you're so good at this."

"Hush. I can't think if you're yammering at me." She bit her lower lip and tapped at the keys, scanning through the information on the screen in front of her as she tried to determine what would be useful and what wouldn't.

Finally, she smiled. "Here we go." She slipped her disk into the notebook computer and saved the information. She removed the disk mere seconds later and straightened, looking at Connor with a smirk. "And we're not doing anything illegal."

"Oh, this ought to be good."

"We're *borrowing* the information. As soon as we have what we need, I'll erase the disk if we don't need it for evidence."

"We obtained the evidence illegally. I don't think it'd be admissible, in any case."

She waved her hand absently as she gathered her equipment and turned to leave the building. "We'll see about that when the time comes. Besides, the side door wasn't locked. It was as though they *wanted* to share this information with us."

He snorted. "I'm thinking the unlocked door was an oversight. Feel free to justify it however you need to, though."

* * * * * *

Liz perused her notebook screen with narrowed eyes. Connor, seated next to her at the table in their hotel suite, looked over her shoulder as she muttered aloud.

"Here's shipping information for Frasier Pharmaceutical. Twenty-six boxes, with a series of numbers following. Leaving Peru and docking in Miami."

Connor reached into Liz's bag and pulled out the sheets of paper they'd copied from Allyson's disk.

"Look. The numbers listed after these U.S. cities are the same as the numbers shown here after the number of boxes going out."

"What are they? Serial numbers? Bar codes, maybe?" Her brows furrowed in a frown. "And what's in those boxes? In his office files, Frasier doesn't list a pharmaceutical or research plant anywhere in South America. Peru takes in shipments of pharmaceutical drugs, but they aren't supposed to be sending any shipments *out* in return."

They looked at each other. "Cocaine," Connor finally said. "I'll betcha a million bucks."

"I wonder . . ." Liz unwound her modem line, connected it to her computer and the phone attachment, and logged online. She launched a search under "illegal drugs" and tapped her fingers impatiently on the tabletop while the search engine retrieved her information. She clicked onto a link for a site set up by an international investigative organization and scanned the contents of the home page.

Scrolling down the list of additional pages, she clicked on one marked "Shipping and Distribution." She smiled grimly as she read the first paragraph. "Well, it all suddenly makes sense."

Connor nodded as he read over her shoulder. "It certainly does."

Liz sighed. "I think I should call Bump." She pulled her cell phone from her travel bag and dialed the number. She smiled as the call was answered without formality or preamble.

"Liz? What are you doing?"

"I'm in Greece."

The sigh was impatient. "I know you're in Greece. Shouldn't you be asleep?"

"Not enough time for that, my friend. I think we've found something interesting. I logged on to a site loaded with illegal drug information. It suggests that drug smugglers often use shippers from other countries that are low on inventory or cash to do their dirty work. The shipping company makes up its cash deficit, and the smuggler or supplier gets his goods delivered." She paused. "And we obtained some other information as well, pertaining specifically to Frasier."

She could hear his grin over the phone. "I've taught you well, haven't I? Why don't you e-mail me what you have, and I'll see what I can do with it."

* * * * * *

"I'm all for being brave, Connor, but this seems to be just plain stupid."

He smirked. "Look at who runs when things get scary."

She bristled at the insult. "I'm not running; I just don't see that it makes much sense to return to the scene of the crime!"

"Aha! So you're admitting it *was* a crime, then?"

Liz scowled as she and Connor approached the Stanopoulis Shipping building they'd visited the night before. He parked their rental car some distance away and opened his door. "Are you coming with me or not?" He smiled at her softly muttered curse. "That's more like it."

Liz shook her head. "What is it, exactly, you're hoping to accomplish here?"

Connor shrugged as they walked under the hot Greek sun. "I don't know. Maybe I'm hoping for a glimpse of Charles Frasier himself."

"What would he be doing here?"

"Checking on details, maybe? He's in Greece—isn't that what Bump said?"

"Yes, but I doubt he's hanging out around here. I mean, what are the odds?" Liz stared at Connor, speculation gleaming behind her brown contacts. "You want to settle an old score? Is that it?" She stopped dead in her tracks.

He turned back in surprise. "What?"

"You want to get a look at the man who stole Allyson from you."

He retraced his steps and stood before her, his large frame shielding her from the sunlight. "Is that what you think?"

She lifted her hands, palms up, in exasperation. "Why else would you care to see him?"

He lowered his voice to a whisper. "Because I think he killed her, and I want to look into his eyes so I'll know the truth myself. I'd like to see him punished; let's call it absolution. It's a chapter I'd like to close once and for all." He continued his walk, pulling her along by the arm. "Aside from all that, I'd like to get a look at a man who can raise a company from a non-entity to a multi-billion-dollar corporation in a mere couple of years."

"I'll tell you exactly how to do it. You start selling cocaine, and you'll be well on your way."

She dug in her heels when they reached the front doors of the shipping company. "You're insane," she hissed. "All along you've been the voice of reason, and now you want to hang out in a viper's nest!"

* * * * * *

"Who are those people?" Charles Frasier asked of the man behind the desk.

The clerk was preoccupied, his head bent, reviewing records. "Sir?"

Frasier motioned impatiently. "Those two, out there arguing. Are they customers of yours?"

"No, sir." The man scrutinized the pair closely. "I've never seen them before."

Charles Frasier stared out the window at the woman's face. Something about her reminded him of someone, and he found his inability to pinpoint the resemblance frustrating.

Acting on impulse, a concept as foreign to him as dusting furniture, he quickly exited the building when he saw the woman's companion leave her side for a moment to retrieve their car. He approached her soundlessly from behind, apparently startling her when he placed his hand on her shoulder.

"This will sound absurd," he said apologetically when she whirled around, "but I feel like we've met before, and I'm having a hard time remembering where." What were the chances that she spoke English? He was wasting his time.

Her brow furrowed slightly, the brown eyes thoughtful. She brushed a handful of thick black hair over her shoulder and offered him a small smile. "I'm afraid I don't remember meeting you," she said in a gentle voice, cultured mildly with Italian accents. "I'm certain I would have," she said with a wink as she patted his arm. She turned to scan the street, apparently searching for her companion.

Something . . . there was something about the woman he *knew*. In desperation, he turned so he stood in her line of vision. "You must think me insane . . . my name is Charles Frasier, and I'm sure I know you from somewhere. Have you spent any time in the U.S.?"

The woman stared at him, her eyebrows raised high. Frasier cursed himself for an idiot and mentally kissed off any chance he might have had with the woman.

The woman blinked and cleared her throat. "I have spent some time in the United States," she finally said. "I have relatives in New York; are you familiar with New York?"

Charles laughed. "I spend a lot of time in New York. Do you vacation there often with your . . . husband?"

The woman smiled. "He is not my husband. He is a friend of my family—a business associate of my brother. I met him here, and later, when his business is finished, we will meet with my brother in Rome."

Frasier smiled. "Your English is wonderful, and your accent lovely, Ms. . . .?"

"Scarlotta." She extended her hand. "Maria Scarlotta. And thank you, Mr. Frasier, for the compliment."

He grasped the hand between his own and drew her subtly closer. "I'm afraid you'll think me forward, but I wonder if you have plans for dinner already?"

She appeared thoughtful. "No, I don't have plans beyond spending time with my friend, but I'm sure he would understand if I needed some time to myself." The look in her eyes was intense. He wondered at her judgment; she didn't know him from Adam, yet was willing to accept a dinner invitation after a few moments of conversation. She was beautiful beyond words. Perhaps luck was paying him a visit in the form of a breathtaking woman with few morals to speak of.

He smiled as Maria Scarlotta produced a small piece of paper from her purse and wrote her name and the name of her hotel with a sure hand.

"What time shall I plan to see you then, Mr. Frasier?" she asked, handing him the paper.

"Let's say seven o'clock; will that work for you? I know of a superb yet intimate restaurant not far from your hotel."

"Seven will be fine." She turned at the sound of a car pulling close and gave him a small wave as she opened the passenger door, sliding easily into the interior. His view of her face was blocked by the dark glass of the car window, but he carried the memory of her image with him as he reentered the shipping building to conclude his business. Before the night was out, he'd decide what it was about her that was so hauntingly familiar.

* * * * *

Several thousand miles away in London, a psychotically furious Phillip Malone pawed through the garbage taken from the room of Maggie O'Scanlon and Zach Williamson. In its contents he found numerous tissues that had presumably been used to blot makeup, a few strands of long, dark, curly hair, and a box of men's blonde hair bleach. He smiled for the first time in days.

Chapter 22

I don't like it."

"You know, Connor, you've said that like, a million times now, and I'll say it again—I don't like it, either." Liz sighed and attempted to quash the surge of irritation she felt by taking a deep breath and closing her eyes. Having done so, she decided she didn't feel any less irritated, but was more disturbed by the fact that the irritation was merely masking the uneasy feeling she'd experienced from the moment Charles Frasier had laid his hand on her shoulder.

"This could be a trap, you know. What if he's on to us?"

"I've thought of that." A headache had formed on the ride back to the hotel when Liz had outlined the details of her conversation with Frasier, and was burgeoning into a monstrosity. "And quit pacing. You're making me dizzy."

Connor halted his frustrated tirade and came to a stop in front of Liz. His hands planted themselves on his hips, and he was preparing to lecture her soundly when he took a good look at her face. His hands dropped to his sides before coming to rest gently on her arms. He led her to the couch and urged her to sit.

"Liz, you can't do this." He touched a finger to the line that furrowed along her forehead, evidence of stress and worry. That he was the root cause of it made him feel ill. His voice gentled and was filled with remorse. "I can't let you do this. We would never have run into him at all if it hadn't been for me, and I'm regretting it more and more with every passing minute. You're doing it for me, for this stupid, crazy trip we've been on, and it's stopping now. Here. I could no sooner let you go to dinner with that man than I could cut off my own arm."

Her lips twitched. "I'd pay to see that."

He shook his head. "I'm not kidding. It's too much. We have no way of knowing what his motives are. I'm not about to sacrifice you just to solve a mystery."

Liz forced a smile. How to say it? *Well, Connor, you see—I have experience analyzing men who are less than faithful to convention. I have no doubt I can put this man right where I want him.* No. Probably wouldn't go over too well. "I'll tell you what. You follow us. Wear a hat—I think I even have a fake moustache or two in my bag of tricks. You'll be with us the whole time. You can observe from outside, or maybe you could even get a table near ours at the restaurant. You wanted a good look at him; now's your chance."

Connor massaged his tired eyes with one hand. "And where is he taking you?"

"I don't know. He didn't say—just dinner somewhere close by. We can even go one step further; I'll wear my surveillance stuff and you can sit there with a little earpiece. I'll scream for help if I need you. You see? It really is foolproof."

"I don't like it."

She patted his knee and stood. "Well, it's really not for you to like. This is a great opportunity, and we'd be stupid to pass it up."

He pulled on her hand and yanked her back down beside him on the couch in a quick, fluid movement that had her blinking. His eyes were narrowed, worry and frustrated emotion clearly etched into his features. "You want to tell me again it's not for me to like?"

Connor, miffed at her. Now, there was something that hadn't ever happened before. She blinked again. "I . . . just . . . I figured it'd be less stressful for you if I took care of things . . ."

He stood, jostling her as he rose, and resumed the pacing he'd abandoned earlier, stopping only to punctuate his statements as he glared. "This is not, I repeat, *not* going to be a part of our relationship, Liz. We are not going to play games. I'm well aware of my duties and obligations here; I won't be manipulated. I'm not one of the men you so effectively staked out and captured!"

So, he wanted to throw that in her face, did he? The fact that he had a point was, well, beside the point. She *had* assumed he could be manipulated and that she'd have no problem doing it. It had always worked; she'd never really questioned her right to do so.

She clenched her jaw, confused at facing a man she couldn't control, and angry that he'd been so blunt. "Yes, and you're just Mr. Perfect, aren't you?" Her words were clipped; she felt the fury and emotion she'd bottled since New Orleans spilling out unchecked. "You got yourself engaged to a woman without even really knowing her, hoping you could shove her into a mold!" She stood in an effort to feel less vulnerable. "Don't you dare lecture *me* on manipulation! I'd say that's a dance you and little Allyson had down pretty well!"

He stood still, looking at Liz with narrowed eyes. He moved to stand in front of her, his quiet frustration much more potent than his outburst had been. "Okay," he said. "You want honest? I'm an idiot. I nearly made a mistake with Allyson that could have cost me everything. My time spent with her is a mockery of the depths of my feelings for you. And here's some more honesty," he continued evenly. "I don't like what you did for a living. The thought of you following cheating men all over town, taking pictures and recording their infidelity, makes me sick. Not because I think you were wrong for doing so—the husbands were the ones in the wrong—but because it's made you bitter, every bit as bitter as I've become. And you've had one bad relationship in the recent past that's convinced you men are all rotten. A relationship, I might I add, that makes me so jealous I'm seeing red!"

She caught her breath and bit back a sob. "You're a hypocrite, Connor O'Brian! You think I like the thought of you with another woman? A woman who looked like me? I hate the fact that instead of just coming after me, you chose a substitute. I hate to think of the time she had you, when you should have been mine." A single tear slipped past her lashes and down her cheek. She cleared her throat, despising the picture of weakness she thought she surely displayed.

She wiped her face and glanced at her watch, sliding away from his reach when he moved to touch her. "I have to get ready. I have a dinner date."

* * * * * *

Liz smiled at Charles Frasier over her water glass. She studied him objectively, noting the expensive cut of his suit and the perfectly styled hair, dark but starting to gray at the temples. His hands displayed a manicure that rivaled her own. He was handsome, in a very tailored sort of way. She could easily see how a young woman, having been raised in squalor by an abusive mother, would be taken in by a man with so much money and such impeccable manners. Too bad those manners didn't include having qualms about committing murder.

She laughed lightly at a charming compliment about her appearance and glanced down at her plate. The delectable Greek cuisine would have been more than appetizing under normal circumstances, but she could barely make herself look at this food, let alone eat it. Nerves had often affected her appetite before, but now they seemed worse than ever—especially given the fact that she suspected her dinner companion of murder. And the more he talked, the more certain she became that he had definitely had a hand in killing Allyson, if he hadn't actually done it himself. Her instincts were rarely wrong.

". . . and so I decided very early on that I'd make something of myself," he was saying.

"Your parents must be so proud," she murmured as she casually pushed the food around on her plate.

The muscles along his jaw flexed, almost imperceptibly. "My parents didn't care much for my welfare as a child; I see no reason to bother them with my presence now." He smiled. "But I needn't bore you with those details. The night is much too pleasant for that."

"Indeed." She smiled in return and raised her glass. "To your success, Mr. Frasier. I find it impressive."

He raised his glass and touched it lightly to hers. "Thank you, Maria. Please, you must call me Charles."

"Very well, Charles." She smiled again. "And I must thank you for this delightful dinner. Such a charming restaurant." She glanced with an appreciative eye at the small, yet elegantly furnished atmosphere.

"I'm pleased that you're enjoying the restaurant," he remarked as he casually tasted a bite of his food, "but you don't seem terribly hungry. Is something wrong?"

"No, no. I suppose I ate more for lunch than I should have, not knowing we would be eating together tonight."

He brushed her remark aside. "No apology necessary. I'm happy to have your company." He studied her under the intimate light, searching her features as though he'd find answers there if he looked long enough. "I'm sorry for staring," he finally said, "but I simply can't shake the feeling that we've met."

If Liz had never seen pictures of Allyson, she'd not have understood his present obsession with her own face. The eye color and wig she currently wore changed things somewhat, but there wasn't much she could do aside from theater makeup to alter her facial structure. She began to wish she'd learned how as his gaze never strayed from her features. He chewed his food slowly, deliberately watching her as patiently as a panther stalking its prey.

He shook his head. "Well, I can't quite put my finger on it, but I will, eventually." He smiled. "I love a good puzzle."

She took another swallow of her water, willing herself not to choke as she considered her options. The fact that she was in over her head was becoming painfully clear. The longer she sat with the man, the more uncomfortable she became. She couldn't recall any other instance when time spent with another person made her want to run screaming in the opposite direction.

What she'd hoped to accomplish with the ridiculous dinner date was, unfortunately, beyond her ability to remember. To think he'd give up incriminating evidence over dessert was laughable; had she really been thinking she could get him to admit he was not only selling his pharmaceutical drugs on the black market, but that he was also distributing cocaine?

She nearly laughed aloud at her idiocy. She could feel the heat from her flushed cheeks, and wished she were a million miles away. Connor had been right; there was absolutely nothing to gain from this stunt.

"Are you not feeling well, Maria?" His expression was one of concern. "Perhaps we should go."

"Oh, no. I'll be fine. I wonder if you will excuse me for a moment?"

He stood as she made her way to the ladies' rest room. Once

safely inside, she leaned against the wall and closed her eyes. What was *wrong* with her? After ascertaining that she was alone in the room, she made her way to a mirror and looked at her reflection. "Pull yourself together, Liz," she told the woman staring back at her. She studied the grim set of the jaw, the tightly pursed lips, the eyes looking for all the world as though they'd like nothing better than to have a good cry. "Later," she told herself sternly.

It was all Connor's fault anyway, she mused. If he hadn't made her so rattled before they left the hotel, she'd have been fine. She'd learned something new that afternoon: tension between her and Connor was a bad thing. Oh, sure, the physical tension was nothing new; she'd felt that from the beginning. If she'd been in a better frame of mind, she might have smiled at the notion. As it was, the best she could manage was a weak grimace. It was clear that if she were ever to relax again in her lifetime, she had to set things right with him. Help him understand that she loved him—that she always had and always would. That his friendship meant more to her than she could express, and that she looked forward beyond anything she could have imagined to furthering their relationship.

Glancing at the door, she thought of the man sitting at their table, waiting for her to return. She smacked her forehead with an open palm and closed her eyes. How to extricate herself? She'd have to think of something, anything to salvage the evening—to prove to herself that her reasons for making a date with the devil's advocate didn't amount to a total miscalculation. Her pride demanded nothing less.

She straightened her spine, ignored the sheen of tears that threatened to spill down her cheeks, and cleared her throat. "You go, girl," she said softly to the woman in the mirror, then turned and left the relative safety of the solitary room.

* * * * * *

Connor sat outside the restaurant in the rental car, his earpiece firmly in place, and listened as Liz spoke to herself in what he presumed was a rest room. He knew he should have set things right with her before she left their hotel room, but she'd been so distant.

He had to admit he didn't know everything he needed to about her; he'd never seen her in conflict, didn't know if she preferred to talk things through or think it out on her own. Attempting to judge her silence earlier, he'd left her alone.

As he sat in the car, however, hearing the quiet evidence of her distress, he knew he should have cornered her, if necessary, and made her spit it all out. He hated letting things fester, and had always been one for getting issues resolved in the open. He *knew* that had she been in a better frame of mind when they'd parted, she'd not be struggling with the role she was currently attempting to play.

As he listened to the final parting shot she gave herself before returning to her date, he groaned and dropped his forehead to the steering wheel, an ache stinging behind his eyelids.

* * * * * *

"So, Charles. You must tell me all about your company." Liz forked a bit of her dinner into her mouth and chewed slowly, determined to keep it down.

"Well," Frasier said, setting his own fork aside, "I must say, I am so proud of the things we're doing. We've raised cancer research to new levels, and I have the best researchers in the world under my employ. It's such a dreadful thing to lose a loved one to a disease . . . if Frasier Pharmaceutical can help in some small way, I'll leave this life a successful man."

Liz nodded. *Yes, it's also a dreadful thing to lose a loved one to murder. I don't suppose you spared much thought for Allyson's family, did you?* Of course, she had to reflect with a mental grimace, Allyson's family hadn't spared her much thought, either. She looked with a critical eye at the man seated across from her. *It's also a shame to lose loved ones to cocaine addictions and overdoses.* Charles Frasier, she firmly decided, was full of garbage. He was no more concerned about saving people from cancer than he was about keeping them off drugs.

She cleared her throat. "Now if we could just do something about the inner-city drug problems in the U.S., we'd have something else to be proud of, wouldn't we?" She smiled endearingly.

He eyed her over his glass of wine. "You sound possessive of the problem, Maria. You aren't a U.S. citizen, are you?"

"No, I am Italian. But such problems are universal, are they not?"

"Indeed they are. I find your good will refreshing." He sat back in his seat. "I'm thinking we could learn some lessons from our Greek friends here."

"How so?"

"There's no legal drinking age here, yet the young do not abuse the privilege. And the adults, for the most part, do not drink to get drunk. There's an edge of responsibility here that we lack in the States. Perhaps what my country needs to do is abolish the drinking age altogether."

Liz smiled. "That the children here do not abuse their privileges speaks volumes about the culture and family values, I believe. Can you imagine what would happen if the drinking age limits were suddenly erased from American society? I wonder if the majority of American youth would embrace the responsibility with the same level of maturity as have the Greeks. One cannot superimpose one aspect of any culture on another and expect the same results. The youth here have grown up in this system. American children have not. There is a difference."

Frasier regarded her speculatively, a small smile playing about his lips. "You are a moralist, then, Maria?"

She shrugged lightly. "I suppose."

Charles ate the remainder of his meal while Liz attempted to eat hers. Discussions of alcohol gave way to pleasant, meaningless exchanges, and before Liz realized how quickly the time had passed, Frasier was replacing his credit card in his wallet and moving to hold the back of her chair while she stood.

"I wonder," he said, his hand at the small of her back, "if you would like dessert—perhaps in my hotel room?"

Liz offered a genuinely tired smile and sighed. "Mr. Frasier, I fear I would be the most tiresome of company tonight. I really must get some rest."

"'Mr. Frasier' again, is it?" He smiled in return as he guided her from the restaurant and out to his waiting car.

He saw her comfortably seated in the back and closed her door, making his way around to his side of the car. His briefcase was on the floor of the car, resting innocently against the dark, lavish interior. As

Liz glanced down while fastening her seatbelt, her eye caught notice of a small, protruding piece of white paper. In a movement born of instinct and done without second thought, she pulled on the paper. It slid easily from the briefcase, proving to be a foot-long strip of bar code stickers. She quickly folded the strip and stuck it in her purse as Frasier opened the door on his side and climbed into the car.

"Well, my dear Maria," Frasier said as the car pulled to a stop a few moments later in front of her hotel, "I hope you've enjoyed the evening. I only wish you would stay with me longer."

"Perhaps another time, Charles." She paused. "You're a fascinating man." *In a creepy, twisted sort of way,* she added mentally as she climbed from the car and made her way into the hotel lobby, resisting the impulse to turn around and make sure he was gone. It required every shred of self-restraint she possessed to leave the bar codes in her purse instead of ripping them out in the elevator for closer inspection.

She was in the hotel room, having shed her wig, hairpins and shoes, comparing the barcode stickers against the sheets from Allyson's disk when Connor walked in. She glanced up as he closed the door. "These numbers match!" she said without preamble, then dropped her head again to study the stickers.

Her eyes widened in surprise as Connor grasped her by the arms and hauled her up against his body, holding her close. She relaxed and slowly drew her arms up around his back, relishing his nearness.

"I'm sorry," he finally whispered. "I'm so sorry."

She closed her eyes. "It's okay. I'm sorry, too."

He drew back enough to tilt her head so he had easy access to her willing lips. He kissed her breathless, stopping only long enough to again whisper against her mouth, "I'm sorry."

She pulled back and looked into his troubled eyes. "Stop saying that. Once is enough. We were both irritated and worried, and we said things we probably should have talked through under more . . . calm circumstances."

He searched her eyes. "Are you okay with everything? With my past, with the whole Allyson mess? Do you know that I love you?"

She nodded and offered a half-smile. "I know. And I am okay with everything—it's just irrational jealousy, you know?"

His smile was self-derisive. "Oh, I think I can relate. I didn't mean what I said earlier . . ."

"Yes, you did, and it's okay." She smiled, her eyes misty.

Thinking of the dinner she'd just endured, he framed her face with his hands. "Are you all right? Did he try anything, did he touch you?"

She shook her head. "No, nothing. He's just . . . he's used to getting what he wants, I think, and his intentions are all wrong. I sensed it the whole time—well, you heard him. He tries to pass off what he does with his company as philanthropic, yet at the same time he's putting drugs onto American streets. I don't think there's anything really mystical about him—he's just plain greedy."

Connor leaned forward again and molded his lips to hers, kissing her softly, less demandingly than he had before. "I love you," he whispered as he quietly broke the contact. "I love you, and I want to take you home."

She opened her eyes, which had closed of their own volition, and frowned. "I love you, too. But we're not done here. And I don't think we're out of danger yet, either. We won't be until we get this thing finished."

He sighed impatiently and rubbed his hand across his face. "So tell me what you have," he said, motioning to the table.

She pulled him into the chair she had vacated when he'd so swiftly entered the room and made her forget everything up to and including her own name. "This," she said, showing him the strip of stickers she'd lifted from Frasier's briefcase. "The numbers on these bar codes match the numbers listed after Cincinnati. My guess is, whatever bottles get these stickers will be shipped to Cincinnati, care of one . . . ," she glanced at the paper from Allyson's disk, "Jumper Jenson."

"Jumper Jenson, huh?" Connor scanned the name listed alongside the city. "Wonder how he got that name."

"Let's not think about it."

* * * * * *

Charles Frasier loosened his tie and sat in a plush chair, the phone to his ear.

"Where have you been?" Phillip Malone was beyond agitated.

"I've been trying to reach you since last night."

"I've been preoccupied. What do you have for me?"

"First of all, someone has access to the 800 number who shouldn't."

"Don't be cryptic. What do you mean?"

Malone gritted his teeth audibly. "I mean that someone called recently and fished around like he'd forgotten the information he was supposed to have. The operator cut it off as soon as he realized something was wrong."

"Do we have the source of the call?"

"No. The signal was scrambled."

"Fine. Let me know if it happens again. Anything else?" Frasier closed his eyes against a tension headache.

"I think O'Brian and his woman are somewhere in Athens."

Charles pursed his lips. "What makes you so sure?"

"They're traveling in disguise again; this time he's got short, very blonde hair and she's probably wearing a long, dark-haired, curly wig. I checked at Heathrow and finally narrowed the search somewhat. There are a few couples exactly matching that description who left London just over two days ago, flying British Air, who went to New York, Oslo, Amsterdam, and Athens. Now, given their pattern for tracking information on Frasier, which couple do you think is ours?"

Frasier thought for a moment. "What information did you say they got off my computer?"

"Everything. Once she got into the system, she would have had access to everything."

"You're sure she did it?"

"Yes. He was accounted for the whole time he was in the building. It had to be her."

Frasier ran a hand through his hair. "Is there something about her you're not saying? Don't mess with me, Malone."

The pause was long and deliberate. Malone finally sighed. "She bears a really scary resemblance to Allyson Shapiro."

Allyson. Of course. Frasier dropped the cell phone. He rose unsteadily to his feet and grabbed the hotel phone, requesting his driver. "Be ready in two minutes. I'm coming down."

Chapter 23

Connor sat at the window of the hotel suite, looking out over the lights of Athens. It was such a beautiful city. He'd have to bring Liz back for their honeymoon. Of course, there was the issue of the proposal. He hadn't done it yet. Not now, he mused. It had to be perfect. He'd wait until they were at home, all settled and free from mysteries surrounding disks, embargoes, and illegal drug dispersion.

He was looking down onto the hotel entrance when a black car pulled up, screeching to a stop. A furious-looking Charles Frasier stepped from the car and stormed into the hotel lobby.

Leave now. The voice sounding the warning in Connor's head brooked no argument, not that Connor was inclined to offer one. He banged into the bathroom, feeling only a momentary stab of disappointment that Liz was already out of the shower and dressed in sweatpants and a T-shirt. Her hair was damp and pulled back into a ponytail hanging halfway down her back, her bangs framing her eyes and giving her face a soft appearance. She looked for all the world as though she was ready to crawl into a warm bed and sleep for several uninterrupted hours.

"We've gotta go," he said without explanation as he began sweeping hairbrushes, shampoo, toothbrushes, and other paraphernalia off the counter into Liz's travel bag.

She stared. "What?"

"Frasier's here. And he looks mad."

Liz grabbed the bag he'd finished loading and ran into their bedroom, thanking all things holy that they'd had the presence of mind to stay packed and ready to go at a moment's notice. It seemed the moment was at hand.

"I wonder how he found out." Her jaw was clenched. She threw on a pair of white canvas tennis shoes and gathered her computer equipment hurriedly, storing it in her bag as carefully as possible.

She glanced up to see Connor standing in the doorway, one bag slung over his shoulder and one in each hand.

"Ready?"

She nodded. With one final glance at the room, she followed him down the hallway toward the elevators. Connor pushed with his shoulder at the door next to the elevators and held it open as she preceded him through and down the stairs. When they reached the bottom, Connor blocked her as she attempted to go barreling out the door. He glanced at her grimly—her blonde hair, her intensely green eyes—entirely aware of the fact that if Frasier got one look at her, he'd see Allyson resurrected.

"Wait here," he said. "Frasier's never seen me. I'll pay the bill for our room and get the car."

Liz glanced over her shoulder at the door leading to the parking garage. "Give me the keys," she said, extending her hand. "I'll get the car and meet you out front."

He retrieved the keys from his pocket and slapped them into her palm. "Be careful." He kissed her hard and was gone.

Minutes later, Liz was attempting to maneuver their car through the insanely congested streets of Athens. "Wish we'd gotten motorcycles like the guy at the rental counter suggested," she mumbled as she swerved to avoid an aggressive motorist.

Connor looked out the rear window for what seemed like the millionth time to check for Frasier. "I don't see him back there yet." He turned back around. "Now," he said, "which passport are you using?"

She gulped, momentarily panicked. "I . . . I . . ." *Who have I been already? I've been Ellen Deveraux, Maggie O'Scanlon, Anna Mendoza, Maria Scarlotta . . .*

"Breathe," he ordered. He reached into the backseat for her shoulder bag. "Is this the one where your passports are?"

She nodded and sucked in a huge gulp of air. He looked at her carefully, concerned. "Are you okay?"

"I'm not . . . I'm not in disguise!" She took another deep breath as she rounded a corner so quickly the car nearly reared up on two wheels.

His eyes widened. "Honey, slow down." He reached over to rub her shoulder. "So you're not in disguise . . . you haven't been Liz Saxton yet. No one will know the difference."

"I don't think I even have my real passport with me!"

He stared. "You've got every other one but your own?"

She nodded again. "I have to get to my wigs, or something!"

"We don't have time, Liz." Connor pawed through her bag, pulling out passport after passport. "Here!" he finally said. "You can be Nina Petrov. She's got blonde hair and green eyes."

Liz glanced at Connor in dismay. "Why would Nina Petrov be going to Peru?"

"Honey, why would Anna Mendoza crack Frasier Pharmaceutical's files? Why would Maria Scarlotta break into Stanopoulis Shipping? There's no reason any of this should start making sense now." He paused and looked up. "We're going to Peru?"

"Well, yeah! They'll be expecting us to go home, so we can't. Besides, if we can get into the warehouse in Peru, we might find something substantial to finally turn over to the FBI. The real FBI." She took a deep, calming breath and released it. "We've come this far. If we stop now, it will all have been for naught."

* * * * * *

Bump knocked at the door last known to be Doc's address. It was opened by a man who looked like death. Dark circles ringed his eyes, and he smelled of everything unpleasant imaginable.

"Yeah?"

"Is Doc here?"

"No. I haven't seen him for days."

Bump turned away from the door after mumbling his thanks, then wandered the streets for a while. He needed that ID number if he hoped to get any information from the service he'd called.

Just when he was ready to abandon his search, he nearly stumbled across a pair of legs sticking out of an alley. He took a good look at the body sprawled awkwardly on the ground and caught his breath. He reached down and felt for a pulse in the neck. It was weak, but there.

Bump reached into his pocket for his phone and dialed 9-1-1. After giving his location, he waited with the young man. Taking the limp hand in his own, he noticed a needle protruding from the arm. He closed his eyes and swore. "Doc," he said quietly, "You're coming home with me."

He turned at the sound of sirens and waved at the paramedics. Standing off to one side, he waited until Doc had been loaded into the ambulance before he asked if he could come along. When they reached the local ER, Bump attempted to give the registering nurse as much vital information as he knew. He shook his head at some of her questions. "I don't know," he said when she asked if the patient had any medical concerns other than the obvious drug addictions.

She scribbled information on her papers. "And what did you say his name was?"

Bump looked dubiously at the woman, searching his memory banks. "It's Jon," he finally said. He watched as she wrote the name in the appropriate blank. "No, not J-o-h-n, but J-o-n." He looked over his shoulder into the ER, where the doctors were attempting to stabilize the man. "There's no 'h'."

She looked at him curiously, but erased the "h" all the same. "Does he have a last name?" she asked.

Bump nodded. "Kiersey, if memory serves." He sighed and turned his attention fully on the nurse. "I'll give you my address and information. I have to leave, but I'll be coming back to get him soon. I'll take care of the bill."

The nurse nodded. "All right," she answered.

"Please call me if he . . ." He looked again at the still form on the table. "Please just call me. I'll be back soon." He scribbled his address and phone number on a pad of paper, then walked out of the hospital, his stride measured and his face hard.

* * * * * *

"Are we sure we're in the right place?" Liz checked the address again and looked around at the overgrowth of vegetation, made more imposing by the fading evening light.

"Maybe we need to walk a little farther." Connor pushed through the underbrush and tried to clear a path for Liz to follow. They had trudged in silence for approximately one hundred yards when Connor stopped so abruptly that Liz smacked into him from behind.

"There it is," he whispered.

Before them, disguised by immense vegetation and jungle-like plant life, stood an enormous building. Beyond it the earth sloped downward to the coast, where several ships were visible in the waning light. Connor glanced over his shoulder at Liz. "Ready?"

She nodded and wiped at her forehead, running her hand through her bangs and back over her hair to the elastic holding her ponytail in place. She examined her hand, damp from its foray across her head. The humidity was intense. "Ready."

It was nearly night. They had slept for most of the flight, which was fortunate. Once they landed, they booked themselves a suite at the airport hotel and dumped their belongings. They then hunted down the address listed in the Stanopoulis Shipping records and waited until dusk to approach it.

They cautiously ventured toward a side door and listened. Not a sound penetrated the walls or the area surrounding the building. Liz took a nail file from her pocket and made quick work of the lock, a feat that had Connor shaking his head yet again. The woman was layer upon layer of odd talents. Should he decide to make a career of breaking and entering, she'd be handy to have around.

They entered the building quietly, their eyes slowly adjusting to the limited light. The warehouse was large—one enormous room surrounded by several smaller areas that apparently served as office space. The main room was crowded with long tables on which sat boxes and containers. Frasier Pharmaceutical containers.

"What do you think?" Liz whispered.

"I don't know. I guess I expected to see huge, exposed piles of cocaine or something." Connor shrugged and made his way toward one of the containers. He extracted a bottle of capsules, scanned the label, and raised his eyebrows. "I didn't know that nervous system neutralizing drugs were manufactured in Peru."

The sarcasm wasn't lost on Liz. If some poor soul ingested a few capsules of this stuff, assuming he was taking a drug to steady his nerves and fight off depression, he'd be in for an unfortunate surprise. She gestured toward the bottle and Connor handed it to her.

She popped the lid off and tore at the silver seal on the top. Extracting a wad of cotton, she gave it to Connor and gently shook the contents of the bottle into her hand. She redeposited all the capsules but one, which she gingerly broke apart, dumping the substance into her palm. Handing Connor the container, she licked the tip of her small finger and dipped it into the white stuff. Touching the tip of her tongue to the residue on her finger, she looked at him decisively. "Yup."

"Now, how do you know what it tastes like?" Connor cocked his head to one side and waited for her answer.

"Bump." She scowled at Connor's snort of derision. "He doesn't use the stuff, he just got hold of some to train us when I first started working for him. And I'll have you know it's a good thing he did, too. That knowledge came in handy for a lot of jobs we did."

Connor shook his head. "I can't believe it. The woman I'm going to marry recognizes the taste of cocaine."

She stared at him open-mouthed. "What did you say?"

"I never in a million years figured you to be exposed to this side of life. I think I'd like to just lock you in a closet somewhere and . . ."

"No, not that part. The other part."

He stopped. "The marry part?"

"Yes, that would be the part."

He looked at their surroundings and grinned ruefully. "I'd planned on a romantic place to ask you after this was all over, but I guess this'll do." He leaned forward, still holding a bottle full of cocaine, and kissed her. "Will you marry me?"

She smiled, her eyes misty. "Yes, I will. Now put the lid on that bottle, and let's go." She ran a hand through his now-blonde hair and winked. Turning around to go out the way they had come in, she made her way across the floor and glanced back to make sure he was behind her. At that moment, she thought she heard him stumble.

She frowned and retraced her steps, her heart in her throat as she rounded the table where they had stood moments before and saw him sprawled on the floor. She flew to his side, touching her palm to his forehead. "Connor?" she whispered, horrified. He was too young to have had a heart attack or stroke, wasn't he? The hair on the back of her neck stood on end as she raised her head. Of course they weren't alone in the building. It had been too easy. Before she could even stand up to look around, she felt a searing pain in the back of her head and caught a final glimpse of Connor's pale face before she passed out.

* * * * * *

Liz squinted against the intense light. The pain in her head was worse than any migraine she had ever experienced. As the room slowly came into focus, she realized that the blinding light was actually nothing more than an extremely low-wattage bulb, suspended by a chain hanging from the middle of the low ceiling. She slowly rotated her head, wincing at the movement and trying to take stock of her surroundings. She was sitting in a straight-backed wooden chair, her hands tied behind her. Her legs were bound to the chair legs.

She opened her eyes wider as she saw a man who was positioned with his back to her, standing over another person she knew must be Connor. She saw only his legs, which were tied to his chair like hers were. The man was barking in rapid-fire Spanish. Connor said nothing. She didn't even know if he was conscious enough to form a coherent thought.

With fingers that were nearly numb, she groped around her waistline and nearly breathed a sigh of relief. Her cell phone was still attached to the waistband of her jeans. Her bag was nowhere in sight, but apparently her captor had missed the phone. She'd take whatever miracles she could get and count herself grateful. Moving slowly so as not to alert the man whose back was still turned, she felt along the buttons of her phone, hoping with all her might that she was pushing the right ones. She had several numbers programmed into her phone, among them family members and Bump. She had to reach Bump.

She stifled a groan and bit her lip, feeling the tears well up in her eyes. Bump wasn't home. She'd tried to call him when they'd reached the hotel. She had only his home number programmed; she'd intended to also make access to his cellular, but hadn't ever bothered with it.

Amber and Tyler were her last hope. She'd not been in contact with them since she and Connor had left Virginia in an effort to keep them safe. She held her breath and pushed the numbers she hoped would automatically dial Amber's home number. Liz remembered a time several months earlier when she'd opened a newsmagazine to find an article outlining a new cellular phone service that provided instant access through satellite systems regardless of the user's location on the globe. She had smirked at the "new" product; she'd had one for well over half a year, thanks to Bump's friends in the telecommunications arena. She closed her eyes at the overwhelming surge of irony. All the while she'd had access to such phenomenal equipment, she'd considered it a waste. She never thought she'd have to use it for such extreme purposes.

She opened her eyes to again examine their captor, and couldn't stifle her horrified gasp of outrage when the man shifted to his left and she was finally granted a clear view of Connor's face. He'd been beaten almost beyond recognition. One eye was swollen completely shut, his lips bleeding and his face bruised.

Connor tipped his head back in defeat as the man who had been repeatedly hitting him turned at Liz's outburst. His one consolation as he'd been smacked, screamed at, and punched had been that Liz was still unconscious and free from harm, albeit temporarily. Now all his efforts had been for naught; she'd caught one good look at his face and roared. He opened his sore mouth to speak to his captor and hopefully deflect his attention from Liz, but she started yelling at the man. *Well, what do you know,* his weary mind mused, *Nina Petrov speaks Spanish.*

"Are you insane?" Liz screeched at the man despite the pounding in her head. "What are you thinking? I come all the way from America with this building contractor at the request of Frasier executives, and you attack us?"

The man sneered. "You enter the building in the dark of night, and you expect me to believe you're here on official business? Why was I not informed?"

"I don't know why you weren't informed! That has nothing to do with me. I'm just here to do my job, and you've beaten this poor man nearly to death! You will answer for this, I swear!" Liz trembled with fear. She didn't dare spare Connor even so much as a glance for fear she'd lose the edge her anger provided and dissolve into anguished tears. She hadn't heard the phone connect, but perhaps there was still hope that Amber would at least hear the present commotion if her voice mail had picked up the call.

Liz's head snapped hard to the left as their captor struck her with the back of his hand. "Don't try to sell your lies to me," he snarled as she blinked back the tears that smarted in her eyes. "Someone will be here to deal with you soon enough."

* * * * * *

"Connor." Liz's voice shook as she strained to make contact with him. The angry Peruvian had stashed them in two adjacent rooms in the office area of the warehouse. Liz's room was completely empty, as Connor's also must be, she assumed. The man had shoved Connor into one room and locked the door behind him, all the while holding Liz with one hand by lifting her arms, which were still tied behind her back at the wrists, painfully high. Before she could maneuver into a more offensive position, he had Connor's door locked and was shoving her into her own room.

She might have been relieved at the momentary reprieve and grateful for the time to think of a way out of the situation had she not heard her captor enter Connor's room for one last, painful-sounding *thump*. Connor hadn't made a noise since. To make matters worse, the man had discovered her phone when his hand made contact with her waist as he shoved her into her temporary cell. He had taken it with a snide smile and slammed her door shut. She supposed she should count her blessings and be grateful that he hadn't found the surveillance equipment strapped to her midsection. It was recording the whole ordeal and would be of some use, provided they made it home alive.

She closed her eyes against the tears that finally streamed unchecked down her face. How stupid were they, really? She had arrogantly assumed they could take on a drug smuggling operation single-handedly and without the help of those in authority. She wished they had turned the disk over to the police before they'd ever left home. Had it been only a week?

"Connor," she moaned. "Please answer me." She slid her body up against the thin wall and pressed her ear against it, hoping for any indication, no matter how minute, that he was alive.

She glanced furtively around the room, looking for an object that might help her cut the ropes binding her hands and feet. She saw nothing, not even a jagged piece of wood or rock. She took a deep, shuddering breath and had nearly abandoned all hope of escape when a key sounded in the lock on her door.

Her sigh of relief was audible until she saw the face of the man who had entered the room.

"You've led me on a merry chase, my friend," Phillip Malone said to her softly.

She flushed in anger. "You'll be held responsible for all this, you know. I think Connor may be dead."

Malone crouched down before her and gazed into her eyes, a small smile spreading across his features. "Good. That'll save me the trouble."

"You are incredibly stupid."

He ignored her. "Where did you learn to hack into high-tech security systems and networks?"

I know who Malone is, Bump, she thought numbly. *He works for Frasier.*

He continued speaking, although she hadn't answered. "Did you give anyone the information you retrieved from my employer's computer files?"

How to reply? If she said yes, he might kill them both in sheer rage. If she said no, he'd finish them off so the knowledge would die with them.

He leaned forward, snarling, and grabbed a handful of her hair, pulling painfully. "Answer me!" he barked, his face inches from hers.

She spit on his face, wanting to tear his eyes out. Still, she said nothing.

He swiped furiously at his face, clenching his hand and punching her once, hard. He smiled in satisfaction as her eyes rolled back in her head and she slumped against the wall.

"It'll match the bruise on the other side of your face," he said softly as left the room.

Chapter 24

Do you think they forwarded the information on to anyone?"

"I don't know, Mr. Frasier. She won't say." Phillip Malone sat in his hotel room feeling much refreshed, having slept for a solid ten hours. He wasn't worried about his captives escaping; Rauel was doing his best to keep them incapacitated. "I'll get her to talk eventually. O'Brian hasn't said much of anything since yesterday."

"What about that Seattle number they called from the hotel in New Orleans?"

"I've got someone on it right now. I should hear from him again in a few hours; he's been staking out the building for days, but the guy's not home." Malone paused. "This is almost over, sir. I'll take care of it."

"Fine. You question her one more time. If she doesn't talk, get rid of them both. They're too much of a liability at this point. I'll be in Greece for two more days. I'll meet up with you at home."

Malone ended the conversation with a smile. It would be easier this time; with the Shapiro woman, he'd had to make it look like an accident. Now all he had to do was rid himself of O'Brian and the woman, depositing them somewhere they'd never be found. Revenge was, indeed, sweet.

* * * * * *

Liz gave a soft cry of relief when she heard a groan coming from the room adjoining hers. "Connor!" Just when she'd thought her eyes couldn't produce more tears, they fell afresh. "Please, say something!"

"Liz?" His voice sounded pitifully weak, but at least he was alive.

"I thought you were dead," she cried, her head leaning on the wall that divided their rooms. She heard a shuffling sound, then a small thud against the wall opposite her position.

"I'm not dead," came the answering groan. "But I wish I were. I'm ready to kill myself for having dragged you into this. I knew better."

"Connor, don't. I did this willingly; we both did. We were stupid, but there's no one to blame but ourselves. I share a huge part of it because I insisted all along that I could handle anything. Please," she continued, the tears still flowing, "don't blame yourself for my sake. I've been sitting here for ages thinking you were dead. I don't think I could bear it." She stopped, unable to continue.

Connor felt sick for her sake, and his own. He closed his eyes and leaned his head against the wall where he knew she must be sitting on the other side. "I'm fine, Liz. I'll be fine." His mind's eye clearly saw the image of their captor backhanding Liz while he just sat there, impotent and unable to act. He felt a tear of his own slip out of the corner of one swollen eye to match the wracking sobs he heard coming from the other side of the wall. He'd never felt such an all-consuming rage as he had when Liz had been hit. He feared that had he been untied, he'd have killed the man.

His head pounding in protest, he looked around the room, taking stock of his surroundings. Except for him, the room was totally empty. He carefully maneuvered himself so his back was against the wall, then slowly inched his way into a standing position, wobbling precariously before a wave of dizziness passed and he was able to balance on feet that had been tied tightly together for over twelve hours. He inched his way along the perimeter of the wall, working his way slowly, painstakingly around the corners of the room.

"Connor?" Liz's sobs quieted as she heard the shuffling movement. "Are you okay?"

"Yeah. I'm going to get us out of here."

She smiled sadly. That would be nice, but she doubted that his noble dream would come to fruition. "I want you to know I love you very much," she said softly.

Connor stopped walking. "Don't do that, Liz. We are going to get out of here, and you can tell me then. We're going to go home, see that these scum are put in prison, and then I'm taking you on an extremely long and lavish vacation. After we're married, that is—which we'll do in about a week, maybe less."

She choked on a small laugh. "So soon? But what about all the arrangements?"

"Forget the arrangements. I don't care if there's not a flower in sight for miles."

Her laugh was true and heartfelt, stretching her face into a painful smile. It was a wonder her jaw wasn't broken, as hard as Malone had hit her. Malone! She hadn't told Connor.

"You're not going to believe this, but Malone works for Frasier. He's not FBI, although we suspected that much," she said, her mirth rapidly fading.

Connor's sore mouth tightened into a grim line. "Well, that would explain things, wouldn't it. How do you know?"

"He's here."

"Great." Connor continued his careful perusal of the room, nearly fainting in relief as he came across something useful in the third corner. It was a jagged, flat stone, closely resembling a Native American arrowhead. He sank down to the floor, felt around for the stone, and went to work.

* * * * * *

Malone took his time with breakfast, lingering over the gourmet food and savoring the task he was about to face. When he finally finished eating, he paid his bill, left a healthy tip, and climbed into his rental car. He whistled as he made his way to the warehouse, planning his evening as he traveled. Maybe he'd catch an early flight out of the country and hook up with the woman he'd met a couple of weeks ago at a company function.

He entered the warehouse casually, not at all prepared for the sight of an agitated Rauel. "Mr. Malone," the man panted, "there's a man here from the U.S. State Department. He says they know we have two prisoners, and we must immediately release them."

Malone's eyes narrowed. "I'll deal with the State Department. You move the prisoners through the back door and down onto the ship."

He paused. "Gag them. If they make a sound, you'll be joining them."

Rauel moved quickly to the prisoners' rooms, grabbing two long pieces of cloth from a shelf as he went. As quietly as he could, he unlocked the door to the man's room and stepped inside. Impossible! The man was gone. He turned swiftly to retreat and never saw the blow that felled him from behind, leaving him in a pitiful heap on the floor.

Connor reached down and grabbed the keys from the man's limp hand, leaving the room quietly and locking his captor inside. He made quick work of the lock on Liz's door and stepped inside, his heart constricting at the sight of her bruised face. Her eyes were huge as she looked at him in bewilderment. "How?" she whispered.

He shook his head and painfully made his way to her as rapidly as he could, motioning her into silence. His fingers were numb and sore from being tied for so long. He tried to free her by untying the knots in the rope, but finding his task hopelessly futile, he instead took the rock that had served him so well and began sawing away at the ropes holding her ankles bound.

"We may not have much time," he whispered near her ear, planting a quick, soft kiss on her neck. He worked steadily at the ropes, figuring that if he could get her legs free she could at least run. He'd deal with her hands later.

They looked up in horror as the sound of voices drew near.

"I told you, I don't know what you're talking about." Malone sounded agitated and more than a little annoyed. "This warehouse is an extension of Frasier Pharmaceutical's South American distribution, and it's all perfectly legal. These boxes contain pharmaceutical drugs recently shipped into the country; they'll soon be distributed throughout Peru and Argentina. Feel free to check the labels, if you like. As for prisoners, that's nonsense! Do you see anyone here?"

"Mr. Malone, I'm with the State Department, and I don't go traveling all over the world for my own enjoyment when I'm on the job. I don't have the time or inclination to mess with you right now, so how about showing me where you have Connor O'Brian and Elizabeth Saxton stashed?" The voice was very, very American.

Liz looked at Connor in relief as the last threads on her ropes gave way, and she lurched to her feet before Connor could help her. She promptly fell against the wall with a loud thud and a groan of pain.

Malone filled the doorway, his eyes huge and panicked, followed closely by a man dressed casually in jeans, a white T-shirt, and a leather bomber jacket. His hair was fashioned in a dark flat-top, and his eyes were an amber color that nearly glowed.

Liz bit her lip to keep from crying out his name; to give away his identity at that point would have been a gargantuan mistake. Malone stared at Liz and Connor as though trying to conjure up a way to save his own hide.

Connor saw the change in Malone's eyes—they took on a desperate, almost feral look as he reached toward the back of his waistband in one fluid movement. Before he could grasp his weapon, Bump rushed against his body, shoving him ruthlessly into the wall and pinning his arm behind his back. He snatched the gun from Malone's waist and tossed it to Connor, who caught it deftly with one hand.

Bump assailed the man he held captive with a litany of words that had Liz's ears ringing and even caused Connor to raise an eyebrow. When Bump finally calmed himself enough to bring his verbal tirade to a halt, he glanced at Liz, his rage-contorted features eventually softening into a sheepish expression. "Sorry," he said.

"No problem," she murmured. "I was thinking the same thing myself." She turned as Connor approached her to untie her hands, which were still bound behind her back. Once her arms were free, she turned to Connor with a ragged sigh and collapsed against his battered but sturdy frame. His arms closed around her and he rested his chin on her head, his eyes closed.

"So, you speak Spanish, huh?"

She laughed, her shoulders shaking against his chest. "Didn't I mention that?"

He smiled into her hair. "No. I'm thinking it'll take me a lifetime to discover all your hidden talents."

Bump allowed them a moment of tenderness before finally interrupting. "Hey, buddy, you want to give me a hand here? Toss me that rope." Connor released Liz and helped Bump tie a furious Phillip Malone in much the same fashion as they had been bound.

"Are you telling me you're not really from the State Department?"

Malone spat at Bump. "I'll have your butt for this, do you understand me? You'll rot in prison, all of you, for breaking into a reputable pharmaceutical warehouse!"

Bump looked down at Malone, who sat in an undignified heap on the floor. "Mr. Malone," he sighed, "this warehouse is full of cocaine that, before long, would have been hitting the streets of America. The fact that I'm not really with the State Department is completely irrelevant. The Feds are on their way; I suspect I'm ahead of them by only a scant thirty minutes or so. Now, why don't you shut your mouth before I shut it for you."

Bump proved to be correct in his calculations; legitimate FBI agents were less than an hour behind him. He looked at Malone with smug satisfaction as a SWAT team stormed the place and began taking stock of the evidence. "Well, now, I'd say you and your boss are pretty much finished, wouldn't you?"

Turning his back on the ashen-faced former head of security for Frasier Pharmaceutical, he placed gentle arms about both Liz and Connor, propelling them toward the exit. "I know a nice hospital not far from here where we can get you two cleaned up," he said, attempting to keep his voice light. "And if they say you can leave, I'll take you both back to your hotel where you can sleep for a week, if you want."

They stepped out of the dark building and into the sunlight, which was softly muted by the beautiful green foliage surrounding the area. Liz placed a hand on Bump's chest and stopped their forward momentum, wrapping her arms around his waist and squeezing. "Thank you," she whispered.

Bump removed his arm from Connor's shoulder and gave Liz a gentle squeeze in return. "You're welcome," he said quietly.

He released her and turned to Connor, his expression serious and concerned. "You did great," he finally said. "Really. If I hadn't been here, you'd have thought of something. You're much tougher than I gave you credit for."

Connor shook his head, searching for words he couldn't find. "No," he said, clasping Bump's hand, his throat raw. "I owe you my life."

* * * * * *

Connor and Liz were released from the hospital with no major internal injuries; Connor had two cracked ribs and a few lacerations on his face that required stitching. Bump made good on his promise and returned them to the comfort of their hotel suite, where they slept for twenty-four hours without interruption. Liz was the first to awaken and treated herself to a warm, refreshing bubble bath. Upon finishing, she exited the bathroom to find Connor and Bump seated in the living room area, along with two other people Liz had never met.

Connor motioned for her to join him on the couch. "These are legitimate FBI agents," he said with a smile. "They've been filling me in on some details."

"Your phone call to Mr. St. James was a stroke of genius, Ms. Saxton," the agent named Craig Gundersen told Liz. "He was able to trace the location of the call because of your phone, and after tipping us off, was on a plane within the hour."

"I thought I was calling Amber," Liz said. She looked at Bump. "I thought you were gone, so I dialed what I figured was Amber's programmed number."

Bump shook his head. "The call was to me, and I'm glad. I was home at the time, and I heard a good fifteen minutes' worth before the henchman there in the warehouse got hold of the phone."

Liz smiled. "Well, I'm glad, too. I don't know what Amber would have done." She glanced at Bump in appreciation. "And you even cut your hair for us. It took me forever to realize that wasn't a wig."

Bump grinned. "It was time for a new look, anyway. And because I did such a good job," he said, winking at Liz and Connor, "the government has decided not to press charges against me for impersonating a member of the State Department."

Connor interjected a question. "Why would you go for a casual look and a flat-top while trying to pretend you work for the government? I still haven't figured that one out. I'd have thought you'd put on a blue suit and dye your hair gray."

Bump snorted. "I was hoping to come across as a former Marine-turned-bureaucrat. You know, scare 'em a little."

"Well, whatever. It worked."

Liz listened with satisfaction as the agents described the current status of Frasier Pharmaceutical. The man himself, Charles Frasier, had been arrested on his yacht in the Mediterranean and charged with violation of the U.S. Embargo Act and possession of cocaine with intent to distribute. He, Phillip Malone, and a host of those working under them had also been charged with burglary, kidnaping, aggravated assault, and the murder of Allyson Shapiro.

Upon hearing the last, Liz turned to Bump. "I take it your trip to Colorado was successful?"

Bump nodded. "Her autopsy report showed proof of abuse that had happened hours before her 'accident.' I also dug up the police report, and there was evidence of black paint on her Jeep that came from a Suburban owned by Frasier. The local auto repair shop had records of touch-up and body work done on that Suburban the day after the accident." He looked at Connor in sympathy. "She was run off the road—there was no way it was accidental."

Connor nodded. "I figured as much. Thanks for looking into it." He was sorry for Allyson; sorry that her last moments must have been truly horrific, and sorry that she hadn't been happier with her life.

Liz cleared her throat. "How did Frasier find out who she was?"

The FBI agent who had introduced herself as Sydney Mario answered. "Mr. Frasier discovered her identity when he became suspicious of her attentiveness to his records and computer files. She was supposed to get any incriminating evidence she could find and turn it over to us. Obviously, she found some. We think she was hanging on to her computer disk until she found the really big evidence, which was, of course, the cocaine information, and planned on turning all of it in together. She should have been providing our offices daily with anything new she dug up." The woman shrugged. "She may have been trying to put on a big show, possibly thinking of selling the information to a large newspaper—who knows? She hadn't worked with the FBI before; this was her only assignment."

Connor nodded. There was really nothing to say.

"I have a question," Liz interjected. "Why did your people never approach Connor about the disk? Frasier's men assumed he had it . . ."

The two agents exchanged a sheepish look. "Our higher-ups figured he didn't have it after the first break-in. They knew Frasier was probably behind it, but when they came up empty-handed more than once, they assumed Mr. O'Brian didn't know anything."

Connor glanced at the agents with a wry expression. "The FBI knew who had broken into my home and didn't bother to tell me about it?"

The woman cleared her throat uncomfortably. "Well, we didn't know for sure. It was speculation."

Bump shook his head and leaned forward in his seat with the intention of changing the subject. He gestured with a handful of papers. "Liz, I took the liberty of calling your sister and telling her where you are. She, in turn, called your mother, who has left six messages for you at the front desk. Amber also gave Connor's whereabouts to his boss, who has been calling her house night and day since Connor's disappearance."

Connor groaned. "I listed Tyler and Amber as emergency contacts on my employment records when I started with the company. He must have dug them out of my files." He gently massaged his tired eyes with one hand. "I forgot all about the audit."

Bump grinned. "Yeah. I have a message here from your boss that says you are to call him as soon as possible to prevent his suicide. I guess you must be quite the human resource guy. Amber said that apparently everyone in your office has been at each other's throats since you left." He grinned at Connor's pained expression and turned to Liz. "You have a message from Amber that says she's more than a little upset you spent only a week with her, and if you don't call her immediately, she'll be forced to call your Aunt Lucy and tell her you've been running all over the world with a man you're not married to."

Liz put her face in her hands. "She'd do it, too," she muttered.

"Aunt Lucy? The same Aunt Lucy who tormented me at Tyler and Amber's sealing breakfast?"

Liz nodded, grinning. "She did torment you, didn't she? Should have known then you'd be part of the family." She patted Connor's knee.

Bump smiled. "Is this an announcement?"

"Yes." Liz gazed up at Connor, an expression of pseudo-rapture covering her features. "He proposed to me in a cocaine warehouse. I'll be the envy of women everywhere."

Bump snorted. "You couldn't think of a better place than that? In the past week you've been in New Orleans, London, and Greece, and the best you can come up with is a cocaine warehouse?"

Connor grinned, his face having lost most of the awful swelling but still covered with bruises in every shade of the rainbow. "Anyone can propose in a glamorous city. I figured I'd go the less conventional route."

Epilogue

Connor watched his wife from the doorway. She sat at the bar, sipping a soft drink and laughing at something the bartender said. He had excused himself to use the rest room while they waited for their table, and was taking advantage of the opportunity to watch her unobserved.

She was breathtaking. She turned the heads of every living, breathing male everywhere they went, and while at first it had made him angrier than a stampeding bull, he had learned to put a damper on his baser jealousies and simply react with pride. She was indeed beautiful, and on the inside, as well.

She swung one foot back and forth, her fingers slowly toying with her glass and the water rings it left on the surface of the bar. She wore a long, forest-green rayon dress that was short-sleeved and flowed in elegant, slender lines to graze the tops of her ankles. It gave him a surge of satisfaction to know that she was his. Other men could glance all they wanted; it was with him that she'd be leaving the restaurant.

He thought of the feelings of frustration he'd experienced over the past few years, the most recent past especially, and marveled at the difference. Life wasn't perfect, but he was convinced it was as close as it could be. He'd fallen in love with and married a friend, and that knowledge was invaluable. He knew that when time had aged their physical appearances and life had done its best to challenge them, he'd still love to be with her, because he loved what was at her core. They shared many interests, and she made him laugh. He counted his blessings daily; she was at the top of his list.

* * * * * *

Liz methodically created more circles with her drink as she lifted and lowered the glass. Life was good. She had a wonderful husband, was looking into working for a computer software company, and they had just bought a house around the corner from her sister.

She mused over events of the recent past. Charles Frasier was all over the news, asserting that his cocaine sales and distribution had been merely to provide the company with the millions of dollars it needed to continue its extensive cancer research. His comments were pathetic to most, and even had he been sincere, he would have had a hard time justifying the end when the means destroyed so many lives.

The company had apparently been smuggling cocaine into the States for three years. When shipments reached Miami, Frasier workers carefully dismantled the cocaine-filled capsules and delivered the drug in nondescript packaging to various cities around the country. The bar codes Liz had come across designated the various shipping destinations. Charles Frasier had been virtually crucified by the media; he would be hard-pressed to find a sympathetic jury when the time came.

She lifted her head, spotted Connor standing in the doorway, and smiled at him with a soft sigh of contentment. Why she hadn't pursued the man five years earlier would be forever beyond her comprehension. Maybe the timing hadn't been right; there were probably things they both needed to learn. At any rate, she was happier than she'd been in ages, and she wanted to shout from the rooftops that she was married to the most wonderful, considerate, and gorgeous man alive.

They were enjoying an extended honeymoon; they had married in the Logan Temple within two weeks of their arrival back in the States, and had been traveling ever since. They began their trip in New Orleans, taking time to enjoy the languid and exotic beauty of the region, and had then traveled to England to visit the Holmes family. Robert Holmes had passed away in his sleep the day following his blessing, and their visit with Sister Holmes and Ben had been sad, at times, but peaceful and pleasant as well. They promised to visit regularly, and Connor had gotten past his jealousy of the fact that Liz still laughingly compared Ben to Gabriel Byrne.

From England they flew to Athens, where Liz currently sat, waiting for Connor to join her. As he made his way to her side, she noticed several women's eyes following him. She bit her cheeks to avoid a smug smile and kissed him softly when he sat next to her.

"What are you grinning at?" he asked.

"I'm grinning because you're mine," she said. "And don't you ever forget it."

"I won't," he answered, brushing a fingertip down her cheek. "I wouldn't ever want to."

He took her hand as they were led to their table near a large window showcasing the extraordinary nighttime view of Athens. Connor waited until she was seated before settling himself into his own chair and picking up his menu. "I forgot to tell you, my mom called this morning while you were showering," he said.

Liz smiled. Since the fiasco in Peru, both her mother and Connor's had called them every other day to make sure they were still alive. "What did she have to say?"

"Let's see. Claire's doing well in Guatemala. She's turning heads left and right with her expertise." Connor's grin was contagious; he was justifiably proud of his little sister.

"Oh honey, that's great," Liz smiled. "She deserves it; she's been working so hard." Claire had an academic history that mirrored Amber's. Liz's sister had raced through school, testing out of many classes and taking on such a heavy load that most people thought she'd collapse. Claire's drive reminded Liz of Amber, and she smiled. "Imagine that—you've joined ranks with those of us who have doctors for sisters."

"I'm so proud of her. She knew when she was seven years old that she wanted to be an archaeologist." He paused, reaching for his glass. "I need to call Bump when we get home," he said as an afterthought. "Mom mentioned that the site where Claire's working has had some security problems lately, a missing artifact or something. I thought Bump might be interested in going abroad for a while—you know, maybe check things out for her."

Liz's mouth quirked into a half-smile. Ever since they had returned from Peru, Connor had been Bump's strongest advocate. Liz was pleased; it made her happy that the man she loved most in the world approved of one of her dearest friends. Bump had developed a certain amount of reluctant respect for Connor as well. "Not bad for a Mormon," he'd said with a grin when Connor had told them how he'd disabled their captor in the warehouse. "I thought you all were pacifists."

"Well, more or less," Connor had said with a wry smile.

Bump had later confided in Liz that he was considering looking into their religion. "Don't get all crazy on me," he said when she'd squealed in delight. "I'm just thinking about it." It was a good enough start, she had mused. She had a feeling he might find some inner peace with "the Mormons" if he allowed himself the opportunity. He'd promised to listen to her version of LDS beliefs after returning from a trip to Chicago. "A certain 'Doctor' needs my help," he'd said with a cryptic little smile. "I need to rescue him from himself."

Liz looked at Connor, smirking. "Bump helping out at Claire's site, huh? I'm surprised you'd trust him around your little sister," she said with a wink.

Connor raised his eyebrows. "If I can trust him around you, I can trust him with my sister. Besides, she has a way about her. She's so unassuming and friendly that before people know it, they're spilling their life stories to her." He leaned forward deliberately, a gleam in his eye. "I think she might even be able to get his name out of him."

Liz laughed. "I'm not so sure. We may just have to accept the fact that we'll never know his real name. In all the time I worked for him, I never found it anywhere—on official correspondence, files—nothing. It's just not there."

"Oh, it's there all right. And Claire will be the one to get it. Mark my words."

Liz's soft laugh filled his heart as he smiled and looked out of the restaurant window and into the glittering Athens night. Life was indeed good.

ABOUT THE AUTHOR

Nancy Campbell Allen, a graduate of Weber State University, has dreamed of becoming a writer since early childhood. In addition to writing, Nancy enjoys reading, book shopping, traveling, skiing, learning of other times, people and places, and spending time with her family. She and her husband, Mark, and two children live in Ogden, Utah, where she is a counselor in her stake Primary presidency.

Nancy enjoys hearing from her readers. Visit her Web site at http://talk.to/nancyallen, e-mail her at necallen@aol.com, or write to her at: PMB #186, 4305 Harrison Blvd., Ogden, UT 84403.

Haven

Carefully, with complete attention to the task, Gwen Evans laid each piece of silver flat and straight on the freshly laundered and crisply pressed white tablecloths. The teaspoons chimed with a musical tone as they settled into their saucers, and the white crockery sparkled. When she had finished she smiled, satisfied that everything was perfect. She took great pride in the immaculate presentation of her dining room, replacing the flowers that adorned each table almost daily, and polishing each knife in steaming water until she could see her face in it. The dark oak beams that ranged across the uneven ceiling were dusted regularly, although Gwen was always nervous standing on the light aluminum ladder she had bought for this purpose, and the china teapots were treated to a chlorine soak each morning after breakfast, for tea stained terribly. It was hard work, but it was these moments when she stood back and imagined the delight of her tired new guests on seeing the cozy room that it became worth the effort.

It would be good to see the room full at breakfast time tomorrow. As beautiful as it looked now, it took a noisy group of happy, untidy visitors to bring it to life. They meant a great deal of work but she loved to see them there, to talk to them, to learn about them, to help make their stay memorable in any way she could. When they were paying for the privilege of staying at her home, she reasoned that it was her duty to see they were well looked after.

It was the beginning of June, and this was the first week this year she had no vacancies. Her guests were all long-term, with no one booked for less than a week. Among those due to arrive soon were two Americans. Gwen reflected that they would particularly love the dining room. The Americans who had stayed here in years gone by usually commented on the room's two natural stone walls built of big, graying local rocks, and the slate-slabbed floor with its woven terra-cotta rug, which brought the only splash of color into the room. She had painted the two roughly plastered walls white to reflect what little natural light was available. They were a foot thick and had been built during a time when keeping out the elements did not mean double glazing and thermal blinds, but solid walls and very small windows.

Then there was the view. Seeing it from in here meant leaning uncomfortably into the cold stone window alcove, but the view stretched across the valley floor to Lake Gwynant, with its steam railway running alongside, and Snowdon, the country's highest mountain, and the tiny tower of an ancient ruin in the distance. She had never tired of the view in all her fifty years of living in this farm-house, and those who had visited her bed and breakfast had found a new tranquillity as they surveyed the scene below—the rough-hewn, bleak mountains dotted with sheep, the stillness of the lake, and the perfection of that stone castle, which might have been built uniquely to bring a focal point to the landscape rather than to watch for the evil hordes of invading English.

Yes, she would put the Americans in Room Three, the one imme-diately above this one, where the walls were again natural stone, and there was a lovely iron fireplace that she had filled with dried flowers. Americans liked old things, she knew; those she had met were always commenting on the history of this or that. She thought the American sisters would like the original features of her two-hundred-year-old home. She hurried upstairs to prepare the room.

The teenage children of the French couple had left it neat, she noted with pleasure as she stripped the beds. They had rinsed out their coffee cups and separated the towels they had used from those they had not. Smoothing the crisp new sheet onto the bed and tucking under the hospital corners as her father had taught her so many years ago, she wondered whether she ought to place a Book of Mormon in this room, as was her practice. The missionaries had been unable to locate a French copy in time to benefit the last occupants, so Gwen had not left a copy of the Book of Mormon in its usual place beside the complimentary beverage tray. Now she paused to consider what she would do. The Americans were members of the Church; they would surely bring their own scriptures, wouldn't they?

Gwen had never been visited by fellow Latter-day Saints before. The two sisters were from Utah, both married, and apparently fearful of coming to a foreign country for the first time. So they had made enquiries, and through friends and helpful church contacts had managed to locate the only bed and breakfast establishment in all of North Wales that was owned by a Mormon. Was it merely luck that it was in exactly the area they needed to visit? Their letter had revealed that they were on a trip intended to search out their family roots, which had been traced to the Beddgelert area, only five miles away.

Gwen compromised finally, not putting the book back in its place but acknowledging the American women's faith by removing the tea and coffee sachets from the complimentary tray and adding extra hot chocolate ones instead. Once she was satisfied that this room would be as delightful to her visitors as the dining room below it, she moved on.

Mr. Anderton would be staying a fortnight as usual, and it would be good to see him again. He always had Room One now, the only single room, and he always left a paper bookmark in his Book of Mormon when he left, as though he had been reading it. More often than not, she would find the bookmark in the index, and then she would know he was only trying to please her.

Edward Anderton was the sort of gentleman who wanted nothing more than to please others. He used to come to Haven with his wife many years ago, and Gwen had seen how Mrs. Anderton had always been the recipient of his natural kindness. If there was only one helping of trifle left, she must have it. If she wanted to spend all day in their room with her knitting, then he would forgo watching the sheepdog trials, which so fascinated him, that he might sit with her. With each passing year Gwen saw Mrs. Anderton grow more infirm, more unthinking in her demands of her husband, more forgetful and complaining, but Edward was never less than self-sacrificing and loving.

When Mrs. Anderton died, he telephoned to ask Gwen matter-of-factly to change his booking to the single room, and she had thought she heard a release in his voice. He had never stopped coming to Haven, perhaps as a pilgrimage in memory of his wife, and after the initial sympathies were expressed, he never mentioned her again. It appeared to Gwen that he genuinely enjoyed his holidays in Snowdonia, and she was happy for him and always more than pleased to see him.

Rooms Two and Four, just across the corridor from one another, were for the hikers. How marvelous it would be to meet them, to see whether they looked like her dear old friend Dora, their grandmother. They had been vague about their arrival time, even unsure of the exact date, but she readied the rooms nevertheless. They had telephoned ahead from Prague, and given that they yet had three train journeys and a ferry crossing to negotiate at that point, Gwen imagined it must be awkward to estimate exactly what time a train would arrive in London, let alone Bangor—the nearest major city—and then there were the buses and taxis to consider as well.

That left Room Five, the big family room. It would be so nice to have a young family here at Haven again. A family of four. Two parents, two children—a boy and a girl, one of each. The perfect family—unless you happened to be a Latter-day Saint, of course, in which case it was just a start. One of those big families she read about in the *Ensign* would fill her entire guest house, and she wondered how much it must cost to go on holiday with eight children. Perhaps, she thought, she would ask the Americans in Room Three. Gwen loved having children here, as if it made up for never having her own, and she so enjoyed seeing the happy relief of the parents when she offered to baby-sit while the two of them went out together. All part of the service at Haven.

When she had finished making the beds and tidying the room, she ran the vacuum over the hall carpet, threw open the narrow window at the far end of the corridor, and headed into the bathrooms. Only the big room was "ensuite," with its own bathroom; the other four rooms shared two bathrooms, which was a good ratio for a bed and breakfast this size. All the bathrooms were cleaned twice a day, lunchtime and late evening. It was a great deal of work, but so important, she felt.

After twenty years the routine was fixed firmly in her subconscious and took her only a few minutes. Then she returned to the lounge, the biggest room in the farmhouse and the heart of Haven, where guests might gather to chat or read the paper and share the news. There Gwen settled into the big, comfortable armchair, stopping only to switch on the tape recorder, which held her recorded scripture cassette, and to pick up the heavy leather-bound Book of Mormon that lay on the table nearby. As the soft voice with the slow American accent began to speak, she followed the words carefully from the Book of Helaman, letting herself become relaxed again and happily looking forward to that afternoon, when the first of her guests was due to arrive.

Haven BY ANNA JONES IS AVAILABLE
AT ANY LDS BOOKSTORE